THE U-BOAT FILLED WITH GOLD

ADELBERT SCHOLTZ

THE U-BOAT FILLED WITH GOLD

A ROMANTIC WAR STORY

RESOURCE *Publications* • Eugene, Oregon

THE U-BOAT FILLED WITH GOLD
A Romantic War Story

Wipf & Stock
An Imprint of Wipf and Stock Publishers
199 W. 8th Ave., Suite 3
Eugene, OR 97401

www.wipfandstock.com

PAPERBACK ISBN: 978-1-6667-4667-9
HARDCOVER ISBN: 978-1-6667-4668-6
EBOOK ISBN: 978-1-6667-4669-3

READ THIS FIRST

This story is a work of fiction. Some of the characters mentioned in this book really lived, but most of the actions and words ascribed to them are nothing but fantasy. The other characters are purely the inventions of the author. If a photograph of a certain person appears in this book then it may be assumed that that person existed. Most of the places where this story unfolds are real places. The units of the Kriegsmarine, the German Navy, which play a role in this story, really existed.

Liberties were taken with certain historical events to achieve a more interesting effect, although care was taken to make this story as credible as possible.

A glossary of German words and expressions with their English equivalents is to be found at the end of the book, together with an explanation of the rank structure of the German Kriegsmarine.

PROLOGUE

Walvis Bay, Thursday, 14 August 1975

My name is Stefan Strauss. I write this story in English but I might, just as well, have told my story in German or Afrikaans. To be honest, I don't even know whether I am Afrikaans or German, or whatever. I start writing this on my sixtieth birthday for the benefit of my children and grandchildren.

It is my intention to impress upon them that it is always the best to choose the right thing to do and to avoid evil. If you promise something, you keep that promise. If you can prevent something bad from happening, you do your best to prevent that. Always tell the truth. If you have to choose between two evils, you choose the one that will cause the least harm. Those are the values taught to me by my God-fearing parents.

I am not telling my story to create the impression that I always acted exemplary. Everybody makes mistakes. But I think I can look myself straight in the face while looking at my reflection in the mirror when I comb my hair. I'm not ashamed of myself.

But let me first explain my background. My late father, Septimus Strauss, was Afrikaans, although he was descended from the German Georg Friedrich Strauss (1697–1749). Georg, an ensign in the service of the Dutch East India Company, came to the Cape from Strassbourg in 1723, where he married an Afrikaner girl, Johanna Mouton, a year later. All their descendants were Afrikaners.

My late mother was born as Sylvia Stein, but our Afrikaans neighbours took that to be the Afrikaans surname of Steyn. She was a German girl from Swakopmund. Her father was a soldier in die Imperial German Army before joining the Schütztruppe in the German colony of South West Africa where he took part in battles against the Heroros and Namas. After his honorable discharge in 1899, after completing his contract of five years with the

3

Schütztruppe – he retired as an "Oberfeldwebel" (sergeant major) – he settled with his family in Swakopmund.

My Dad was born around 1881 in the former Cape Colony and as a young man he joined a Boer commando to fight the English during the South African War of 1899–1902. Because he was a subject of Her Majesty, Queen Victoria, he was charged with high treason after the war and he, therefore, fled to South West Africa. He later owned one half of a fleet of fishing trawlers that was being kept at the harbor of Walvis Bay. He supplied fish to the local fish processing plant. He was also a self-trained diesel mechanic who serviced the engines of the trawlers himself.

My mother's elder brother, Helmut, was my Dad's partner and he owned the other half of the trawler fleet. He was a trained electrician and he cared for this aspect of the trawlers. My Dad and "Onkel" (uncle) Helmut became friends in 1908 and they decided to acquire a fishing trawler jointly.

They were so successful that they managed to obtain new trawlers from time to time. My Dad soon fell in love with Helmut Stein's younger sister Sylvia and they got married in 1909. They have two sons: my elder brother Simon who was born in 1910 and me who arrived in 1912. Our home language was simultaneously Afrikaans and German and I visited the German School in Swakopmund since this school had an excellent reputation.

Because my Dad had fought the English and his in-laws were German he was in no way enthusiastic about the fact that the South African troops of Generals Louis Botha and Jannie Smuts invaded the country in 1915 after the start of the First World War and took possession of the country on behalf of Great Britain.

Walvis Bay was already part of the Cape Colony but the rest of the country was part of the German Empire since 1884.

As the South African troops advanced deeper into the country my father and uncle Helmut took agents and saboteurs with their fishing trawlers to spots behind the South African lines. That was to no avail and the German troops were eventually beaten. Deutsche Südwestafrika came under South African rule and became South West Africa.

I tell this story against the background of my recollections and with the use of available documentation and the log books that I have kept over the years. I do this for the benefit of my children and grandchildren who expressed the wish to know more about all my experiences. The narrative is in the present tense, as if I am experiencing everything live.

THE STORY OF STEFAN STRAUSS

(IN HIS OWN WORDS)

Walvis Bay, Thursday, 5 January 1933

My Dad and my brother Simon help me with my luggage while I board the the SS Usambara in the port of Walvis Bay. My Mom, as well as Onkel Helmut and Tante (Aunt) Gertrud, his wife, are also here to bid me farewell. This passanger liner of the Deutsche Ost-Afrika-Linie docked here early this morning and is due to depart for Portuguese West Africa tonight, en route to Europe.

My destination is the German city of Bremen where I plan to study nautical engineering at the "Seefahrtschule" (Nautical School).

It is a rather long story how I got to this point.

My brother Simon was sent to Cape Town by my parents where he qualified as a diesel mechanic after two years at the Technical College. It is the idea that he takes over my father's role at some or other stage. He also took a year's course in accounting so that he could manage the financial affairs of the business.

After I had finished school I was also sent to Cape Town to become a qualified electrician in order to succeed Onkel Helmut in this aspect of the fishing fleet.

After a course of two years I also followed a year's course in accounting so that I could understand something about money matters. I completed that at the end of last year.

There is presently no room for me and Simon in my Dad's and Onkel Helmut's fishing business and I had to think about temporary alternatives until the time comes when I and Simon can replace my Dad and his brother-in-law. Therefore, I begged my father and Onkel Helmut to send me on a course to qualify as a nautical engineer.

Especially Onkel Helmut fellt positive about this option. Because he and Tante Gertrud don't have children of their own they treated me and Simon as if we were their own children and they even made us their heirs. Onkel Helmut enquired with various ships' captains in the harbor of Walvis Bay about my prospects of becoming a nautical engineer. With my background, the sea was simply in my blood.

The Seefahrtschule in Bremen in Germany was eventually agreed upon and this is where I am now heading. There I plan to follow a course of three years to gain a diploma in nautical science. Since I am already a qualified electrician and book-keeper I was given credit for one semester and I may complete the course in five semesters instead of six.

Shortly after we have deposited my luggage in my cabin the ship's horn is sounded as a sign that the visitors aboard must leave the ship. My folks bid me an emotional farewell and leave the ship across the gang plank.

My Mom admonishes me again: "Please, don't forget to write regularly."

Me: "Every Sunday night. And then I post the letter on Monday morning."

I get onto the deck to wave them good-bye as they leave.

After the mooring ropes have been released the ship sails slowly past Pelican Point to exit the bay. We hug the coastline till we reach Swakopmund where the captain blows his horn to greet the people on the pier. I recognise my folks who promised to drive the distance of twenty-seven miles to wave to me for the last time. I wonder how long it will take before I see them again, if ever.

Dinner is being served after the ship has turned away from the coast and I am seated at a table for four persons. I have hoped to be have Germans as table company, but my table companions are pleasant Afrikaans-speaking young men. Two of them, David en Willie Scholtz, are twins and the third man is a distant cousin of theirs, Gerrit Scholtz.

Willie is on his way to Berlin to study atomic physics (whatever that is). David wants to become a medical practitiner – also in Berln. Gerrit is heading to Amsterdam to obtain a doctor's degree in hisory. It's a mystery what he intends doing with that. I find the three men pleasant company, though. And I look forward to seeing more of them during the voyage.

Atlantic Ocean, Sunday, 8 January 1933

We are meeting Father Neptune today. As everybody knows, he is the boss of the oceans. And whenever a ship crosses the equator, he is invited aboard to initiate all mariners who cross the this line for the first time.

Of course, I and the three members of the Scholtz clan are part of those who have to meet this illustruous figure. The ship slows down briefly to allow a guy with sea-weed in his long white hair and beard and with a trident in his hand to appear on the main deck. He commandeers a few seamen to assist him.

All the newcomers to the equator have to line up and receive a douse of shaving cream from the visiting deity, which has to double as foam from the waves.

After old Neptune has disappeard again the captain calls for refreshments, including frothy beer from a barrel. All the Germans aboard start singing – as they often do – and I join in with the songs that I have learnt at school. Even the stiff Gerrit Scholtz unwinds and joins in with the festivities. The shipboard band, consisting of two accordions, a trumpet and a clarinet, accompanies the singing.

It appears that these Germans are in good spirits, in spite of the fact that they have lost the Great War in 1918. We hear from them that they are hopeful that a great future awaits Germany under the leadership of a certain Herr Adolf Hitler, who may become "Kanzler" or Prime Minister, one of these days.

In Swakopmund and Walvis Bay the Germans often spoke about this Hitler and they regarded him as a hero. I wonder what type of man this Hitler is. Will I ever have the chance of meeting him?

Rotterdam and Bremen, Tuesday, 17 January 1933

At last! We are sailing into the port of Rotterdam this morning, the busiest port in Europe. The past three days have been horrible to some passengers as we cruised through the "Bizkaia" – the German name for the Bay of Biscay, north of Spain and west of France, where the stormy seas threw the ship up and down.

The farewell dinner with the captain last night was attended by only a few passengers. Most were too seasick to leave their bunks. I'm a good seaman from a young age because I, more or less, grew up on my father's fishing trawlers. I am, therefore, used to a moving vessel.

It takes a while to move through passport control and customs and to get my luggage onto the train to Amsterdam. At Rotterdam's train station, I bid farewell to my friends, the Scholtz twins. They travel through to Berlin, while Gerrit and I take the train to Amsterdam. There I have to catch the express train that takes me directly to Bremen where I ought to arrive during the late afternoon. I could have stayed on the Usambara because she later docks in Bremen, but it's faster with the train.

The train has been sliding slowly over the last few kilometers after reaching the outskirts of Bremen and she comes to a graceful stop at the Hauptbahnhof, the main station, exactly on time. It's a Tuesday afternoon and the sky is covered with clouds. Some of my fellow travelers announce that it looks like snow.

I grab all my belongings — two suitcases plus a backpack — and walk to the exit while following the other passengers. Outside the station, I get a taxi that takes me through the city to my place of residence. On the way there, the driver takes me through the middle of the "Altstadt" – the old city, the medieval core of Bremen. He proudly shows me the "Markplatz" (Market Square) with buildings that are centuries old.

13

We reach the Weser, the river that divides the city into two parts and we drive across a bridge to the other side. At last, we reach my boarding place in the suburb of Neustadt, which I have acquired through the administration of the Seefahrtschule – a room in the apartment of an old lady, the widow Sarah Stockhausen.

Her late husband was a ship's captain and her place of residence is therefore near the harbor in the Weser and the Seefahrtschule. I share the bathroom with her and she takes care of my breakfast, dinner and laundry. I have to provide my own lunch, which I can take at the cafeteria of the Seefahrtschule.

Bremen, Wednesday, 18 January 1933

Tante Stockhausen woke me early on this Wednesday morning. When I looked through the window, I saw that the world is white from the snow. At the breakfast table, she serves me bread rolls, cheese, a boiled egg and strong coffee. Also, she explains how I should walk to get to the Seefahrtschule at 30 Neustadtswall. I have to tread carefully, because one easily slips on the snow.

This is my first opportunity to really talk to Tante Stockhausen and it is clear that the dialect she is using is quite different from standard German. I ask her about this and she explains that the North Germans mostly speak Plattdeutsch ("flat" German), or Platt, even though they were taught standard or "high" German at school. I find that if she speaks slowly, I can understand her quite well because Platt – so it seems me – corresponds a little bit with High Dutch. I do not find High Dutch strange, because the minister in the church in Windhoek, which we sometimes attended, always read from the old Dutch Official Translation of the Bible.

The school is accommodated in an imposing building and I report to the administrative office, along with the correspondence I have received from the school that deals with my admission. The friendly girl behind the counter lets me complete a registration form and she provides me with a student card. She also says that I have to get acquainted with the Herr Direktor, Herr (Mister) Joachim von Czapiewski. She phones through to his office and it turns out the Herr Direktor has time for me.

When I enter his office, the Herr Direktor gets up from behind his desk to come and shake my hand. He, fortunately, speaks standard German.

"Aaah, Herr Strauss! Welcome to our Seefahrtschule. It hasn't happened yet that we receive a student from the distant, strange and terrifying Africa here and, therefore, I asked the lady at the counter at Administration to ask you to come here. I needed to see who you are."

"Thank you so much, Herr Direktor."

"Herr Strauss, how is your German? Will you be able to follow the lectures at least?"

"Herr Direktor, German is my one native language. The other is Afrikaans. My mother is German-speaking. Her father was an Oberfeldwebel in the Schütztruppe who had to protect the former German colony of Südwestafrika. I believe I'll be able to understand the lectures at least."

"I hear that you're not struggling with German. Fine. Tell me, why did you decide to study here – and not somewhere else?"

"Herr Direktor, unfortunately there is no such type of school in South West Africa. Nor throughout southern Africa, either. I had to take a course in electricity in Cape Town in South Africa. I also completed a course in bookkeeping there. My family are some of the few families in South West or in South Africa who are making a living from the sea. My father and his brother-in-law are the joint owners of six fishing trawlers that are being kept at the port of Walvis Bay."

"Oh, your father is, therefore, a 'Reeder' (ship owner)?"

"You can probably call it that way. And, therefore, I want to learn everything about shipping and the machinery of ships here."

"So that you can probably take over your father's business at a later stage? Wonderful. You couldn't have sought out a better place to study than exactly here. This school has been around for more than a century. We started as the Navigation School in 1798 and we're still going strong."

"My father's brother-in-law spoke to more than one ship's captain to hear where I can get the best training. Everyone agreed that this school is the best place."

"We have a proud tradition. I was initially a student here myself until I joined the 'Kaiserliche Marine' (Imperial Navy) shortly before the Great War and became an officer. Later in the war, I captained a U-Boat (submarine) after initially training on a battleship. After the war, little remained of the fleet and that's why I came to join this Seafaring School later on. I am in love with ships and the sea. And today I'm Direktor."

"That's great. I suspect the lectures have already begun. How should I join them?"

"Yes, the lectures started the day before yesterday. You need to get acquainted with your lecturers and instructors as quickly as possible."

"Thank you so much, Herr Direktor."

He gets up and that's the sign that I have to leave. I return to the administrative office to learn what the timetable looks like for this semester and who my lecturers and instructors are. It turns out that I will attend lectures on the history of seafaring with Herr Doktor Sebaldus Severus Schnautzius. I walk over to his office to see if he's available.

Fortunately, Herr Doktor Schnautzius is in his office and he's available.

"Aaah, Herr Strauss! Our new student from the distant, strange and forgotten continent of Africa! I expected you earlier. But, fortunately, here you are at least now. My next lecture is tomorrow morning at eight o'clock. Until ten o'clock. Make sure that you get hold of my book on the history of seafaring from the time of the Phoenicians to this day. The academic book shop further down the street has it on their shelves. Thank you so much!"

And with that, my visit to this lecturer is over. I will also have to meet the lecturers for mathematical navigation and navigation tools.

When I got home again later in the afternoon in a frozen state, Tante Stockhausen grabs me and pours me a cup of strong coffee. And she starts chatting and chatting and chatting. It is about the history of Bremen, a member of a trade league during Medieval times, namely the Hansa, consisting of cities on the North Sea and the Baltic. It is about the Seafaring Academy for whose students she has provided accommodation in the past. It's about her late husband who was a ship's captain on a passenger liner. It's about contemporary German politics and according to her, all the Germans are holding their breaths to see what Herr Adolf Hitler is going to do with the country if he is perhaps requested to take over the reins as new Kanzler.

I listen politely and nod my head often. I also occasionally say "Yes" or "Hmm" to show that I'm paying attention.

It's clear to me that this aunty is starved of conversation. It won't work if I want to sit here in my room to study, because she will probably want to talk to me the whole time. I decide that I will, therefore, have to do my studying in the Seefahrtschule's library.

The preparation for dinner interrupted the conversation with Tante Stockhausen somewhat and at about nine I at last manage to go to the bathroom and prepare for the night. It strikes me that I didn't even take the books that I have bought during the day from their paper bag because the Tante kept me so busy the whole time.

Bremen, Saturday, 21 January 1933

It's Saturday and I give a sigh of relief. I survived my first two days of lectures at the Seefahrtschule. I am a member of a class of around sixty students and I wonder if I will ever master everyone's names.

Today I want to explore the area. As far as I could find out, Bremen has a proud past and was already an affluent city during the Middle Ages. Although the city is located about sixty kilometers from the coast, there is a major port in the Weser that handles sea-going ships. I simply have to go and see this port and the ships. I also learned that there are shipyards and I'm not going to skip those either.

During breakfast, Tante Stockhausen starts babbling and babbling again and I feel that it will be bad manners to excuse myself and go out. She keeps me busy until lunch and then invites me to enjoy lunch with her as her guest, although it is not part of my boarding. I only get bread rolls, butter, cheese and coffee, anyway.

Actually, I listen with attention to Tante Stockhausen, because she's a goldmine of information about Bremen, Germany and the world of shipping. She recounts that the Peace of Versailles, at the end of the Great War — which Germany, according to her, only lost due to the treason by the Communists and the Jews — placed a ban on large warships for Germany. Submarines, or U-Boats, with which the Germans almost managed to starve England by cutting the country off from the rest of the world, are strictly forbidden. However, it is an open secret that German shipyards have established branches in Holland and Spain where submarines are being built. German torpedoes are manufactured in Sweden. The boats were sold to Holland, Finland, Russia and Turkey, amongst others. Before the boats were delivered, German crews were trained on them. One of these days,

Germany should start building submarines again, here in Bremen or in its suburbs, Bremerhaven or Wilhelmshaven on the Weser Estuary.

"Herr Strauss, you ought to think about joining our 'Reichsmarine' (Imperial Navy) later if you're done with your studies. My informants tell me that Adolf Hitler has secret plans to rebuild the Navy if he were to come to power. There will also be U-Boats again. How do you feel?"

"Dear Frau Stockhausen, it is my plan to return to my 'Heimat' (homeland) again after my studies and help my father and my uncle with their boats. With my knowledge and expertise, we should be able to build up the largest fishing fleet on the west coast of Africa, in due course."

"Here, a great future is also awaiting you. You will be able to apply for German citizenship, if I am not mistaken, because your grandparents and your mother were born here. Do you agree?"

After lunch, Tante Stockhausen announces that she is going to rest somewhat and protect herself with her "Oberbett" (eiderdown)

against the cold winter weather. I use the opportunity to grab my coat and scarf and sail into the city to go and view the harbor.

Bremen, Sunday, 22 January 1933

Today is Sunday and at breakfast I announce – even before Tante Stockhausen can start her chatting again – that I would like to attend a service in a church.

"You can come with me. I want to show you the 'Dom' (cathedral) today. It is a beautiful medieval building, although it is nowadays a Protestant church. Surely, you're Protestant, nicht wahr?"

"Yes, my mother was a member of the Lutheran Church in Swakopmund and my father also joined. He was actually born in a Reformed family, but there is as yet no Reformed congregation in the town of Walvis Bay and so we always attended the church in Swakopmund – except if the fishing was in full swing and we had to catch on a Sunday."

"Oekee, get your coat and your scarf. Also take an umbrella because it looks like rain. Maybe, some more snow."

During dinner, I ask Tante Stockhausen: "Why does Hitler hate the Jews so much? During the sermon this morning, the pastor reminded us that Jesus and his disciples were all Jews."

"Yes, they were Jews. That's right. But please, remember that the other Jews wanted to have Jesus killed. Jews had a very hard time in Europe during the Middle Ages because the Church wanted to punish the descendants of the killers of Jesus. Hitler and the Nazis are only following the example of the Church."

"But it's not right to punish people for what their ancestors did many centuries ago."

"Perhaps not. But then we must remember that the Jews always hated us Christians."

"That was because we hunted them down, as you told me."

"All the Jews are criminals, crooks, cheats and corrupt liars. That's why the Inquisition of the Roman Catholic Church persecuted them, to rid Europe of this scourge. Hitler is just completing the work of the Catholic Church."

Bremen, Monday, 30 January 1933

No one attends lectures or practical classes on this Monday afternoon. All the students and even some of the lecturers flock to the city center. "Reichspräsident" (Imperial President) Paul von Hindenburg, a field marshal of the Great War, requested Herr Adolf Hitler to form a new government. After the previous elections, no party was able to achieve a majority in the "Reichstag," the Imperial Parliament. However, the National Socialists, or Nazis, emerged as the strongest party from the elections and could form a coalition with a like-minded party to dominate Parliament.

There is a parade of the "Sturmabteilung" or SA, the storm troopers of the Nazi Party. They wave banners and flags and a brass band escorts them. The crowds cheer them on.

During dinner, Tante Stockhausen is very excited and alive. She cannot hide her big smile and repeatedly tells me that Germany can expect a wonderful time ahead. Surely, this Hitler will fix things.

"Another thing he's going to fix is the fact that we have to pay so much so-called reparations to the English and the French because we lost the war and they purportedly suffered so many losses. Hitler promised that this nonsense was going to stop. He's not going to let a single 'Groschen' (penny) be paid over to the English and the French anymore."

"I also think it's nonsense — these reparations."

"Surely, he will also deal effectively with the Communists. They just want to strike all the time and cause damage and stoke revolution. These idiots just have to go and look how bad things are in Russia since the Communists took over there. Everybody is starving. I'd be glad if Hitler suffocated the Communists and Socialists and cut off their water and lights."

"When I was in the city this afternoon, everyone in the whole of Bremen seemed to think so — except for the bunch of Communists who surely went into hiding."

"Young man, you are experiencing historical times! I'm sure many of these wicked Communist and Jewish cowards are now going to flee. We can definitely get along without them! Want another helping of Sauerkraut?"

It strikes me that Tante Stockhausen stopped addressing me as "Sie" – the polite form of address and equivalent to "thou". I've become a "Du" (you) now — surely because she likes my company.

Bremen, Friday, 16 June 1933

Today I wrote my last paper in navigation and looked forward to the summer holidays. Just as I was leaving the exam venue, one of the supervisors called me:

"Herr Strauss, Herr Direktor von Czapiewski would like you to visit him in his office."

"Why? Did I commit some kind of crime or break a rule? Am I going to be expelled? Am I in trouble?"

"Unfortunately, I can't answer your questions. Just go and hear what the Herr Direktor himself has to say."

I slowly proceed towards Herr von Czapiewski's office as my head reels on why he wants to talk to me. When I get to his secretary, she asks: "Are you Herr Strauss?"

"Yes."

"Stefan Strauss?"

"That's me."

"Unfortunately, you'll have to wait a while. The Herr Direktor is busy at the moment."

She continues to type and dance on her typewriter. I sit down on the tip of an empty chair somewhere.

After half an hour, during which the sweat drops marched down my spine and soaked my shirt collar, the Herr Direktor's door opens. Herr Doctor Schnautzius comes out. He barely looks in my direction and steps away with a frown on his forehead. I wonder if I was the subject of discussion.

The Herr Direktor smiles in my direction and invites me into his office. I wonder if the smile is a sign that he is already enjoying the trouble I am in.

He immediately says: "Herr Strauss, what are your plans for the holidays?"

"Herr Direktor, actually, I haven't exactly made any plans yet. I'll probably stay around here in Bremen and take a look at the surrounding countryside. Maybe I will buy myself a second-hand bike as a mode of transport. I can't afford to visit other places or other countries."

"How do you feel about a holiday on a sailboat to Scandinavia?"

"It would be great to sail on a sailboat because I love the ocean. But where am I ever going to have the chance to participate in such a holiday?"

"Do you have any experience of sailboats?"

"No, unfortunately not. I only know fishing trawlers. But I would very much like to learn everything about sailboats, just as of any other kind of vessel. But it, surely, will cost a fortune to join a yacht club."

"I'm looking for a crew member for my sailing boat. Are you interested?"

It's as if a shock of thousands of volts is sliding down my damp spine and I almost can't help calling out: "Of course! Obviously! You don't have to ask twice."

"We're leaving next week — that's me, my wife, my two sons and my daughter. My two sons are still young, but they are already experienced sailors. But we need a sixth crew member. The girls take care of the meals and we men make sure that we move forward and move in the right direction. I'm sure we'll be able to teach you in a matter of days how to handle a sailing ship. Are you with us?"

"Her Direktor, I don't know how to thank you for this opportunity. Of course, I grab hold of the chance with both hands, with all ten fingers and with my teeth as well."

The Herr Direktor laughs: "Strauss, then that has been taken care off. It is not necessary to break your teeth. Make sure that you report to the Nicoletta at the Vegesack Harbor with your passport and luggage next Tuesday morning at six o' clock. I can't pay you a salary for your work, but you get free accommodation and meals."

"Herr Direktor, but why exactly me?"

"Because I need an extra crew member."

"But surely, there are many other men you could have asked — someone who already knows sailboats? Why especially me?"

"I thought about you who probably can't go anywhere over the summer holidays, because you come from that far-away desert country of South West Africa and your people are out of reach. Then I felt sorry for you."

I leave the Herr Direktor's office quietly, but when I get outside the building I can't help to start running and swinging my arms in the air.

During dinner I tell Tante Stockhausen about my luck.

"Stefan, do you know how to get to the Vegesack Harbor?"

"That's right on the Weser, isn't it?"

"Yes, it's along the Weser, but about twenty kilometers downstream, toward the coast. You'll have to take a bus to get you there."

"I've got to be there at six o'clock already. Are there any busses running at that time?"

"How do you think the workers get to their workplaces? Many of them have to clock in early. How about another potato?"

Bremen, Tuesday, 20 June 1933

It wasn't possible to sleep last night. Tante Stockhausen, who is just as excited as I am, came to call me for breakfast around four o'clock so that I could walk with my luggage to the bus terminus in the city shortly before five o'clock – or actually, run because I don't want to be late. Some of the bystanders show me where I can catch the bus to Vegesack.

The drive takes about half an hour with plenty of stops in-between. I get off the bus at ten to six and walk to the quayside where the sailboats are moored. I don't see anyone I can ask where the boat is to be found. It takes a bit of stressful reconnaissance and detective work before I finally see the Nicoletta. At least I manage to go on board at exactly two minutes to six.

Herr Joachim von Czapiewski welcomes me: "Strauss, you're just in time. As you can see, we are already busy hoisting the sails and loosening the moorings. If you had come three minutes later, you would have had to swim to get on board."

"Fortunately, I'm a pretty good swimmer, Herr Direktor. I had many opportunities to swim and dive into the cold waters of Walvis Bay."

"Come on, let me introduce you to the other crew members. Mutti (Mommy), this is Herr Stefan Strauss from South West Africa – one of our best students. Herr Strauss, this is my spouse, Frau Nicoletta von Czapiewski. Our boat bears her name."

We shake hands and I manage an elegant bow, as I've seen the important people do.

"Here's my son Johannes."

We shake hands. I guess he is about sixteen.

"This is my daughter Cornelia."

We shake hands. She looks about fifteen – an innocent young girl with braids and yet she is beautiful. I instantly fall in love, overpowering love. Heads-over-heels. Totally. The touch of her hand when we greet sends a spark of at least six thousand volts through my arm and almost causes my brain to burn out. I believe a few fuses did get damaged because my vocal cords are suddenly paralyzed.

"And here's my youngest son, Franz."

We also shake hands and I mumble something inaudible. He seems to be around twelve years old.

While the others continue to hoist the sails and loosen the fastening ropes, Frau von Czapiewski takes me to my bunk — a simple wooden cot in the space below the deck with a mattress of straw. There is bedding at least. She shows me where the tiny bathroom facilities are and where the "Kombüse" (ship's kitchen or galley) is. By now, at least I know that a house has a "Küche" for a kitchen and that a ship or a boat's food is being prepared in a "Kombüse".

I ascend the ladder to the top deck again to see if I can lend a hand somewhere. Johannes asks me to help him to pull on a rope so that we can hoist the second sail to the top. I notice that the boat has two masts.

Johannes: "This kind of sailboat is called a schooner. It's because she has two masts and long sails."

Fortunately, the wind blows from the south and it's possible to sail away on the Weser without the diesel engine. The river's current seawards also assists us to float forward. After about three hours of careful navigation between all the windings and bends and other ships and boats, we finally reach Bremerhaven, a suburb of Bremen that lies on the coast and which actually does not border on Bremen itself. There are other towns and municipalities in-between.

I go to stand next to Herr von Czapiewski who is handling the steering.

"Strauss, you will soon be taught on the open sea how to do the steering. We are four men on board and each one gets a six-hour shift to stand guard and steer the boat. Fortunately, you know by this time how to handle navigational tools – such as the compass, the sextant, the chronometer, the sea maps and the like. We rely on you not to get lost or to let us get ship-wrecked."

"Herr Direktor, I'm eager to master the art. At least, I often navigated one of my father's fishing trawlers."

"If Franz can do it, then surely you can too."

I notice that the Herr Direktor is less stiff towards me and I am no longer addressed as "Sie." It makes me feel good.

Cornelia calls us at ten o'clock for breakfast after we have reached the open sea and left the estuary of the Weser behind us. All six of us sit at the table in the cramped galley. Herr von Czapiewski tied the steering and he declares that it's safe to leave the boat to its own devices for a few minutes.

Cornelia sits opposite me and I can admire her fine facial features. At fifteen, she's not a woman yet, but I can see that she's going to become a beautiful lady. Right there and then I decide that

I will have to look well after her so that one day I can make her mine when she is old enough. However, she doesn't seem to notice me and only speaks the minimum to me. I believe she feels shy in the presence of a strange man who will be spending the next few weeks with her on this boat.

After breakfast, I keep Herr von Czapiewski company again where he handles the steering once more so that I can learn as much as possible about handling the boat. He teaches me the names of all the different ropes, sails and other parts of the boat.

"Herr Direktor, where are we actually headed? And how long are we going to be gone?"

He laughs: "Strauss, for those questions I've been waiting. Our first stop is Cuxhaven, just northwest of Hamburg. I want to go and see what the naval base there looks like nowadays. During the Great War I was an 'Oberleutnant zur See' (sublieutenant) on the battleship Kronprinz Wilhelm that sometimes visited that port. That was before I was transferred to the U-Boat section. Let me quickly show you a picture of this battleship — the most powerful battleship of the Kaiserliche Marine at the time."

He continues: "After that, we sail all along the west coast of Denmark on the Skagerrak until we reach Esbjerg. Then we lay on at Skagen. That's the northernmost tip of Denmark. And then we cross the Kattegat to visit Göteborg in Sweden. From there we sail to Kristiansand in Norway. This we should reach in three weeks' time. And then maybe we can advance up to Bergen further north in Norway and maybe view one or two fjords before we cruise straight back to Bremen across the Skagerrak. We should be gone about five to six weeks."

"Herr Direktor, this cruise is something I never even dared to dream of. Now I get the chance to see interesting places in Europe and at the same time greatly revamp my knowledge of the sea and seafaring. I must have a good look at those places because it may my only opportunity ever of visiting those spots. Thank you so much!"

"Bitte" (please).

Skagerrak, Monday, 26 June 1933

Today is the first opportunity I get to chat to Cornelia on our own. We have been at sea for six days already and we're on our way to Esbjerg on the west coast of Denmark. It is my turn to take the shift at the helm between the midday hour and six o' clock. Cornelia serves me a mug of hot coffee at four o' clock and I seize the chance to get to know her better.

"Where are you at school?"

"I'm in the Hermann Böse Gymnasium in Bremen."

"What's your favorite subject?

"I love biology. But I also like German literature."

"Have you thought about what you want to become one day when you're done with school?"

"I don't actually know yet. Maybe a nurse. But then I want to work with kids. Or maybe a German teacher. Then I can work with kids too. There's still enough time to decide."

The conversation seems to be drying up here and to keep it going, I tell her about my school days in Swakopmund. She seems to be interested in my stories and I inform her about the pranks I and my friends have played.

For instance, we messed with the spirit of poor Herr Paul Pöhlmann, among others. He was rather old and easily got nervous. He gave us history. We quietly tied a rope to his table's legs and dragged the table closer to us as soon as he wanted to put something on the table. Then the book or the pen or whatever obviously fell to the floor. One of us then quickly jumped up to help him and in the process pulled the table back up to its old position. The poor old guy easily became flustered and then began to stutter.

She giggles.

"Old Herr Pöhlmann taught us about the Franco-Prussian War. One of the smart-heads in our class, Klaus Schultz, one day told him about an episode of which old Herr Pöhlmann knew nothing. Klaus told him that the fighting had run onto a deadlock on a certain day and that no side could budge the other a single centimeter. Then the chancellor, Otto von Bismarck and the French prime minister – a man with an unpronounceable name – decided to determine the result with a game of chess. Of course, Bismarck won and so the battle's outcome was determined."

She laughs: "Did Herr Pöhlmann swallow the story?"

"He wasn't sure what to make of the story and he promised to do some research on it."

Cornelia asks: "What kind of town is Swakopmund?"

I explain that, on the one hand, it is a typical German town. Many buildings could have stood equally well in a town in Germany. The Lutheran church, for example, has a "Zwiebelturm" (onion-shaped tower). But, on the other hand, it is also a town along the cold Atlantic Ocean and in a barren desert where nothing grows. There are only sand and stones — and yet there are wild animals such as gemsbuck, jackals, lions and thousands of birds living off the fish in the sea. Seals also occur at certain spots.

I add: "A lot of people there still celebrate Kaiser Wilhelm the Second's birthday on January the 27th."

"The poor old Kaiser. He is still alive and he now lives at an estate at Doorn in Holland after fleeing Germany at the end of the Great War. Many of his old ministers and friends still often visit him."

By now I've finished my coffee and I return the empty mug. When she disappears, I think that I have broken the ice today and got the start of a friendship with her going. However, I still have to take it bitterly slowly because she is still young. The question, however, is: how will I keep in touch with her when this dream holiday comes to an end? When I think about this prospect a cold, hard fear grips my heart because I don't think there will be any possibility to keep contact with her. But then I remember that there is still lots of time to be near this heavenly creature because this holiday is not yet over. I decide that I must make the most of the available time by being a well-behaved young man who wants to impress Cornelia's folks.

I wonder as well: how will this aristocratic family accept me? I'm a poor craftsman whose father owns a few boats. My German grandfather wasn't even an officer in the Army — only a sergeant major. The "von" in the family name of von Czapiewski shows that they are of noble descent. Maybe someone in their family has some or other title like "Herzog" (duke) or "Ritter" (knight).

Bremen, Wednesday, 2 August, 1933

After six wonderful weeks, we return to Bremen. For the last time, I have to help to fold the sails, to loosen and store the ropes, to arrange the flags, to clean the inside of the boat and to help with the fastening process. Herr von Czapiewski is the last one to leave the schooner after securing all the hatches.

We all travel to the city by bus. Although I fervently wished to sit next to Cornelia, she sits next to her brother Johannes and I have to share a seat with Franz. By now, I'm Franz's hero with all my stories about South West and how my father and uncle discreetly helped the German forces against the Union troops. The fact that I have already flattened a gemsbuck with a gun, he finds the pinnacle of excitement.

He also could not get enough of my story how I, my father and four more crew members almost lost one of our boats in a sudden storm on the open sea. It was just my father's good seamanship that prevented us from sinking or being beaten to pieces against the coast. It was my job to man the manual pump with which I had to prevent sea water from collecting in the hold and let the diesel engine crunch to a halt.

According to Franz, it is his and Johannes's ideal to become U-Boat commanders one day, just like their father.

The day before yesterday Franz told me in confidence that his sister had admitted to him that she finds me attractive. It was also important to note that she sometimes touched me while we were sitting at the table and elsewhere – while I pretended not to notice anything because I don't know how her parents would react to that.

There were many occasions where we both could chat on our own while I manned the helm. Afterwards, I repeated every conversation over-and-over in my mind. We talked about ordinary topics and I realized that it would be totally premature to mention

39

to her how I felt about her. She needs to get older first before we can get to that point.

Just before dinner, I reach Tante Stockhausen's apartment. She's so happy to see me that she almost grabs me around the neck, but she stops herself and just greets me by hand.

During the dinner I have to tell everything, although – of course – I stay silent about my friendship with Cornelia. Although Tante Stockhausen has never ventured outside of Bremen, she knows of all the places we visited because her late husband, the ship's captain, told her about them.

"Stefan, you surely couldn't have gotten a better training as a seaman by sailing on a schooner over the Kattegat, the Skagerrak and the North Sea. I'm sure you'll find the rest of your course to be kids' games."

"I learned not only something about shipping, but also about history. Herr Direktor von Czapiewski was an Oberleutnant zur See on the battleship Kronprinz Wilhelm that participated in the Battle of the Skagerrak off the coast of Denmark in May 1916. The British call it, I believe, the Battle of Jutland. Although there were fewer German ships that British men of war participating in the battle, the British lost more ships than the Germans. Therefore, the Germans insist that they had won the battle. The British's loss of tonnage was almost double that of the Germans and more than twice as many British seamen perished as Germans. The Herr Direktor took us through the exact area where the slaughter took place. We all wondered what became of all the wrecks on the seabed."

"My late Wilhelm was also there at that time as an officer on a cruiser and he survived it fortunately. After the war, he joined the commercial fleet and later became a ship's captain."

Bremen, Monday, 28 August, 1933

The new semester starts today. It is actually the beginning of the academic year after the summer holidays – unlike South West or South Africa where the academic year always starts in January or February. If I stayed with the class I joined in January, I would have had to do the following subjects during the coming semester: electricity, radio and shipping finances. However, these are courses I have already completed before coming to Bremen and for which I have received credit.

As a result, I fall in with the freshmen for this semester and follow the subjects I missed a year ago because I dropped in at the middle of the first academic year. The following subjects, therefore, await me: international maritime law, welding, metallurgy and timber technology.

During the four weeks that have passed since my return to Bremen, I longed for Cornelia every day. I simply couldn't get her out of my mind. I bought myself a second-hand bicycle and explored the surroundings of Bremen, including Bremerhaven and Wilhelmshaven with their shipyards. I even pedaled through to the Netherlands for a few days and viewed the surroundings of Emden and Delfzijl with their ports and I slept in guest houses. At night I wondered what Cornelia was doing at that time. Was she perhaps thinking of me? Unfortunately, it was impossible to find out.

By now I am familiar with the set-up at the Schifffahrtschule and I, therefore, easily fit into my new class. There are again about sixty students in the group.

Bremen, Friday, 1 September, 1933

I receive the message this afternoon that I must please go to the Herr Direktor von Czapiewski's office as soon as my practical class in timber science ends. Because I already know him well by now, I don't feel distressed when I report to his office. His secretary says that I can go in right away. The Herr Direktor indicates that I may sit.

"Herr Strauss, or should I rather say, Stefan, thank you for coming. Let me come to the point straight away: please come to our home at five o'clock tomorrow afternoon. There's a family feast. Cornelia is having her birthday and she turns sixteen. We only invite family members, but Franz insisted that we consider you as an honorary member of the family and that you should also be invited. Can you come?"

"Herr Direktor, thank you very much for the invitation. It is an honor for me to be considered part of the family. I'm eager to come."

On the way home, I cannot help but to rejoice and yell and yodel. Here's a chance I can get back into Cornelia's presence! But then – there are sure to be so many other guests that I'm going to get very little time with her. But two minutes with her is better than zero minutes, as it is at present.

Bremen, Saturday, 2 September, 1933

Tante Stockhausen helps me to think of a fitting gift for a girl of sixteen. I explain that it is the daughter of the Herr Direktor, with whom I spent part of the summer holidays, who is having her birthday party and that I am now almost considered a member of the family.

At breakfast we therefore discuss a few possibilities. Tante Stockhausen says at last: "Get your jacket and then we go to town so that we can look around in the shops and I can help you choose a suitable gift. But you have to help me with the dishes first. And then you may also clean the kitchen with a broom and empty the waste paper baskets into the garbage bin."

The fact that Tante Stockhausen asks me to help with the homework is a sign to me that she accepted me as the son she never had. She also almost feels like a second mother to me because she actually takes care of me very well and she's always worried about my health and my state of mind. She makes sure that I sit next to her in church every Sunday.

In the Altstadt we get a nice pendant with a stone on a silver chain and a nice colorful picture card on which I can write a message. The shop assistant wraps the gift in pretty colored paper for us. The gift is actually a little above my budget, but Tante Stockhausen reminds me that I should thank the family von Czapiewski in a fitting way for the free holiday. She also reminds me that I paid less for my room during my holidays, as she did not provide meals and she did not have to deal with my laundry. So, I've saved some "Reichsmarks" (the German currency) that I can spend right now.

On my way to the residence of the von Czapiewski family, I pick a bunch of autumn flowers in a park. An angry lady who walks her puppy starts to argue with me, but I just ignore her with a stupid grin on my face.

I make sure that I arrive twenty minutes early in the hope that there won't be many guests occupying Cornelia as yet. When I ring the doorbell, it's Cornelia who comes to open by herself. I squeeze the bunch of flowers into her hands and hand over the gift with the card to her. She puts them all down on a table in a hurry, hugs me and gives me a kiss.

It feels as if the world suddenly started to turn faster around its axle and it makes me feel dizzy. My eyes stare straight ahead and I can't focus easily, either. It's as if strong magnetic fields are drawing all the iron in my blood onto a single lump and that leaves my head without oxygen.

I do notice that Cornelia grabs me by the arm and drags me inside the home. We go directly to the kitchen where she gets a flower pot, fills it with water and arranges the flowers in it.

"And now I have to see what gift my good friend brought!" Her voice sounds like silver bells.

She takes out the pendant and cries out: "It's beautiful! It's beautiful! Thank you very much!"

And right there, I get a smacking kiss again – unfortunately only on my left cheek. Nevertheless, it feels as if a blowtorch's flame is directed at that cheek and I become crimson in the face.

"And now you have to hang it around my neck. I don't know how to open the chain's lock."

With shaking hands, I do what is requested. Directly after I've finished the task, the front door bell rings and Cornelia shoots away to open the door again.

It's people I don't know. Cornelia hugs everyone and gives each one a smacking kiss — just as she did with me. So, I have to conclude that I'm not exactly special in her eyes. Although – she just called me her "good friend".

The Herr Direktor and the rest of his family emerge. The Herr Direktor exclaims when he sees the new guests: "Welcome,

Onkel Hermann! Welcome Tante Hermione! Welcome to my two cousins!"

I conclude it's the Herr Direktor's uncle and aunt with their two adult daughters who have now arrived. I'm introduced to the newcomers

The Herr Direktor announces: "This is Herr Stefan Strauss from South West Africa. He is one of my star students and a good family friend. And this is Hermione Gräfin (Countess) von Czapiewski."

The Gräfin holds her hand so that I can kiss it. Fortunately, I know by now that my lips may not really touch her hand.

The Herr Direktor goes on: "And this is Hermann Graf (Count) von Czapiewski."

We shake hands as I make an elegant bow.

I also greet the two noble daughters, Helene and Heloisa. Their hands must also be kissed. I wonder if they're ever going to get husbands because they seem rather dull and unattractive to me. It's hard to believe they and the beautiful Cornelia are related.

The count's family moves along. My head is reeling and half my brain cells get short-circuited. My eyes blink at a rate of five hundred winks per minute. My knees want to buckle. How on earth did I end up among these elevated people? Will Cornelia, who has such noble relatives, ever be interested in me?

More guests show up and each time Cornelia greets them with hugs and kisses. She is particularly pleased when her grandparents arrive.

We get drinks – wine, beer and stronger beverages – which I avoid, because I can't afford to lose my self-control under the influence of alcohol. Fortunately, there is also fruit juice.

The count approaches me in a corner: "You are Herr Strauss, if I am right?"

"Yes, that's me, mein edler Herr."

It suddenly strikes me that I don't know how to address a count. Is he an excellency, a highness, a lord, a highness, or what? At least he doesn't seem to feel insulted that I addressed him as "mein edler Herr" (my noble Sir).

He continues: "I learned that your grandfather was with the Schütztruppe in South West Africa?"

"Yes, he was a 'Kompaniechef' (commander of a company)." I don't disclose the fact that he was actually just a sergeant major who only had command over a company of soldiers for a fortnight when the "Oberleutnant" (lieutenant) in command fell ill. I tell this half a lie, because I've noticed that the officers in the armed forces had previously come mainly from the nobility. It is therefore almost as if any officer must also be of high descent.

"Did he participate in any battles?"

"He fought against the Hereros and the Namas. He also was a recipient of the Iron Cross, Second Class."

"In other words: he was a war hero?"

"You can probably call it that way, but he got this decoration during the war against the French in 1870."

"Are you, by any means, contemplating a career in the armed forces?"

"The possibility has been raised. I am currently studying at the Nautical Academy and it may just happen that I later join the Reichsmarine. The plan, however, is that I have to help my father, a 'Reeder', with his fleet after my studies. My country, South West Africa, doesn't have a navy. Our neighbouring country, South Africa, also does not have a battle fleet. However, I don't know if the Reichsmarine will ever accept me because I'm not a German citizen."

"But your parents and grandparents were born in Germany?"

"Just on my mother's side. Maybe that could help me."

"Where does the family come from?"

"From Westphalia. From Barmen in the Wupperthal."

Dinner is being served on a long table. Cornelia, as the birthday girl, sits at the head of the table. I, as the only non-noble, sit at the very bottom point. Fortunately, Franz keeps me company on my left. A cousin of Cornelia on her mother's side sits on the other side. This chap ignores me. There is in any case no chance for me to get nearer to Cornelia tonight. At least I get the chance to admire her at a distance.`

Bremen, Friday, 15 December, 1933

As we sit down for breakfast, Tante Stockhausen asks: "Stefan, what are your plans for the Christmas holidays? Do you have any ideas?"

"Dear Tante, actually I haven't made any plans yet. I was so busy doing my best with my studies that I just concentrated on that. Today I am writing my last paper in international maritime law and I'm quite nervous about it. Maybe we can pay attention to it tomorrow."

"Just as you like. You know, of course, that you are welcome to stay here all the time until the semester starts again in January. I'd quite love it if you could celebrate Christmas with me."

"I'm sure you can make something special for my first Christmas in Germany."

"Then tomorrow you also have to help me to bake 'Stollen' (almond cake with raisins). We can't celebrate Christmas without that."

"I hope you have the same recipe my Mom always used. Her Stollen was of prime quality."

"Let's see."

After breakfast, I set off to the Seefahrtschule where I have to complete my last exam paper for the semester. As I sit and grapple with the paper, Herr Direktor von Czapiewski comes into the exam room and speaks a few words with the supervisor. After that, he comes directly to my seat.

"Stefan, sorry to bother. Would you please come and speak to me as soon as you've done here?"

"Oekee."

This, obviously, breaks my concentration. Am I going to get another invitation to go on holiday with him and his family? Will I get another opportunity to enjoy the presence of his beautiful daughter? I struggle to complete my paper because the image of the fair Cornelia constantly intrudes upon my consciousness.

At about twelve o' clock I hand in my answer script when the supervisor calls: "Time, gentlemen!" I walk to the Herr Direktor's office.

When I'm inside and sit down at his invitation, he starts: "Stefan, you did very well during this past year which is now nearly finished. I believe that you're also going to get good marks for this morning's paper. Next semester, the following subjects await you: metereology, oceanography, the control of shipping routes and the management of crews. I'm going to lecture oceanography and it's my wish that you do superbly well in it."

"Herr Direktor, I've always had a great love for the oceans, though I've only got acquainted with the Atlantic Ocean as yet."

"You know that there are traditionally seven seas on earth. There are actually many more, that is, when one considers the Mediterranean, the Baltic, the North Sea, the Skagerrak, the Arctic Sea, the Sargasso Sea, the Caribbian Sea, the Arabian Gulf, the Chinese Sea and so on. Each has its own features. Actually, we still know hopelessly too little about the oceans and of the ocean bottom — and also about the ocean currents — but I believe you'll find it an interesting subject."

"Of that, you can be sure."

"Another thing: you are to come and visit us on 'Heiligabend' (December 24) and on Christmas Day. My wife feels sorry for you for having no family around here and she insisted that we invite you."

"Herr Direktor, I would very much, very much, like to have accepted the invitation, but I am saddled with a dilemma."

"Yes?"

"Frau Sarah Stockhausen, my landlady, just asked me this morning that I spend all of Christmas with her. She is a lonely widow and I have already promised her that I would like to keep her company over that time."

"Stefan, I would never have expected of you to break a promise — especially not to a lonely old lady. Of course, you stay with her over Christmas and brighten her life somewhat."

"I'm grateful you understand, Herr Direktor."

"Oh, yes, I understand. I haven't spoken to my wife yet, but I'm sure she'll agree with my new plan. You are to come and visit us on 'Silvester' (New Year's Eve) and New Year's Day. You simply sleep over because we can't expect you to sneak back home after midnight on New Year's Day. How do you feel about that?"

"Herr Direktor, of course, I gratefully accept this invitation."

When I walk away from there, I feel as agile and flight-footed as a springbuck or a gemsbuck. Within a few short moments, I'm back in Tante Stockhausen's apartment again.

I grab her: "Dear Tante, is it possible that you could teach me how to dance?"

"Where did you get this silly idea, this nonsense? What makes you think I know something about dancing? Why, on earth?"

"I have to go and spend Silvester and New Year's Day with the Herr Direktor and his family. People always dance on Silvester. And I don't know how."

"And now, this old lady with her stiff legs has to give you dancing lessons?"

"You've showed me pictures where you and the Herr Kapitän danced. Of course, you can waltz and dance the polka and turn and swing on the beats of a march. With my family name of Strauss it's actually a shame that I haven't learnt to dance yet. My very, very, very distant relative, Johann Strauss, the Waltz King, would have been very ashamed of me."

"Oekee, oekee. You surely don't leave me much of a choice. Then you will have to go and buy yourself some real dancing shoes. Smooth leather soles. And I'll look out on the radio for fine dance music and then we start tomorrow afternoon. But first of all, we go into town tomorrow morning – to get your shoes and also to buy the ingredients for our Stollen."

"And if we can't find appropriate dance music on the radio, then we're just dance to the beat of a bunch of songs we can sing together."

Tante Stockhausen's eyes shine brightly.

Bremen, Monday, 1 January 1934

It's a strange bed in which I wake up. However, I immediately realise that I find myself in the guest room of the von Czapiewski residence after celebrating with my "Ersatz" family (stand-in family) Silvester last night.

The festival of yesterday, on the Sunday night, was somewhat of a mixed success. I arrived during the afternoon with extra clothes, nightwear, toothbrush and my dancing shoes in my backpack. Cornelia opened the front door when I rang the bell. To my disappointment, she didn't greet me with an embrace and a kiss as with her birthday. At least, she smiled quite kindly and took me to the guest room where I could deposit my backpack. After that, I had to help in the kitchen, the dining room and the living room with preparations for the evening's celebrations. So, there was little enough chance to talk to Cornelia, except when we prepared the dinner table together.

At seven o'clock, dinner was served. A cousin of Cornelia, Luise, with her boyfriend Alfred, joined us in the meantime. Luise I've met fleetingly at Cornelia's birthday party. At the table I came to sit between Luise and Franz.

Frau von Czapiewski insisted I enjoy a glass of red wine with the meal.

When I hesitated, she asked, "Stefan, how old are you?"

"Gnädige Frau (dear lady), I'm twenty-two one of these days."

"Well, yes, then you're old enough to enjoy alcohol. Even Johannes and Cornelia get something tonight."

During the meal I committed my first blunder. In order to conduct a polite chat with Luise next to me, I asked her how she spelled her name. I added that in Afrikaans we follow the French spelling, "Louise". And then I added that she could consider herself fortunate in that she did not find herself in South Africa, because the Afrikaners would have pronounced her name simply as "luise", a direct pronounciation of her name.

She asks: "What is 'luise'?"

"It's small creeping creatures hiding in animals' pelts. In German, it's called a 'Laus' (lice)."

Nobody thought it was funny. I decided to keep my big mouth shut after this.

After the dinner table was cleared and the furniture was pushed to one side in the dining room, the dancing began. There was but little chance of dancing with Cornelia, because her father, her two brothers and Alfred all wanted to take turns. Of course, I also had to dance with Frau von Czapiewski and with Luise – although the latter did not feel very enthustiatic about me. I was intensely grateful for the lessons Tante Stockhausen gave me and I managed to step on no one's toes and to keep the rhythm of the music. Franz was the one who managed the music by playing the family's collection of records with waltzes, polkas, and marches on their turntable.

It was heavenly, of course, to take Cornelia gently in my arms as we danced. She looked like a fairy to me — almost too good to be true.

And then midnight came. Herr von Czapiewski brought two bottles of "Sekt" (sparkling wine) along and gave each one of us – except for Franz – a glass full. All of us exclaimed "Zum Wohl!" (cheers!). In my over-enthusiasm to drink a toast with everyone, especially with Cornelia, I bumped my glass with so much enthusiasm against her glass that our glasses both broke and the Sekt splashed onto Cornelia's dress. Fortunately, the dining room has a wooden floor where the moisture could be cleaned up more easily than from one of Frau von Czapieswki's expensive carpets.

I suspect the red wine from earlier the evening somewhat affected my judgment and that's why I committed this blunder. My host and hostess, fortunately, had the grace to laugh it off. Cornelia was angry that her pretty dress was messed up and she disappeared directly afterwards, not to reappear again. We all went to bed a little later after helping to clean the floor and getting it dry.

And now breakfast is to be served at some time or another. How am I going to prevent another blunder?

After I have dressed myself, I set off to the kitchen. I encounter only Cornelia there while she's brewing coffee for the rest of the house.

Me: "Dear Fräulein (Miss) von Czapiewski, I hereby offer my sincere apologies for last night's accident. I should have been more careful."

"Oh, Stefan, such things do happen. I was angry at that moment, but no permenent damage was caused except for my dignity that was somewhat bruised. But I've slept it away and I forgive you. My dress can be washed again and then we rinse away the damage."

"Thank you so much!"

"All right, here's your coffee. I don't know if you need strong black coffee after last night's Sekt, but drink it this way anyway."

"I didn't drink any Sekt last night because I messed up your dress with the contents of my glass."

"Anyway, here's your coffee."

When I accept my mug of black coffee, she disappears into the house to take the other people's coffee to them.

I realise, I have to try to somehow repair the mess I've caused. During breakfast, I quietly ask Franz: "When does your mother have her birthday?"

"On the twenty-fourth of February. Why?"

"Oh, I just wanted to know."

When I get home again shorly before lunch, Tante Stockhausen immediately wants to know how the festivities have turned out. I tell her about the two blunders I've committed.

"Stefan, that's nothing, really. When my Wilhelm and I started dating, I forgot his mother's first name. And then I called her 'Tante Rosine' instead of 'Tante Rosalie.'"

"She surely didn't like being called a raisin, did she?"

"Definitely not. Can I give you some more peas?"

Bremen, Wednesday, 21 February 1934

Directly after the lecture on oceanography has ended, Herr Direktor von Czapiewski addresses me: "Stefan, it's my spouse's birthday on Saturday. We are inviting a few family members. You are also welcome. Be there at six o'clock. Can you come?"

I mumble a thank you and promise to come.

When I leave the classroom, electric lights started flashing and blitzing everywhere around me. What an opportunity! This is a promise that I certainly will keep. I often wondered how I could present a fitting birthday gift to Frau von Czapiewski. With Tante Stockhausen's help, I have already bought a set of six champagne glasses as a birthday present. Now I can go and hand them to her personally on her birthday and apologise again for breaking two of her glasses with Silvester. And, of course, this will be another opportunity of seeing Cornelia!

Bremen, Saturday, 24 February, 1934

I show up early at Frau Nicoletta von Czapiewski's birthday dinner. To my disappointment, it's Franz who opens the front door — and not Cornelia. At least he's happy to see me again. Frau von Czapiewski approaches and I kiss her hand quite gallantly before presenting her with the gift.

"Stefan, it's not necessary to be so formal! I'm not a duchess or a princess! However, thank you very much for your gift. What is it?"

She opens the parcel and cries out: "This is really not necessary! But, thank you anyway!"

"Gnädige Frau, I was really disturbed by what happened on Silvester. At least I have to compensate you in a way."

During the dinner I am seated next to her elderly father, Nikolaus Freiherr (Baron) von Nimwegen. So there's no chance of being able to talk to Cornelia and I can only admire her on the opposite side of the table – except when she and Johannes sometimes get up and play waiter and waitress.

Grandpa von Nimwegen is quite sociable and tells me he was an "Oberst" (colonel) during the Great War. He fought against the Russians under Field Marshal Paul von Hindenburg and General Friedrich von Scholtz as an artillery officer. At the Battle of Tannenberg, his regiment decimated thousands of Russian soldiers. When peace was concluded with Russia in 1917, his regiment had to go and help against the French.

"Your grandfather was also a man of war, am I right?"

I persevere with my white lie again (while feeling guilty): "He was a company chief in South West against the Hereros and the Namas. However, he retired in 1899 and he did not participate in the Great War."

"And what do you think of our new chancellor, Herr Hitler?"

"I don't actually follow German politics. But I hear good things about him. Unemployment has dropped and people are looking towards the future again. He surely deserves a chance to get things straight and let the country find its self-respect again."

Bremen, Friday, 15 June 1934

It is my firm intention not to disappoint the Herr Direktor today. I am writing the oceanography paper this morning, the subject he lectured upon. He encouraged me not to disgrace him by failing and so I made an extra effort with this subject.

During the semester I repeatedly told Tante Stockhausen what we learned in class and what I read up in my books. She could tell interesting anecdotes about how her late Wilhelm had roamed most oceans of the globe.

Just as I hand in my answer script, the Herr Direktor approaches me: "Stefan, you're obviously going to sail with us again next week."

"Thank you so much, Herr Direktor. When must I report to the Nicoletta?"

"Come Monday afternoon just before dinner. Then we all sleep in the Nicoletta and sail out early the next morning."

"If I may ask, where are we going?"

"Holland, France and England."

"Fortunately, I can speak a little Dutch and I also had English at school."

"Excellent. You're going to be our interpreter in Holland."

Bremen, Monday, 18 June 1934

Tante Stockhausen helped me to be well prepared for my holiday by having a look at my clothes. Lost buttons on shirts and trousers were sewed on, socks with holes were mended and she made sure that I buy a good raincoat. I also had to buy two new shirts.

It's still rather early when I arrive at the Vegesack harbor and I hope that I'm the first one to reach the Nicoletta. However, I find the Herr Direktor and Johannes already there. The Herr Direktor oversees the filling of the fuel tank for the diesel engine and taking on fresh water for human consumption. Johannes carries a bunch of parcels, which he takes from from their car and a trailer. I start to help him with this task immediately after I have greeted him. It's mainly groceries, food and personal luggage that we load into the boat.

When I get aboard with a box in my arms, I greet the Herr Direktor. He replies immediately: "Yes, good day. Stefan, it's your job to watch the boat untill Johannes and I return. We all will return with the bus later. Because you're staying here, I don't have to lock up everything again."

The loading and tanking last for about another hour. I promise to get everything in their proper places in the meantime, because by now I know the boat quite well.

The von Czapiewski family appears in the course of the afternoon. I greet the two female members of the family with an embrace and little Franz with a solid handshake. I don't greet the Herr Direktor and Johannes again because we've already seen each other earlier.

When dinner time arrives, Frau Nicoletta von Czapiewki produces a basket with food. There is ham, cold chicken, bread rolls and fruit. A bottle of white wine is also produced and I promise myself that I am going to keep my mouth closely shut after swallowing a glass of wine. I don't want to make a fool of myself again — especially not in front of the fair Cornelia.

My good intentions, unfortunately, evaporate swiftly because the von Czapiewski family decide to greet the setting sun with a bunch of seaman's songs as we all sit on the deck. The result is that I am forced to open my mouth and sing along.

It happens that I get to sit next to Cornelia. Her proximity, the setting sun on the water and the wine makes me feel exhilliarated — as if all the batteries in my body are fully charged, the electric currents are swirling through me, keeping all the lights burning.

I've been in Bremen for almost a year-and-a-half now and I decide that I like the place a lot. I have almost forgotten to long for Walvis Bay and Swakopmund. Suddenly I feel guilty because I forgot to write home last night. I'll just send postcards from all the ports where we dock.

Bremen, Tuesday, 19 June 1934

Althoughe we went to bed early, we only wake up at breakfast time this morning. It is almost the longest day of the year and the sun has been hanging two hand breadths above the horizon since it roze at five-o-clock.

We loosen the mooring ropes and drift off with the current on the Weser, towards the sea. A light wind grips the sails and it gives us a little more momentum.

The Herr Direktor steers the boat during this shift and little Franz has to relieve him this afternoon. My watch is from midnight onwards – the graveyard shift.

While the others are busy elsewhere, Cornelia and I sit on the deck near the stern. We babble about everything and anything. She tells me about her schoolwork and I discuss my studies. Suddenly, Herr von Czapiewski turns around where he is at the helm and says:

"Stefan, I almost forgot. I've already marked all the papers after the exam in oceanography on Friday afternoon and evening. Yours as well."

He remains silent for a few moments and the tension suddenly builds up within me. Is he afraid to tell me that I did badly?

"Stefan, come and stand here (and he points to a spot on the deck next to him and I do so). I want to shake your hand. You were the best in class. But I'm disappointed in you. I expected you to have gotten one hundred percent, but that didn't happen, unfortunately. But ninety-five percent isn't too rotten either."

Cornelia jumps forwards and gives me a hug. I'm suddenly dumb, speechless, without words. There has to be some blown fuses in my brain in the part that controls my vocal cords.

Bremen, Wednesday, 25 July 1934

We've returned to Vegesack this morning. After that, it took quite a bit of time to get everything ready so that the boat could be left safely behind. The Herr Direktor and his wife and two sons went towards the city with the bus to fetch their car with the trailer. Cornelia announced that she wanted to help me watch over the boat in the meantime, until the last pieces of remaining groceries and luggage can be taken back.

Five minutes after the others have left, the most beautiful girl in all of Bremen asks me to sit down with her on the lock-up trunks for the tackles on the deck at the bow end. It's as if an electric shock is being administered upon my heart, because he suddenly starts bouncing and dancing faster under my rib cage. I even feel afraid he's going to jump out from under my ribs. Therefore, I sit down, about two meters from my dream girl.

She holds her arms folded in front of her chest: "Stefan, I want to chat to you. It took a lot of persuasion to convince my father and mother that I could stay behind here with you. My excuse was that I still had to clean up and dust everything for the last time and wash the floor of the Kombüse. But actually, I wanted to be alone with you. And now I want to know: what are your intentions with me?"

I am totally taken by surprise. What can I answer? Can I even dare to tell this woman how I really feel about her? Isn't it going to frighten her off when I reveal to her the deepest secrets of my heart?

Luckily, I manage to ask her after frowning fiercely: "Why are you asking me this?"

"Because I want to know."

"Why?"

"Look here, your stupid man, it's me asking the questions. Stop eluding me by asking questions yourself. I want a straight answer. What are your intentions with me?"

I swallow a few times and at last I manage to speak: "My intentions with you are absolutely honorable. I have no wish to ever harm you."

"Is that all?"

"What else can I say?"

She stays quiet and watches me with a smile that hovers around her beautiful mouth corners. After a while, she goes on: "There's still a lot you can add. For example: why do you stare at me so much when you think I don't notice it?"

I shrug a little bit because I thought she would not notice it. I manage to say after a few sobs: "You are the most beautiful woman any man can dream about. You are the pinacle of the female species. If I were a painter, I would already have made a dozen paintings of you. Unfortunately, I can only make engineering drawings."

"And what more?" She sounds very resolute and I hesitate and tremble a little bit.

"I will fight for you if any person wants to hurt you."

She stays quiet again as she looks straight at me. After ten long seconds, she asks, "What next?"

I feel distressed: "Why do you nag so much? Haven't I said enough?"

"No."

I keep quiet and view this goddess staring at me with a playful smile around her pretty mouth.

She speaks again: "Stefan, everyone could see that you are madly in love with me. Head over heels. You constantly watch me with those idiotic glances. Am I correct?"

I can't help it and I have to concede: "Yes, actually you're right."

"Now, yes, what are you going to do about it?"

"Keep hoping and praying."

She laughs slightly: "What are you hoping for and what are you praying for?"

I feel trapped in a corner and I feel I have to be honest with her: "That you're not going to disappear from my life."

"Is that all?"

I plead in distress: "Isn't all that enough?"

It seems as if fiery sparks are shooting from her eyes: "No. Do you have any plans with me? Answer me!"

I think rapidly. "You're still too young. You only turn seventeen later this year. You're still in school. I dare not make any plans at this stage."

"What's going to happen when I finish school one day and turn eighteen?"

"I can only hope that at that time you don't get tired of me and chase me away. Or that you get interested in another young man."

"How are you going to react if something like that happens?"

My soul feels as if has been beaten with a hammer and electric sparks. I feel tormented while she tortures me with her questions and messes with my feelings. At last I succeed in answering her after I have taken some time to think: "I'll tell myself that I'm surely not good enough for you and then I will just continue with my sorry, sick, sad existence. Maybe I will hop onto the first available ship and sail to Alaska. Or Brazil. Or maybe China..."

"Do you think I'll ever chase you away?"

"How in the name of the devil am I to know? Females are sometimes capricious creatures!"

"Stefan, now I have to be honest with you. I'll never chase you away. I hope and pray a lot, too."

I'm pleasantly surprised and ask: "Yes?"

"That you're not going to meet another woman and forget about me."

"The odds for that are exactly zero comma zero."

"How do I know?"

"I have been worshipping you since I first saw you when we sailed out with this boat last year. An ancient Greek sculpturer would have used you as his model to make an image of a goddess. That's why I worship you."

"That's pagan. We're Christians, remember."

"Well, I'll put it differently: if I cannot worship you... then I will anyway worship you. I dream of you. I think about you every day. I fantasize about you. If I can't get you, I won't feel like living anymore and I will just get lost in the wide, wild world and become a pirate."

"Stefan Strauss, stop being so ridiculous. Stop this nonsense."

"I can't help it. You pulled it out of me and squeezed me into a corner. It was like you tortured me with an electric blow torch. I simply had to admit that my whole heart belongs to you — if you want it."

The tears start to drip over my cheeks and I shake as I sob.

The love of my life comes to sit next to me and puts her arm around my shoulders: "I like those tears. They tell me you're deadly honest with me. That's all I wanted to know."

I sniff. She pulls out a female handkerchief, a little bigger than a postage stamp, and dries my tears. I feel relieved that I was able to blurt out the truth.

"There, my treasure. I'm just a young girl, but I have the heart of a woman. A woman who recognizes love when she sees it. And this woman (and she's pressing with her index finger against her throat) also knows what it's like to respond to love."

I get hold of her and we remain sitting for a long time as we stay silent. The moment is so overwhelming that I cannot talk anymore. My whole consciousness is filled with the feeling of a warm soft body pressed tightly against mine — something I've been longing for.

After a quarter of an hour, she gets up and announces: "We still have a little bit of coffee in the galley. I'm going to brew some for us."

When she comes back with the coffee, I have my tears under control again. She carries on: "Stefan, I want you to come and visit me. I'm sure my parents will allow it. Then we can see each other regularly and then we don't have to long so much for each other. And then we see what happens when I finish school some time. Is that all right with you?"

"Of course. I can perhaps visit you every Saturday afternoon and maybe we can do things together."

When I stumble into Tante Stockhausen's apartment during the late afternoon, the tears run over my cheeks again. Fortunately, the Tante isn't home now — surely busy shopping or having a "Kaffeeklatsch" (cozy coffee drinking) with one of her friends. I wouldn't have been able to stand it if she saw me in this condition. It's tears of heartache, but also of happiness.

Bremen, Thursday, 26 July 1934

At breakfast, Tante Stockhausen wants to learn all about my holiday. It's easy to tell all about my experiences – except for what happened between me and Cornelia yesterday. It is still too personal that I can talk about it and I first have to process the whole event in my mind and think carefully how to approach the new situation. Fortunately, I am calm enough now to share the news about the holidays with her.

Therefore, I tell her that when we've reached the North Sea we turned westwards. Our first stop was the city of Emden on the border with Holland. Then we saw Texel in the Netherlands and I had to act as interpreter with my knowledge of Dutch, although the people around there all understood German. Texel is an island in the North Sea and is also a base of the "Koninklijke Marine", the Royal Dutch Navy. I, the Herr Direktor and his two sons were very interested in the Dutch warships, especially the two submarines that lay there.

Tante Stockhausen: "They're obviously submarines designed and built by German engineers, although this was done at a Dutch shipyard,"

"Exactly."

I tell her that our next port was Ijmuiden. This is where ships moving to Amsterdam's harbor enter the interior of the country through a canal. We docked there and drove to Amsterdam by bus and went to explore the place. A miracle happened when I bumped into my old friend, Gerrit Scholtz, who had travelled with me on the Usambara to Europe last year. We happened to see each other on the street. He was very interested in my doings and actions and in my friends. It was almost strange to speak Afrikaans again. We went to drink coffee together and fortunately his German is good enough that he could chat with the Herr Direktor and his family.

Tante Stockhausen: "Such coincidences do happen. I'm sure you will encounter each other some time in future again."

I also tell her that we skipped Belgium and sailed directly to Calais on the French coast. It is a port city where one can take a ferry to England. Hence we went to Le Havre, an important French naval base where we viewed the French battleships, cruisers and destroyers. The Herr Direktor assured us that there are plans for Germany to build such ships again. He ought to know. After all, he's Direktor of the Schifffahrtschule.

Tante Stockhausen: "My Wilhelm also performed service on large ships in the Great War. It's high time we get these types of ships again."

My story continues and I mention that from there we crossed the Channel to view three UK ports. We first went to Southampton, the busiest commercial harbor. Directly after that, we sailed up to Portsmouth. It's one of the Royal Navy's most important bases and we also saw some of their great ships — also an aircraft carrier. Then we visited Harwich – a less important naval station.

Tante Stockhausen: "That's also something we need to get – aircraft carriers. A single aircraft taking off from an aircraft carrier can drop a torpedo that causes a battleship or a cruiser to disappear under the waves. Where else were you?"

I relate how we sailed back to Holland. We went to Rotterdam where the Fijenoord Shipyard is and that's where the submarines are being built that we sell to other countries. That technology will soon be used here in Kiel and elsewhere to manufacture our own U-Boats.

Tante Stockhausen: "That's what I've been telling you for a long time. And now you've seen it with your own eyes! The firm that builds the submarines is called 'N.V. Ingenieurskantoor voor Scheepsbouw' and the head office is in The Hague. "

I tell her that our last stop was Den Helder. It is also a base of the Dutch Navy. The Dutch are an old seafaring nation that, with their ships, built up a vast trade empire. Even Çsar Peter the Great of Russia came to see how the Dutch built their ships.

Tante Stockhausen: "It seems to me as if it wasn't actually a holiday in the first place, but an espionage cruise. You've actually went to see what the enemy is doing. Am I correct?"

"If you want to see it that way."

"Do you now consider yourself to be a seasoned seafarer?"

"I'm now more than halfway done with my course. Hopefully I will get my diploma next year this time and then I have to make plans about my future. But I think I'm a good seafarer now. The Herr Direktor has a schooner — a sailboat with two masts. I now know how to handle her and I feel very much at home on her."

Bremen, Saturday, 28 July 1934

While I ring the bell at the front door of the Herr Direktor's home on this Saturday afternoon, I suddenly feel the urge to run away. On my way here I repeated my prepared speech to myself but now I suddenly feel afraid. It is as if I cannot get any breath. What wil happen if the Herr Direktor and his wife chase me away or regard me as a being far below their social class and, therefore, not good enough for their daughter?

It is too late. I cannot retreat because somebody opens the door. It's Johannes. He is quite surprised to see me but he, nevertheless, invites me in.

I ask: "Is it perhaps possible that I may speak to the Herr Direktor?"

Johannes: "About what? Do you consider terminating your course?"

"No, man. It's something else."

"Oekee. Please get a seat here inside. I will call my father."

The Herr Direktor enters three long minutes later. While I was waiting I sat on the edge of the chair, ready to flee should it become necessary, drops of sweat glide down my spine again.

"Ah, Stefan! It's nice to see you on this Saturday. Do you want to discuss the next semester's work with me? It will be a busy semester. Are you ready for the course on diesel engines, part one? Are you able to go on with nautical architecture and steering mechanisms? I believe that you will be able to perform well if I take your current record into consideration."

I swallow – and swallow again: "Herr Direktor, I actually want to discuss something else." My voice suddenly sounds strange to me – almost as if it isn't me who is talking.

"Well, what is it? Please don't tell me that you want to drop out of the course? That will be extremely sad because you are a very promising student. I am confident that you will end the coming semester between the top three – that is, if you're not the best."

"No, Herr Direktor. I am eager to continue with my course and I look forward to the next semester." My voice again sounds strange. It might be because my throat suddenly became bone dry.

"Well, what is it? You know that you are already almost a member of our family. You may discuss anything with me."

I suffocate. I suffer. I sweat. I almost start shedding tears.

"Stefan, what is the matter? I can see that you are extremely agitated. Are you perhaps ill?"

I manage to stutter: "No, Herrrr … Direktor. I… I am not ill." I stay silent for a few seconds while I seek the right words: "Herr Direktor, actually I want… to… to ask a great favor."

"You may ask me anythong if it deals with your studies. You certainly do know that."

"It's actuall something per… personal. Something very… very… important to me."

"Yes?"

I look around me. I look down at my shoes. I look up at the lamp hanging from the ceiling.

"Come on, man! You make me extremely nervous if you stutter and suffer and swallow like that. Please, make your point!"

The words erupt from my mouth: "Herr Direktor, may I come and visit Cornelia occasionally?"

"Ooooh, that is what you wanted to ask. I see… Is there anything brewing between you and my daughter of which I have to know?"

I lick my lips. I sniff. I am on the verge of tears. What will happen if Cornelia's father forbids me to visit her? That's something that I will never be able to survive.

"Herr Direktor, we are… we are good friends. We enjoy… enjoy… each other's company. I promise that I will behave myself very, very well. But I… I would like to get to know her a little better."

"You stay seated, just there. I want to call my wife."

While I sit and wait it is as if small elecric motor is switched on in my stomach and it causes my stomach to turn and churn and crunch anti-clockwise.

Frau Nicoletta von Czapiewski enters the living room five long minutes later with her husband. I stand up in her presence as my parents have taught me and I only sit down again after she has taken a seat.. She doesn't even greet me and promptly asks: "Stefan, do I understand you correctly? Do you want to come and visit Cornelia from time to time?"

"Yes… hmm, yes, Gnädige Frau."

Cornelia's mother: "Our daughter is only sixteen. She has to complete two more years at school. You are already an adult man of twenty-two. Don't you think that the age gap is a bit too much? You differ six years. And how does Cornelia feel about this?"

"It was her… her idea that I come here to ask… ask your permission."

The Herr Direktor: "I will call her presently to hear what she can tell us herself. But in the meantime I want to tell you something of our family history so that you can understand that my daughter occupies a special place in my heart. Yes, very special."

Frau von Czapiewski: "It was an extremely difficult time when she arrived and it is actually a miracle of the dear 'Herrgott' (the Lord God) that our family survived everything. Joachim, you do the talking."

"All right. Stefan, I have already mentioned to you that I was an officer in the Kaiserliche Marine during the Great War. Directly after I have obtained my diploma at the Seefahrtschule in 1908 I joined the Navy. I completed the officers' training course in record time and at the beginning of 1913 I was a Leutnant zur See on a battleship. I was promoted to Oberleutnant zur See in 1915. In 1916 I took part in the Battle of the Skagerrak, of which I told you last year when we sailed over that area.

"Although we sank more ships than the British sank of ours, our fleet was crippled thereafter. The admirals were too afraid to venture out again, fearing that we would loose too many more ships. Our remaining battleships and cruisers, therefore, lay in the ports of Wilhelmshaven and Kiel and collected rust. I got married in that time to my Nicoletta and Johannes was born in 1917.

"In the meantime, a number of our frustrated officers and seamen applied for transfers to our fleet of submarines because that was the only department of the Navy where things were happening. After a course of six months I was promoted to 'Kapitänleutnant' (naval Lieutenant) and given command of a U-boat. The middle of 1917 was a wonderful time for us submariners. We sank hundreds and hundreds of British and American ships. Litteraly hundreds of them. Britain was on the verge of starvation because they could not import enough food from their colonies.

"But, during middle 1918 it became clear that Germany was losing the war. We submariners became very downhearted. We lost more submarines than could be replaced by new ones. The tactics of the Allies to neutralise us became more and more effective. Look there against the wall. There's a photo of my U-boat."

I look at the picture because I am interested in all types of ships and boats.

"On 11 Bovember 1918, when an armistace was agreed upon, all the submarines were ordered to surrender at the English submarine base of Harwich, which we recently visited. I was under water at the time when this radio message was sent and I could not initially receive it. At that precise moment I was engaged in helping a British torpedo boat to disappear beneath the waves. I was actually technically breaching the armistice agreement.

"After we had reached the surface we received the news that we had to surrender. I held a meeting with my men and we all agreed that we don't want to donate our submarine to the British – especially not after we disposed of this torpedo boat after the armistice was signed. We sailed in the direction of Wilhelmshaven and scuttled the U-boat two nautical miles from the coast. At night. We rowed in our lifeboats to the coast in the dark and from there we all disappeared into all directions.

"Cornelia was born in the meantime on 2 September – just before I departed on my last patrol. I wanted to reach my family at all costs. After I and my crew had landed surreptitiously we learnt that the crews of the battleships and cruisers in Wilhelmshaven started a strike. The high command of the Navy wanted to see what could perhaps be done to a hopeless situation and they ordered a last battle against the British. The seamen, though, went on a strike. Many were arrested but that left the ships without crews and they could, accordingly, not put to sea.

"And then the crews of the ships in Kiel also struck. Within a short period of time the whole country was in a state of uproar. The Kaiser abdicated and fled to Holland. A republic was hastily established and fights broke out between the Communists and their opponents. Nicoletta and I decided it was too dangerous to stay in Wilhelmshaven and I stole a yacht in the harbor at Vegesack. It was little more than a derelict and I suspected that her owner must have been deceased at that time – perhaps ending his life at sea.

"With that yacht I, my wife and our two infants fled to Norway. We procured provisions across the Dutch border at Delfzijl and sailed from there to Bergen in Norway. The Norwegians were very sympathetic and gave us refuge. I was appointed as an officer on a freighter and I sailed for the next four years between Bergen and America. In he meantime, my family stayed in Bergen. We all learnt to speak Norwegian.

"Stefan, you must understand: Cornelia is very special to us. To flee with a baby of two months old is certainly not a joke. Fortunately, we survived without a scratch.

"And now I want to call Cornelia herself so that she can tell us how she feels about your request."

Exactly at that moment Cornelia appears: "It's oekee. I've heard everything that you have discussed. Vati (Daddy), do you want to know how I feel about Stefan?"

The Herr Direktor and his wife look somewhat perplexed that their daughter overheard us, but her father says nevertheless: "My daughter, all right, tell us how you feel. Is it acceptable for this young man to pay you visits? Is he in any way welcome?"

Cornelia comes to my side and places her hand on my shoulder: "Vati, the two of us are special friends. I've invited him to come and visit me. Provided that Vati and Mutti are satisfied with that."

Frau Nicoletta von Czapiewski: "Joachim, in that case, we certainly don't really have a choice. What do you think?"

The Herr Direktor: "Granted. Stefan, you may come for a visit on a Saturday afternoon. Untill six o' clock. Both of you are to sit here in the living room on different chairs. Your studies may not suffer due to your friendship and, therefore, I only allow visits on a Saturday after lunch."

Cornelia: "Vati, it is still vacation."

The Herr Direktor: "All right, during the vacation you may also see each other on a Sunday. Stefan, on a Sunday morning during the vacation you attend church together with us and you enjoy lunch with us. Please note: that is only during the holidays. You are truly almost a member of our family and, therefore, you are always welcome in our home. But you are not to enter a single step with your feet into Cornelia's bedroom. Neither the rest of your body. Verstanden (do you understand)?"

I venture for the first time in a considerable period to open my mouth again: "Herr Direktor, Frau von Czapieswki, does this arrangement come into effect tomorrow?"

Cornelia: "Yes, you fool. Didn't you listen to what Vati said? You may also stay here till six o' clock tonight. Today is Saturday."

Me: "I have already arranged with Tante Stockhausen, the lady who lodges me, to accompany her to church tomorrow. But I think she will understand if I explain that the Herr Direktor has invited me to attend church together with his family and to enjoy lunch with them."

The Herr Direktor and his wife leave their seats and he announces: "All right, it is Saturday afternoon now. Stefan, you have our permission to see Cornelia. But then only under the conditions we have stipulated."

Cornelia takes a seat on the chair next to mine after her parents have left the living room and she takes my hand.

"Vati did't forbid us to hold hands."

"You ought to feel ashamed that you spied on us. That cannot be good manners, don't you agree?"

"Johannes told me that you are here. I knew immediately why you came. It, therefore, involved me. And I have the right to know what was being said about me."

"I have experienced two extremely difficult converstations within three days. Fortunately, I have survived both."

"I felt sorry for you when you struggled so much. But I understand that you were very afraid that my father would forbid you to see me. I would not have allowed that, in any case."

"Thanks."

"Now, Herr Strauss, what are we going to discuss untill you have to leave at six?"

Bremen, Friday, 1 September 1934

During breakfast I ask Tante Stockhausen: "Could you please help me to find a suitable present for the Herr Direktor's daughter for her birthday?"

"Young man, why do you go so often to the home of the Herr Direktor? I there something I have to know about?"

"Yes. The Fräulein von Czapiewski has her birthday the day after tomorrow. She becomes seventeen then."

"How does she look? Plump? Or as slender as a lamp pole? Red hair? Skewed teeth? Freckles? How is her figure? Like a flat wooden board with two peas?"

"No, not one of those describes her. She has light brown hair and brown eyes. In addition, she looks like a young Greek goddess. She has much more than two peas in front."

"And you cannot keep your two front paws off her?"

"I am only allowed to hold her hand."

"Aha! I see, I see. Then we must look for a gift that is fitting for a minor goddess. Must it have a pagan theme?"

"No, her folks are good Christian people. I am supposed to accompany them to church tomorrow and afterwards I stay there the rest of the day."

"I know what you have to give her. Because she is a young goddess it is necessary that her beautiful face must appear on a beautiful photograph. We have to find a nice portait frame no later than this morning. And then you hire a photographer who is to visit her this afternoon together with you and he takes her portrait. He must develop it straightaway this afternoon and then you present it to her on Sunday. And you keep a copy of the same photo in your Bible."

"Dear Tante! That is a piece of inspiration that came from heaven. It almost seemed as if an angel perched onto your shoulder and whispered this wonderful plan into your ear."

1 September 1934

"Gmff! I can think for myself. I don't need little angels to do my thinking for me."

Bremen, Monday, 31 December 1934

Yesterday and the day before yesterday were a Sunday and a Saturday and I really enjoyed my visits to Cornelia on both days. And today, Monday, it is Silvester and I am again visiting the family von Czapiewski and we are gathered around the dining room table for dinner. There are a few male and female cousins, including Luise who felt less than friendly towards me a few months ago because I mentioned to her that her name, when pronounced in Afrikaans, referred to unpleasant insects. She has forgiven me in the meantime.

Everybody is celebrating because it seems that Germany is rapidly becoming a prosperous country. This is being ascribed to the resolute leadership of Adolf Hitler, although not everybody shares his hatred towards the Jews.

The best of all is that I may sleep over and continue my visit tomorrow a while. By this time, it is taken for granted that Cornelia and I belong together. Her father gave me permission to address him as "Onkel Achim" because I have become part of the family for all practical purposes. I address Cornelia's mother as "Tante Nicoletta".

During breakfast this morning, Tante Stockhausen wished me all success with my romance. She is just as excited as I am regarding Cornelia – especially after I have shown her the portrait of Cornelia.

I look at Cornelia's portrait where it has a place of honor against the wall of the dining room. She liked the idea of her portrait being taken and the protrait was placed in a nice frame. The photographer took six beautiful photgraphs of her and the best one was enlarged to be placed in that frame.

I also feel quite satisfied about my other circumstances. My marks at the end of last semester were very good and I was acclaimed as the best student in our class.

After dinner, we clear the table and Cornelia and I wash the dishes – she washes and I operate the drying cloth. The others shift the furniture in the dining room to one side to provide space for the dancing. Cornelia promised me that I may dance at least every second dance with her. Her Dad, Johannes, Franz and her two male cousins also deserve their chances with her – but I am first choice.

At the stroke of midnight we fill our glasses with Sekt and I am careful not to break any glasses again. Cornelia and I use the opportunity to drink our own toast on the year that awaits both of us – a year in which I am to complete my studies after I have done courses in diesel machines II, signals, logistics and gained two months' practical experience on a freighter.

Wilhelmshaven, Friday, 29 March 1935

We don't have any lectures today because the students of the Seefahrtschule, together with the instructors, occupy four busses – on our way to the "Kriegsmarinewerft" (Naval Yard) at Wilhelmshaven, sixty kilometers north of Bremen. Today, we are going to be witnesses of the resurrection of Germany's proud maritime tradition.

We are made to feel very welcome by the commander of the naval yard, "Kapitän zur See" (navy Captain) Eberhard Ehrenschneider. He addresses us:

"Welcome here, meine Herren! We are going to show you the biggest engineering feat of the Third German Reich. This is the result of the fact that we are executing our Führer's plans to strengthen our armed forces considerably. The Reichswehr, as you surely know, is now the Wehrmacht. The Reichsmarine is now called the Kriegsmarine."

"The huge engineering feat that I referred to is the building of the hyper-modern battleship, the Scharnhorst. We are taking you shortly to the place where she is being built.

"We also build a number of lesser men of war – destroyers, torpedo boats, mine sweepers and so forth. We will also start with U-boats one of these days.

"I want to disclose a minor military secret to you. The steel we are using to build these ships was secretly bought from the British at a great discount. At the end of the Great War, our battle fleet was ordered to surrender at Scapa Flow, the naval base in the Orkneys. Before the Brits could take possession of our ships, their crews scuttled their ships. The Brits didn't like all those wrecks lying around and started to dismantle them. And then we helped them to get rid of those wrecks by buying up all the steel they salavaged. Of course, they didn't know at the time that we Germans were the actual purchasers. We used dummy corporations in Holland, Sweden and Russia to negotiate the sale of the steel. The Brits were only too glad to get rid of the wrecks in this manner.

"After you have had the opportunity to see how the Scharnhorst is progressing on dry land, we invite you to come and enjoy some refreshments."

This outing is of great importance to me. I have ridden my bicycle more than once to Wilhelmshaven, but I have never seen such a big project as this because it was taking place at a spot where the public was not allowed. When I go to visit Cornelia tomorrow again I will have much to discuss with her father.

Bremen, Wednesday, 3 April 1935

Our class today receives a visit of a recruiting officer of the Kriegsmarine, "Korvettenkapitän" (Lieutenant Commander) Gerd Gärtenbach. This takes place during the time in which we were supposed to have had a lecture on logistics.

The gentleman explains that we as future marine engineers are exactly the people whose services are sought by the Kriegsmarine. At the moment, a large number of ships are being built of which the engines need to be maintained and repaired and that guarantees a career for each one of us – provided we complete our course and receive our diplomas. We have, though, also acquired enough knowledge about seafaring in general to be deployed as deck officers and we can easily be promoted to become captains of U-boats, fast patrol boats and mine sweepers or officers on a battleship, a cruiser, an armoured ship or a supply ship. There are, likewise, many positions available on land at various headquarters, navy yards, harbor protection units, coastal artillery units, store depots and transport units. He has been informed that we are at this very moment busy with a course in logistics and that may come in handy when store depots and transport units have to be managed.

We need not decide immediately. He distributes pamphlets with more particulars. Each one of us also receives an application form that we can complete if we wish to be admitted to a training course for officers.

I find this offer an overpowering temptation – this will immediately ensure my career at sea. It will also mean that I won't have to say good-bye to Cornelia. She still has to spend more than a year at school and I cannot take her prematurely away from here.

On the other hand – my parents and Onkel Helmut have invested much money in my studies with the idea that I apply my knowledge and skills at home. I grapple, therefore, with a dilemma, a bloody fat and obese and weighty dilemma.

Bremen, Friday, 5 April 1935

It is Friday afternoon and I am supposed to be busy in the workship with a diesel engine. I have, though, requested leave of absense from my instructor and I am on my way to the "Marineintendantur" (office of the naval intendant) of the Kriegsmarine in Bremen. In my hand I hold the application form to be admitted to a training course as an officer in the Kriegsmarine, together with a copy of my up-to-date academic record. I completed the form last night with the enthusiastic help of Tante Stockhausen.

The Tante remarked: "Stefan, I know that you are supposed to return to your Heimat after the completion of your studies in order to run your father's fleet later on. But you also told me more than once that there is no room for you and your brother at this moment. Tell me again, how old is your father?"

"Fifty-four."

"There you have it! He'll think of retirement at the earliest in ten years' time. And in the meantime you have to find work somewhere else, just as your brother. Where is there a better spot to obtain very valuable experience than with the Kriegsmarine? Must I bake you another pancake? With apple slices? I still have some dough and I cannot keep it."

"Please."

"If my Wilhelm was still alive, he would surely have encouraged you to join. By the way, does the form require you state what your 'Staatsangehörigkeit' (citizenship) is?"

"No."

"Place of birth?"

"Yes."

"Then you simply write 'Swakopmund' without mentioning where it is. It will certainly never dawn upon the idiots in government service to find out where Swakopmund is. It sounds German enough, in any case."

"Right."

And now I am on my way to hand in the completed application form. I know that Onkel Achim and Cornelia will support me with this giant step I'm taking.

At the reception desk I show my application form and I enquire where I have to hand it in. I am directed to the office of Korvettenkapitän Gärtenbach – the guy who addressed our class the day before yesterday. When I arrive at his office I find two of my class mates who are already waiting in the passage outside the office.

While I am waiting I wonder more than once whether I am doing the right thing. Won't I, perhaps, disappoint my father and Onkel Helmut? How will they react if I inform them on Sunday night in my weekly letter about the step I have taken? Will they feel that I have abandoned them?

But, on the other hand, I cannot imagine myself leaving Cornelia behind. If I don't find employment somewhere in Germany and I go back to Walvis Bay or somewhere else in that part of the world it will be impossible for her to remain part of my life. While I am awaiting my turn to have an interview with the recruiting officer I get yet another vision of Cornelia's beautiful face. That settles it – I just have to join the Kriegsmarine. There is absolutely no other option.

When my turn comes at half-past-three, I am required to sit in a chair opposite the German officer behind his desk. He peruses my application form in silence and occasionally makes a mark with his pencil at a certain spot.

He suddenly lifts his head: "Why do you want follow a career as officer in the Kriegsmarine? It is not clear enough to me from your application."

"I love the sea and ships. I more or less grew up on my father's fleet of 'Fischkutter' (fishing trawlers)."

"Did your esteemed father fight at sea during the Great War?"

" In a certain sense, yes."

"Yes?"

"He and his brother-in-law, who is co-owner of the fishing fleet, often took agents and saboteurs at night to points behind the enemy lines."

"And this was from that place, Swakopmund, where you were born?"

"That's correct." (I hope that he understands them to be Russian lines, not the lines of the Union troops).

"Never heard of the place. Where is it?"

"At the mouth of the Swakop River."

"Oh, I see. Which foreign languages do you speak?"

"Latin. I was taught it at school. And also English" (I stay silent about Afrikaans).

"I doubt whether you will ever encounter a battle situation where you have to fight Latin-speaking people."

"I agree. They were erradicated by our Germanic forebears."

"When was that?"

"Many centuries ago. Even before the Middle Ages."

"Oh. On which types of ships or boats have you sailed?"

"On a Fischkutter. Also a schooner and a freighter across the Atlantic Ocean. I was also a passenger on a passenger liner."

"It doesn't count to have sailed on a passenger liner, except if you've been a member of the crew. Ever been on a U-boat?"

"I saw two of them in a Durch naval base. There was one in the harbor at Le Havre. I also visited the shipyard in Rotterdam where they were being built."

"It sounds as if you regard yourself as some sort of a spy?"

"I'm only curious."

"But you wish to be trained as a U-boat officer?"

"That's correct. I have had a conversation with somebody who served as the captain of a U-boat during the Great War and that is something I also want to do."

"How do you feel about National Socialism?"

"I don't have a great interest in politics. But I do have the impression that Herr Adolf Hitler, our 'Führer' (Leader), is succeeding in getting Germany again on its feet."

"Can you certify that all your ancestors were of Aryan stock?"

"Without the slightest doubt."

"Heil Hitler!"

I stay silent at this point because I don't know how to respond, except to nod my head.

"Your application is approved. Here is your service number in the Kriegsmarine, as well as your call-up orders. From this moment onwards you are an 'Offiziersanwärter' (officer candidate). Your training starts on 10 September at the Naval School at Mürwik in Flensburg. As soon as you report there you are to be promoted to the rank of 'Seekadett'. You will receive your travelling orders in due course. Good day! Heil Hitler!"

I get up, bow in his direction and leave the office. I take a deep breath when I enter the passage outside the office and exhale slowly again. This idiot of a government official, to quote Tante Stockhausen, is under the impression that I am a born German citizen! Otherwise he would have torn up my application.

A little voice inside my head speaks up: "Stefan Strauss, you were not totally truthful. You hoodwinked that guy to believe that your father did war service and that you are a German citizen – which you are not with your South African passport."

Fortunately, tomorrow is Saturday and then I will pay Cornelia another visit. She and her parents will surely be interested to know that I have chosen a career in the Kriegsmarine. I will certainly show them my service number and call-up papers that Gärtenbach issued. I hope to be totally truthful with them.

Bremen, Saturday, 6 April 1935

It's Franz who opens the front door of the von Czapiewski residence: "My sis is still applying her make-up. You are somewhat early."

"Hallo. I will wait here in the living room in the meantime."

Onkel Achim comes in. He must have heard my voice. I immediately blurt out my service number in the Kriegsmarine: "I must report at Flensburg in a few months' time to be trained as a U-boat officer."

"How on earth did you manage that? According to law only German citizens may serve in our armed forces."

"The stupid and idiotic Korvettenkapitän with whom I had an interview yesterday did not take the trouble to find out exactly where I was born. On the application form I wrote 'Swakopmund'. He only mentioned that he had never heard of the place, but accepted that it must be somewhere along the coast of Germany."

"Exactly what is your citizenship actually?"

"I have a South African passport because my home address is in Walvis Bay. It belongs to South Africa. But I am also a native of South West Africa since I was born in Swakopmund."

"When were you born?"

"In the year of our Lord, nineteen-twelve."

"But then you were born under the German flag, after all! South West was a German colony untill 1915. Should you ever get any problems in this regard, you may always claim German citizenship on account of this."

"Ach, yes…"

The little voice inside my head gets turned on again: "Stefan Strauss, ou may feel relieved because you didn't hoodwink that guy, after all."

Cornelia glides in at that very moment, as if she is as light and graceful as a Zeppelin: "What are you two discussing so earnestly?"

Onkel Achim: "This friend of yours is going to be trained as a Kriegsmarine officer one of these days."

Cornelia: "Where?"

Me: "Flensburg."

Cornelia: "That's not too far from here. A little more than three hours per train. One changes trains at Hamburg. Then you can come here over weekends!" Her cheerful voice again sounds like an electrical dynamo on full revolutions and her lovely smile reminds me of electrical sparks flying around.

Onkel Achim: "He won't be free during weekends – only occasionally. But that is better than nothing. And then he will most probably come and stay here. Stefan, you will certainly not lodge with Frau Stockhausen any more at that time?"

Me: "How will that be possible if I sit in Flensburg?"

Cornelia: "When do you start? Will you be able to complete your studies?"

Me: "The intake is only in September. I will be able to enjoy a long, lazy holiday after my final exam."

I show them my call-up orders and my service number on paper.

Cornelia: "Vati! Are we going to sail again somewhere on the Nicoletta as soon as the holidays start?"

Onkel Achim: "Fortunately, I will be able to manage that. I start at the beginning of August at the naval base of Wilhelmhaven with my old rank of Kapitänleutnant. I have already tendered my resignation as Direktor of the Seefahrtschule. The Kriegsmarine made me an offer, which I couldn't ignore. They promised me that I would receive promotion within six months as soon as I have settled down in the Kriegsmarine. And, besides that, I plant my feet far too little on the deck of a ship. Perhaps I am offered a position on the Scharnhorst after she is launched and fitted out completely."

Cornelia: "And our summer vacation on the Nicoletta?"

Onkel Achim: "Yes, that goes ahead. Stefan, perhaps you should tell us where you would like to sail. Any thoughts from your side?"

Me: "How about the eastern coast of England and Scotland, up to the Shetland Islands?"

Cornelia: "Then I can practice my school English."

Onkel Achim: "Sounds rather acceptable. Do you realise that the Orkneys house one of the biggest British naval bases – Scapa Flow? But, first of all – Stefan, here is my hand! I congratulate you in advance with your future appointment as an officer. I am sure that you will make a great success of your career because I am well aware of your love for the sea and everything that moves on or in it. You are also a top student at the Seefahrtschule."

After Onkel Achim has shaken my hand, Cornelia gives me a hug and a kiss – clearly in sight of her father.

Cornelia: "Tonight's dinner must be a festive occasion – wine, fish, grilled chicken and everything else that goes with those."

Later, after everybody has calmed down again and I sit and chat with Cornelia on our own, she declares: "I cannot wait for the day when you arrive here with your uniform. We will go for a stroll in town so that everybody can see that I have an extraordinary boyfriend! My school friends will become green and yellow and toxic with jealousy."

Kiel, Saturday, 15 June 1935

Yesterday, I completed my last bit of academia – a paper in signals. The Herr Direktor invited our class to travel to Kiel today where we are to witness the launching of Germany's first official submarine.

For me it is a very special expedition because Cornelia is sitting next to me in the train. My class mates are rather envious of me for having such a beautiful girlfriend. On top of everything, she flirts slightly with everybody sitting with us and everybody likes her. She does that while holding my hand where we sit.

Suddenly, I feel jealous because Cornelia enjoys joking and laughing with the other guys. But, then my heart softens, because this sunshine girl makes everybody happy around her. She simply has a happy disposition and I am grateful for being part of her life. As she is becoming more mature, some previously hidden characteristics appear and I find it a very interesting journey of discovery to observe her development.

The launching of U-1 is to take place on the midday hour and the members of our class who attend the occasion arrive quite on time.

Apart from the U-boat that is the prinicpal player on the scene today, there is another important role player: Adolf Hitler, the Führer, who is to perform the launching and deliver a speech. He is being accompanied by a bunch of admirals, generals and other important folk where he marches along the naval yard. This is my first chance today to see this man in his very person.

I am part of the crowd that gives him enthusiastic applause for his fiery speech in which he promises that Germany is on the point of overcoming the humiliation of 1918. Although the Allies have forbidden any U-boats they are powerless to prevent the launching of this piece of modern weaponry. Dozens of U-boats are due to follow.

Germany's first "Unterseeboot" (submarine) after the Great War with the fitting name or number of U-1 is allowed to slide into the water with pomp and ceremony while a brass band performs marches. She is almost ready to be handed over to the Kriegsmarine and only a few finishing touches have to be concluded. Her first captain is already appointed, namely Kapitänleutnant Klaus Ewerth. He is one of those present.

She is a rather ugly craft, but it is not the idea that she should look handsome. She is supposed to stalk her prey invisibly, under the surface of the sea, and to send it to the bottom of the ocean with a torpedo.

While we are marching back to the station to catch the train to Bremen, Cornelia remarks: "One of these days you are to become the captain of such a jam tin. Are you not afraid of suffocating inside that thing?"

"Not if I take your photo along with me. It cannot be deemed to be a jam tin – it is actually a tin full of sardines. That is how the crew members live inside her, tightly packed together."

"What do your parents think about your plans to become a U-boat officer?"

"They understand and they approve."

"I am sure that you will write to them about everything that happened today?"

"Of course."

Bremen, Monday, 2 September 1935

Today, it is Cornelia's last birthday as a school girl and she turns eighteen. She looks like a mature woman – and an excellent specimen of the species, as well. The girl with braids that I met more than two years ago doesn't exist anymore. Because today is a Monday, the occasion was already celebrated yesterday with a few of her friends who arrived during the late afternoon.

Onkel Achim doesn't limit my visits to a Saterday afternoon anymore and, therefore, I am again at the von Czapiewski residence on this Monday. Tante Stockhausen helped me as usual to find a fitting present – a beautiful wrist watch.

Cornelia utters a wish: "You have told me a lot about your Tante Stockhausen. It is high time that you introduce me to her."

I, therefore, do not have a choice and we stroll over to my lodging place. Tante Stochausen is fortunately at home and she immediately presses Corneilia to her heart.

"My dear, thank you very much that you came to brighten the life of an elderly person with your presence. I recognised you immediately on account of your photo. I think I know everthing about you because Stefan kept me abreast of all your doings. It's wonderful to see you in person. I must also congratulate Stefan with his excellent taste in girls!"

Cornelia: "Don't you think that I also have excellent taste concerning men?"

"Without the slightest doubt. I know this young man almost three years now. He almost feels like an own son to me and I am very proud of him. I am very sorry to lose him one of these days as a lodger when he is to report at Flensburg. Have you already congratulated him properly with the fact that he received the prize for the best student in his class during the recent diploma ceremony?"

2 September 1935

"He received a kiss of exactly eleven minutes. I timed it with my new wrist watch."

Flensburg, Tuesday, 10 September 1935

The day before yesterday (Sunday), I evacuated my lodgings at Tante Stockhausen's home and took all my belongings to the von Czapiewski residence where everything will be stored. That will be my home address from now on.

Tante Stockhausen grabbed me around my neck with tears in her eyes: "You really feel like my own son – a son that I never had. Will you occasionally remember this old lady and write a little letter? You may also come and visit me when you get a pass and stay with that angel Cornelia."

"I promise."

The whole von Czapiewski family takes me and Johannes to the main station of Bremen to catch the train. Johannes completed his "Abitur" (matriculation) in June and he also wishes to get submarine training.

Onkel Achim says again for the last time: "The Marineschule in Flensburg is situated in the suburb of Mürwik to the north of the town centre. It lies on the coast and is a large complex. Somebody will surely meet you at the station and take you there. There, you will be provided with everything you need. Don't cause any scandals while you are there!"

Cornelia: "If you don't write every week I will be very angry."

At the station I find six of my previous class mates and we decide to sit together in the train, while I include Johannes in our group. The journey takes almost four hours and we change trains in Hamburg where the rest of the aspiring submariners join us. Flensburg is near the border with Denmark and almost next to the most northern spot in Germany.

At our arrival at the Flensburg main station we, fortunately, see a guy in a naval uniform awaiting the train. About twenty young men congregate in a circle around him – the eight of us from Bremen included.

Although the man initially stood watching us without a word, it transpires later that he is, after all, able to talk: "Listen carefully, you collection of rotten fleas on the back of a hungry dog! I am 'Oberfeldwebel' (Warrant Officer, class II) Knopp. It is my task to take you by truck to the Marineschule in Mürwik. There you will receive more instructions. Follow me. Verstanden?"

Nobody responds and the man looks disappointed, but he stays silent again. He starts marching and we follow him with our few pieces of baggage. Outside the station we find two military trucks and we get aboard, two groups of ten men in each one – without orders from Knopp. We travel through the town centre in a northerly direction and after about half-an-hour we reach an imposing red brick building complex.

While we disembark, Knopp gestures silently that we have to follow him. He takes us to a big dormitory with about twenty-four beds. Everybody rapidly annexes a bed and leaves his few possesions on it. The seven of us who came from the Seefahrtschule stay together in one group. Johannes joins us.

While we are standing around and feeling lost, Knopp suddenly appears and yells: "Here!"

He takes us to an office where two clerks are sitting behind tables and they inspect our call-up papers. A photo is taken of each one and it is pasted onto an identity document. I see on my card that I have become "Seekadett Strauss, Stefan". My rank is on the same level as that of an ordinary sailor.

From there, Knopp takes us to the quarter master's store where each one receives a complete set of uniform pieces, overalls, boots, shoes, sporting clothes and other necessities. Knopp blows on a whistle and shows everybody who has completed the process of kitting out to join a long row outside – still without uttering a word.

After the last one of us has joined the row, Knopp deems it prudent to use his vocal cords once again: "Dinner at eighteen hunderd hours. In uniform!"

One chap dares to speak up: "Herr Oberfeldwebel, where?"

"In the bloody dining hall, you stupid obscene bags of shit, guts and fluids! Or do you wish to grouse here from the fucking floor?"

Nobody dares to ask where the dining hall is. Knopp waves to us that we must return to our baracks and we start sorting our pieces of uniform and other equipment. We succeed in getting dressed in our uniforms and to lock our civilian clothes in the lockers next to our beds. A bell in the tower of the main building rings and we amble outside, searching for the dining room. Fortunately, there are other men who are following all sorts of other courses who stream directly to the dining hall. We follow them.

Flensburg, Wednesday, 11 September 1935

We are woken at six o' clock by the bell in the tower of the main building. I am disappointed to be rudely drawn from my slumbers because I was having a wonderful dream, which was interrupted. I was dreaming that I was caressing Cornelia's soft breasts – something that I have often wished to do in the past, but never had the courage to do.

We all do our best to get dressed as fast as possible – summer uniforms. We don't know what to do further and we gather in a group outside.

At half-past-six, Oberfeldwebel Knopp comes marching along and stops ten paces from us. He merely roars: "Overalls!"

We all tumble into our dormitory to get rid of our uniforms and get dressed in overalls. A few minutes later, we gather again outside, rather stressed and terrified of this Oberfeldwebel who rarely talks, but whose tongue is as sharp as the tip of a needle.

Knopp blows on his whistle and yells: "Alphabetic order!"

Chaos ensues as we try to hear from each other what our family names are and to decide how we must stand in the row between Apfel and Zwiebel.

Knopp: "A must be on my left hand side, you slimy balls of snot."

This causes some more chaos because Apfel is on his right hand side.

Knopp blows again on his whistle and shouts: "Straight line! You look like a dog's leg!"

We do our best in an effort to please him.

Knopp: "Those lot on my right hand side – you are standing askew!"

The lot on his right hand side shuffle forwards.

For the first time, Knopp talks longer than a few seconds and he reads a list of our names to do a roll-call. The relevant man has to respond. It seems that two men who are supposed to be here didn't turn up.

Knopp: "Breakfast at half-past-seven!"

We start to leave the row at random and Knopp's whistle sounds shrilly, while he yells: "Who in hell gave you lot wretched reptiles the right just to walk away?"

We jump back into the row, hopefully in the right order.

Knopp: "Perhaps I shoud teach you lot retarded toads how to march properly. First of all, I must show you how to do a right turn, although you were supposed to have done it in the Hitler Jugend."

He demonstrates the movement en thereafter he provides us with the instruction that we must use our left feet first when we start marching.

We almost succeed in making the right turn simultaneously and to start marching as he commanded. He shouts the rhythm and leads us to our dormitory.

Knopp gives the order to halt and we fall over each other as some stop sooner than the others. Knopp turns red in his face and shrieks: "You lot are worse and more stupid than a heap of toddlers in a third rate whorehouse! Go and gorge your breakfast and get back here at eight-o-clock. Verstanden?"

A few of us mumble and growl: "Yes."

Knopp: "Do it together and audibly, you stupid and sinful pieces of shit! Verstanden?"

We yell enthusiastically "Yes!" – more or less together.

Knopp: "Yes, who?!?"

We: "Yes, Herr Oberfeldwebel!"

Knopp turns around and marches away. We only dare to leave our places in the row after he has disappeared around a corner.

After breakfast we go outside again in the right order and we wait for Knopp. He leaves us standing for half-an-hour before he turns up.

"Platoon, attention!"

We jump at attention.

"Platoon, right turn!"

We do that.

"Platoon, forward march! Left! Left! Left! Keep that up."

He leads us to a lecture hall and we go in and sit in alphabetic order without Knopp ordering us to do so. I laugh a bit at Knopp who regards himself as very important but the younger guys are clearly afraid of him.

Suddenly, Knopp bellows again: "On your feet! Stand at attention!"

We do that. Five officers come ambling in and the most senior of them, a "Fregatten-kapitän" (commander) lets us sit again and he addresses us: "Welcome, meine Herren! I am Fregattenkapitän Kurt Slevogt and I am the chief of the 'U-Bootschule' (submarine school), a part of the Marineschule Mürwik.

"All of you are volunteers who applied to be trained as officers of our U-boat flotilla. Thank you. Germany needs your services urgently. You are only the second intake for this training course after we have commissioned our first submarines. You will be trained as naval officers, but the emphasis will be on U-boats.

"But, first of all, you must complete the basic training for officers. You must learn how to march. You will be made familiar with hand-held weaponry. You will receive training on sailing boats to get a feeling for the sea. You must know about the organisation of the Wehrmacht. This part of the course you will follow together with the other cadets in other departments of the Marineschule. After having completed the basic part, you will be promoted to 'Fähnrich zur See' (Midshipman, class II).

"During phase two of your training you will especially be taught about the design and building of submarines, their propulsion systems, their navigation, the use of torpedoes and naval guns, the management of a submarine's stability under water, communication and escape routines.

"I understand that here are seven men who have already completed the course at the Seefahrtschule in Bremen successfully and have received their diplomas. Perhaps we may learn even something from them. I am sure that they are already on top of some of our subjects.

"I wll hand you at this stage to our four submarine instructors and I ask that everyone lifts his hands as I call out his name. The senior instructors are Korvettenkapitän Werner Fürbringer – and Harald Hülsmann. The other two instructors are Kapitänleutnant Hans Rudolf Rösing – and Fritz Freiwald.

"I wish you all success with your training! Heil Hitler!"

The man sitting next to me whispers in my direction: "This commander has far better manners than Knopp."

Me: "Yes, he treats us like human beings – not like dirt."

Wilhelmshaven, Monday, 6 January 1936

My course in Flensburg is to resume the day after tomorrow, Wednesday, after we have completed the first part of our basic training just before Christmas. Today is still vacation for me. Onkel Achim takes me and Johannes to his workplace, the naval base of Wilhelmshaven to witness an historic event – the commissioning of a proud German warship, the Admiral Graf Spee, a ship that has been built and equipped in Wilhelmshaven.

The official name for this type of ship, the third member of a class of three, is "Panzerschiff" (armoured ship). She is too small to be a battleship, but she is also too thickly armoured to be deemed a conventional cruiser. Her tonnage is more than 16 000 tons and her chief armament are six huge 280 millimeter guns that are housed in two turrets – in contrast with heavy cruisers of which the main armament is usually guns of no more than 100 millimeters. She also has eight smaller guns, torpedo tubes and heavy armour to protect her against enemy fire. She is a fast ship thatt is supposed to able to sail at more than thirty knots.

The Kriegsmarine takes official possession of the ship with a parade today. Her master is Kapitän zur See Conrad Patzig, a veteran of the Great War. Onkel Achim, Johannes and I cheer with the crowd when the ship's horn is blown as a sign that she is ready to leave the harbor. We feel proud to be members of the Kriegsmarine.

By this time, I have almost forgotten Walvis Bay and South West Africa. I am a member of the German Wehrmacht and one of these days I will become an officer in the U-boat branch – an elite section. On top of all that, my lovely girlfriend is a member of the German aristocracy. Life couldn't have been better.

Bremen, Friday, 1 May 1936

Our class members reach an important milestone today: we receive a real rank, namely that of Fähnrich zur See. The rank is shown by a silver shoulder strap on the summer uniform and a golden star on the lower sleeve of the winter uniform. To celebrate the occasion, we are granted five days' leave, together with the two adjoining weekends. That means that Johannes and I are able to depart by train this Friday afternoon to Bremen.

During our journey we consider the road that we have travelled this far. Knopp taught us to march properly and to swear like sailors. Fortunately, he didn't instruct us in the art of boozing like sailors.

For Johannes and me, the part of navigating with sailing boats was really easy because both of us had much practice on the Nicoletta.

1 May 1936

We were fortunate to have been given leave between last Christmas and New Year's Day. Johannes and I immediately took a beeline to Bremen. We had to tell the von Czapiewski family everything about our course – including Oberfeldwebel Knopp's way of working with us. I visited Tante Stockhausen on Christmas Eve and her eyes were filled with tears when she saw me again. She naturally invited me and Cornelia to enjoy the Christmas lunch with her and consume some of her Stollen afterwards. Silvester was celebrated, as usual, with the von Czapiewski family.

We heard that Cornelia's father was promoted within three months to Korvettenkapitän at the naval base at Wilhelmshaven. He liked the idea of being back in the Marine, but to his chagrin he only had an administrative position in an office. He would have preferred to have served on a ship. His background as Direktor of the Seefahrtschule prompted his deployment to a headquarters.

Cornelia opens the front door of Johannes' parents' home shortly before dusk after we have rung the doorbell. She is even more beautiful than I remember her. She hesitates a moment, unsure of whom she should hug first, but then she decides that I should get the favor of receiving the first hug and kiss. The rest of the family members are on the scene shortly thereafter and we are taken inside.

Tante Nicoletta: "Dinner tonight will be formal. You three members of the Kriegsmarine are to attend with full parade uniforms. Cornelia and I will see to it that you get a fitting treat."

Cornelia: "Just tomorrow, you two young men are to go for a walk through the city with me. I want to hold onto the arms of you two heroes on both sides. Everybody must see that my elder brother and my boyfriend are on their way to become warrior heroes!"

During dinner, Franz asks: "Do you get any opportunity to participate in sport?"

Johannes: "There is a sporting parade every Saturday. Our group of twenty submarine men are divided into four groups or teams of five men each. We compete against teams from other departments of the Marineschule. We participate in tug of war, swimming, rowing, regattas with sailing boats and running. Our team – that is me and Stefan and three other guys – are often the winners. That is because Stefan is certainly the strongest of us all."

Onkel Achim: "Stefan, where did you learn to swim in that desert country of South West Africa? Did you dive into the sand?"

I laugh: "Not into the sand. Into the tranquil waters of the sea at Walvis Bay. I can even dive somewhat. I have even suggested to the commander of the U-boat school that a course in scuba diving ought to be appropriate and he liked the idea."

Cornelia: "What does the environment around the submarine school look like?"

Me: "The Marineschule is a large building complex of which we only use a small part. It's north of the town center. We are situated on a small hill next to the beach and there is a harbor directly in front where a number of small craft are moored. The bay at Flensburg opens onto the Baltic. The south-eastern coast of the bay is German territory and the north-western coast is part of Denmark. One may actually describe the bay as a fjord."

Franz: "Do you get any free time?"

Me: "Only on Sundays. Then we may attend church if we wish. For that, we have to march in squads with cadets and midshipmen of other courses. Otherwise, we must sit around in the barracks, writing letters or studying."

Onkel Achim: "Are there opportunities to mingle with the other midshipmen?"

Me: "We eat in the same mess hall but the members of our group mostly stay on our own. We regard ourselves as the elite, a step better than the other lot who are being trained to do administrative work, man the coastal artillery, shoot with naval guns, do minesweeping and so forth. We are supposed to be able to perform any task aboard a U-boat."

Bremen, Saturday, 1 August 1936

It is marvelous to wake up in my old bed in the home of Cornelia's parents. Yesterday, Friday, was a special day for our group because we were all promoted to the rank of "Oberfähnrich zur See" (Midshipman, class I). We all got two pips on our shoulder straps, which were previously empty.

And then we were again granted passes – five working days and the two weekends on both sides. It was a joyous homecoming last night. We celebrated the fact that Cornelia had completed her Abitur and that she is now being trained as a nurse in the "Sanitätsdienst" (Military Health Service) of the Kriegsmarine at the "Marinelazarett" (naval hospital) in Wilhelmshaven, as well as Johannes' and my promotion. Cornelia becomes eighteen in a month's time but, unfortunately, Johannes and I won't be able to share in that occasion.

Cornelia brings me coffee in bed and she sits on the edge of the bed while sipping her coffee. Her first words are, even before she has said "hello" or something: "When are we getting engaged?"

I get such a fright that I spill some coffee on my payama shirt and burn my chest: "What did you say?"

"When are we getting engaged? Or are you so dumb, stupid, idiotic and retarted that you cannot realise that we are meant for each other?"

I place my mug of coffee on the chest of drawers next to my bed, take Cornelia's coffee from her hand, put that also down and pull her up to a vertical position.

"Watch, here I go onto my knees before you while I hold your hand. Both of us are in our payamas, but I would have preferred to have been dressed more appropriately. I would also have preferred that we were seated on a bench in a lusciously green forrest where I could kneel before you. But, unfortunately, you

113

chose this unromantic, inappropriate, unfit and mundane environment for this extremely important, influential, essential, weighty and serious event. In any case, notwithstanding and nevertheless, I want to ask you in earnest: Will you marry me sometime?"

Cornelia pulls me upright and gives me a first class kiss: "I think this is a very romantic environment to provide a response to such an important question. No one of us has combed our hair yet. None of us has even washed his or her face yet. We are standing here in our nighties with the result that where we touch each other it is a very direct touch."

"But what is your answer. You haven't answered me yet."

"Stupid! As you might have noticed, you will remember that it was I who first asked this very important question. I expect a direct answer. Now, immediately, on the dot, suddenly, promptly: When do we get engaged?"

"How about tomorrow?"

"Too soon. We must make a big occasion of it. One needs time for that."

"I won't get another pass before Christmas."

"All right, then we do it at Christmas time. That is to say if you have at least the desire to become engaged."

I don't answer and I grab my dream girl around her body, pull her tightly against my body, place my lips on her lips and before I can stop myself I place my left hand on one of her soft breasts. She groans with pleasure.

We finish our cold coffee only after I have released her.

During breakfast, Onkel Achim interrogates Johannes and me about our course. We explain that our instructors instructed us very patiently regarding their fields of specialisation of warfare under the oceans. A few of the chaps who haven't completed the course at the Seefahrtschule, including Johannes, requested me to give them extra lessons so as to make sure that they understand everything with regards to diesel engines, electrical motors, navigation, communication etcetera. Because I am the eldest in the group I was, as it were, automatically accepted as informal leader.

We explain that we initially didn't get any practical experience on real submarines. Mock-up conning towers of U-boats were erected on old minesweepers. The minesweepers then took to sea and we had to practice all the procedures on these mock-up conning towers. A month ago, we had the opportunity of experiencing a voyage of a fortnight on a real U-boat – mainly as spectators. With my knowledge of diesel engines I was able to help somewhat in the enigine room when a small problem arose.

Bremen, Thursday, 24 December 1936

Johannes and I got home last night for our Christmas holidays. And now I am sitting together with Cornelia in Tante Stockhausen's living room to celebrate Christmas Eve after we have attended church with her. The old lady shed tears of joy when we knocked on her front door.

While she is serving us both with a plate ful of "Knödel" (dumplings), Cornelia announces: "Dear Tante, you are to have lunch with us tomorrow. Stefan will come to fetch you. It is an extra-special, extra-ordinary and extra-remarkable Christmas lunch and we want you to be there. You are as it were the only famly Stefan has in Bremen – except for us, of course."

"My luvvy, thank you very much. I would like to come. I will sit ready straightaway after breakfast for Stefan to come and fetch me. But why is this Christmas so special? Do I guess correctly?" – and she simulates a movement with her right hand of pushing a ring over the ring finger on the left hand.

Cornelia smiles: "Correct."

Neustadt in Holstein, Monday, 4 January 1937

It is the first Monday of the new year and our group of twenty prospective submariners report at the Navy's training base at Neustadt in Holstein, a town on the coast of the Baltic to the east of Flensburg.

This time it is not the sourly and bombastic Oberfeldwebel Knopp who welcomes us at the station. It is a jovial "Stabsfeldwebel" (chief petty officer) Jürgen Jung who awaits us.

"To this side, meine 'Herrschaften' (gentlemen)! We have waiting for you a long time. As soon as we arrive at the base you are to be fed dinner. You will be allowed to enjoy a beer with your dinner, should you so prefer. Please beware that you do not slip on the mud while getting onto the trucks. Let us do it orderly and efficiently. Please get into alphabetical order and then we proceed in line to the vehicles. I won't expect of you to march because you are carrying your heavy luggage. Please, to this side!"

This friendly welcome makes us feel all right.

Neustadt in Holstein, Tuesday, 5 January 1937

After Stabsfeldwebel Jung requested us to form a long line, he divides the line into two sections with the result that everybody in the second half of the alphabet is standing behind those who belong to the first half of the alphabet. He guides us like a shepherd dog guiding a flock of sheep to the officers' mess for breakfast.

After breakfast we assemble again outside.

Jung: "Meine Herrschaften! It is to be hoped that you have found the breakfast at Neustadt acceptable. If you feel nourished and have inbibed enough coffee, we are to move to the lecture hall. Let's do it orderly and efficiently by marching properly. I believe that you know by this time how to do it after having joined the Kriegsmarine more than a year ago. All right, detachment! Right turn!"

In the lecture hall we are greeted by Kapitänleutnant Heinz Beduhn: "Welcome, meine Herrschaften! I am the commander of this base. You are the second group of aspiring submarine officers that is being handled here. The previous group concluded their course last July and they presently serve as officers in our U-boat flotilla. We have learnt much from our experience with them and we believe that we will be able to present you with an improved course. We plan to increase next year's intake drastically because our Kriegsmarine plans to build dozens and dozens of new U-boats.

"We will mainly concentrate on the propulsion systems of U-boats. You have already acquired an elementary knowledge of diesel engines and electrical motors – except for those who have done a diploma course at the Seefahrtschule in Bremen. We have heard that Oberfähnrich zur See Strauss was the top student there. He is also a qualified electrical technician. Herr Strauss, perhaps you can lend us a hand with the training in this regard.

"Herr Strauss, do you mind standing up for a moment so that I and the other instructors may see who you are?"

I stand up and sit down again.

"Thank you. Now we all know who Herr Oberfähnrich zur See Strauss is. Apart from the propulsion systems on which are will be working, you will also do a diving course. Only the elementary part because you didn't join the Kriegsmarine to wriggle and fidget and play under water. But it will be a good idea if you know how to handle diving apparatus because you are being trained to work beneath the waves, even if it is only in a steel cylinder with a front end and a back end. But it might happen that the U-boat in which you are, might sink and then you have to know how to escape from the wreck and reach the surface.

"I would also like to have an interview with each one of you. Here is a roster with the times when everyone has to come to me. Alphabetically. We start immediately after we have concluded here and we ought to finish this afternoon. In the meantime, Oberfeldwebel Jung will take the rest of you around to show you where everything is. Thank you!"

My turn to talk to the commander is directly after lunch.

"Please sit, Herr Oberfähnrich Strauss. I have received favorable reports about you from the Seefahrtschule and from Flensburg. I am sure that you will become a good submarine officer. I gather that you almost grew up on the sea."

"Indeed, Herr Kapitänleutnant."

"But it is not quite clear to me exactly where you got acquainted with shipping during your youth."

"My father and his brother-in-law, the brother of my mother, own a fleet of six fishing trawlers and I and my brother worked on them from a young age and we even steered the boats."

"But where? On the coast of the North Sea or the coast of the Baltic?"

"On the coast of the Atlantic Ocean."

"Yeees, we all know that the North Sea is actually part of the Atlantic Ocean but the Atlantic Ocean is very big. It stretches from a region just below the North Pole to almost the South Pole. Exactly where?"

"Walvis Bay."

"Where in hell is that? Never heard of it."

"It is geographically part of South West Africa, but it actually belongs to the Union of South Africa." (I feel good about telling the truth.)

"In other words: You are not a German? A spy in the pay of Great Brittain that has close ties with the Union of South Africa?"

"My grandfather on my mother's side was an Oberfeldwebel in the Imperial Schütztruppe who fought against the Namas and the Hereros. My mother is, therefore, German."

"But of which country are you actually a citizen? South Africa?"

"Walvis Bay is a little bit of South Africa on the coast of South West Africa. Actually the only natural harbor in the whole country. I, therefore, have a South African passport. But I was born under the German flag."

"Did your mother travel to Germany to give birth to you?"

I smile: "No. I was born in Swakopmund."

"Never heard of the place."

"It is a German town in South West Africa, north of Walvis Bay. I was born in 1912, before the Great War when South West was still part of the Imperial Reich."

"Oh, so you are, after all, a German! That explains your perfect German. It even sounds as if you sometimes use a little bit of Plattdeutsch. You actually gave me a fright. You certainly are aware of the fact that we don't like the British very much."

"Neither do my parents. My Dad and my uncle took agents and saboteurs with their boats during the Great War to spots behind

120

the South African lines and they had to create chaos. It didn't help very much but that shows you in which type of home I grew up."

"Fantastic. Our Kriegsmarine may, therefore, rely on your loyalty?"

"Absolutely."

"Thank you for your time. Heil Hitler!"

I get up, salute and leave with a smile.

Bremen, Saturday, 3 July 1937

The moment I woke up this morning, I jumped out of bed to prepare for a very important day. This afternoon, the wedding reception of me and Cornelia is due to take place.

Johannes and I arrived the evening before last night by train, together with Onkel Achim, Tante Nicoletta and Franz. The last mentioned three attended the parade in Flensburg where our group of submariners were promoted to the rank of "Leutnant zur See" (ensign). The previous two months, we served as midshipmen on submarines after having completed the course at Neustadt in Holstein.

Yesterday, Cornelia and I were married legally at the "Standesamt" (registry office). And today our marriage is to be solemnised in church. Onkel Achim tasked the Protestant "Marinepfarrer" (Navy Chaplain) of the naval base at Wilhelmshaven to deal with this aspect and it is due to take place in the medieval Dom of Bremen. The reception is to be held at a well-known hotel in the city centre of Bremen.

It is to be a military wedding in the cathedral. Onkel Achim in his uniform as Korvettenkapitän will escort the bride into the church. He will wear all his decorations, of course, including the Iron Cross, First Class. My best man is Johannes and he will naturally, just as me, be wearing his uniform. Our six class mates who hail from Bremen will form a guard of honor.

It isn't possible for my parents from far-away Africa to be present and they will be represented by Tante Stockhausen.

Bremen, Sunday, 4 July 1937

I wake up in the most wonderful circumstances imaginable – a near-naked minor goddess who lies next to me in a double bed and stares at me with a wicked smile.

Yesterday's wedding reception was very pleasant. More or less every member of the von Czapiewski and von Nimwegen families were present. I cheated somewhat by introducing Tante Stockhausen as Frau Sarah *von* Stockhausen to all, the widow of Kapitän *zur See* Wilhelm *von* Stockhausen. She played along and she was easily accepted by the high and mighty as their equal.

After the festivities were concluded rather late last night, I and Cornelia retired to our hotel room, which I have booked in advance. It was our plan to sleep here only one night and then to travel to Skagen in Denmark by train where we are to catch the ferry across the Skagerrak to Kristiansand in Norway.

When we retired to our hotel room last night I was rather very nervous – almost as severe as I was when I had to ask Onkel Achim's permissin to visit his daughter. Cornelia could see my tension and asked what the matter was.

"My dear, now I must confess. I am terribly unsure. I don't know the way forward."

"About what do you feel unsure?"

"About what I and you are supposed to do now."

"We are going to do what all newly-weds do."

"Yes, but what precisely is that? How is it done?"

Cornelia laughs: "Stefan, my man! You are already twenty-five years old. You must surely have heard about the flowers and the bees?"

"Yes. I am fairly familiar with the theory. But the practical side of this makes me nervous. I am afraid that you are going to laugh at me if I don't know what to do."

Cornelia laughs again: "Stefan, I cannot help but to laugh. But it is not to laugh at you. It's a laugh of love, of pure pleasure about what is awaiting us."

"Yes, I know something extraordinary is supposed to await us, but I am very dumb with that. The only thing that I know is that we are supposed to exchange saliva – or so I have heard. I am totally in the dark regarding the precise procedures, actions, attitudes and movements."

Cornelia laughs some more: "If you want to describe it that way! All right! Yes, that is where it all starts. With a series of passionate and long moist kisses. But do you really want to tell me that you don't know how to proceed from there?"

"I think that I am extremely stupid regarding these things, even if I know the theory. I was only trained to work met engines, electrical wires, batteries and submarines."

"Don't worry, my man. You are now in capable hands. And remember, there is no fixed procedure. Every time is supposed to be different. It's different from steering a submarine where an exact sequence of movements have to be repeated every time. But we are not machines – we are a man and a woman of flesh and blood with all sorts of urges and needs. In case you haven't realised, I am a trainee nurse and I was thoroughly trained in the theory of this part of life. I must simply apply my knowledge. Allow me to be your instructrix. I am on top of the whole story."

"Is it necessary for you to be on top? I thought I had to be on top?"

"No, you stupid. You simply use the apparatus with which you were born. I know that you have it because I could feel it more than once when you held me in a furious fiery clutch."

And now we newly-weds wake up after we have comsummated our marriage last night. Cornelia says: "We still have enough time before we must go and have breakfast and catch the train. Let us practice again all the movements and actions and postures and procedures that I have taught you during the night. Let's see if you are on top of everything."

Wilhelmshaven, Monday, 12 July 1937

Our time in Norway was hopelessly too short for both of us. It was impossible, though, to get more leave than a five-day workweek and the two weekends on boths sides. We arrived home last night and spent the night in our new flat in Wilhelmshaven. Father-in-law Achim has already procured it for us in June. It suits us nicely because Cornelia is being trained as a nurse at the Marinelazarett in Wilhelmshaven and I was ordered to join the U-30 in Wilhelmshaven today. My position is second "Wachoffizier" (watch officer), the officer who has to oversee the radio personnel and the crews of the two guns on deck, as well as acting as commander when the "Kommandant" and the first watch officer are both off-duty.

But, first of all, I must meet the commander of 2 U-Boat Flotilla, Fregattenkapitän Werner Scheer. I knock on my father-in-law's office door where he is employed in the harbor captain's division en he explains where I can find this man. When I am invited into his office, I standd at attention, salute and call out: "Herr Fregattenkapitän, Leutnant zur See Strauss reports for duty. I must join U-30."

Scheer responds to my salute and invites me to sit: "Strauss, welcome. I have received a signal about you. You were appointed as an officer merely a week ago and the position of second watch officer on U-30 was assigned to you. I also know that you have attained a diplima at the Seefahrtschule, here in Bremen. Let's hope that you will be a useful officer."

"Thank you very much, Herr Fregattenkapitän."

"There is, though, a problem. A rather thorny problem. U-30 hasn't arrived yet. She experienced a difficulty with her electrical system and she is floundering somewhere on the North Sea. We sent a submarine tender to her with the necessary technicians, tools and parts aboard. Also some provisions because their food stocks are low, the poor hungry souls. Hopefully, they will be able to locate the problem soon so that U-30 can reach the harbor. Otherwise, the tender will have to tow her in."

"And what do I do in the meantime?"

"You do the same as all member of the Kriegsmarine do in these circumstances."

"And what is that, if I may ask?"

"You sit around and wait for better days."

"Does that mean that I may stay at home untill U-30 arrives some time?"

"Of course not, Herr Leutnant, of course not! You come here to my office every morning to hear if we perhaps have some or other task for you and otherwise you walk around through the whole base, the Marinewerft included, and you get familiar with the place. Talk to everybody who has time for you – the people at the harbor captain, the people at coastal defence, the anti-aircraft gunners, the dry-dock, the submarine defence."

"I am sure that will be edifying."

"Something else: have you ever read our Führer's book, 'Mein Kampf'?"

"I don't have much interest in politics. I am chiefly interested in the sea with everything floating on top of it or inside it."

"Go and buy a copy. It is in two volumes. It is actually essential reading for every officer of our Wehrmacht."

"Will do so."

"That will help you to understand in which direction Germany is heading with National Socialism."

"Thank you for the advice." (I decide to go and buy the book but I don't have a great desire to read it. Something I cannot understand, is Hitler's well-known hatred towards the Jews. Jesus and his apostles were, after all, Jews and I have never seen a crooked Jew. I can remember old Mister Goldberg in Walvis Bay who was the most friendly and honest shop-keeper one could imagine, even if he was a Jew.)

"And, Herr Leutnant, I would like to know how the people at the training centres see the task of the U-Boat Branch."

"Herr Fregattenkapitän, they are rather frustrated. It seems as if the people at the OKM (Oberkommando der Marine – high command of the Navy) don't recognise the value of submarines. The admirals all want to build battleships and cruisers so that we can shoot the Royal Navy to pieces. The problem is that the Kriegsmarine will one of these days only have four battleshipos after the Bismarck has been commissioned. The Royal Navy, on the other hand, possesses four times as many batteleships. The French also have more battleships than we have. We will always be on the losing side. On the other hand, if a single submarine, which can be built at a fraction of the price of a battleship, stalks a battleship she can sink the battleship with a single salvo of torpedoes."

"Your are right, perfectly right. Fortunately, our submarine fleet is being enlarged at a steady pace. Our commander, Kapitän zur See Karl Dönitz, is a very energetic man and he repeatedly pesters Admiral Raeder, the chief of the OKM, to increase the size of the submarine fleet. We have, though, another problem. We don't have enough senior officers to fill important positions in the submarine branch. It is the idea that somebody with my rank, that of Fregattenkapitän, ought to command a flotilla. At present, we have five flotillas and all the other commanders are people with lower ranks. A submarine commander is supposed to be at least a Kapitänleutnant, but many of our boats are being commanded by an Oberleutnant zur See. I foresee that you may become the captain of a U-boat within two or three years – especially with your training."

"Thank you for the confidence you have in me."

"And now, Herr Leutnant Strauss, you must excuse me. I have work to do. Thanks for the visit. Start with the exploration of tha base. Heil Hitler!"

Wilhelmshaven, Tuesday, 13 July 1937

After my interview with the commander of 2 U-Boat Flotilla yesterday, I return to the office of my father-in-law Achim to report about our conversation.

"Stefan, I would have liked to accompany you on your tour of exploration through the base. But, unfortunately, I don't have the time. Please, walk around on your own. Perhaps you should go and have a look at the warships in the harbor. There are quite a few of them."

"Vati, thanks. Will do so. May I also discuss another minor problem with you?"

"Go ahead."

"Last night, while Cornelia and I were unpacking our things in our apartment – by the way, I want to thank you again for the pieces of furniture that you have bought as a wedding present for us – I happened to find my South African passport. And I discovered that it expires at the end of this year and has to be renewed, otherwise I will become an illegal immigrant in this country."

"Donnerwetter! Yes, that's something we have totally forgotten. You ought to ask leave of absence tomorrow or the day after that while you are waiting for the U-30, and travel to Berlin to visit the Embassy."

"Thanks for that advice. But how am I to go about as citizen of a foreign country in the German Kriegsmarine? If the 'Behörden' (authorities) discover that I have a South African passport I will be chucked out of the Navy without ceremony. I will be deported and I will not be able to take Cornelia with me. How do I handle this?"

"Get your passport fixed up first and then we can talk again. I will think of something in the meantime."

After we have drunk some coffee I step outside and start my exploration of the port. I am pleasantly surprised to see three of Germany's armoured ships, which are actually super-heavy cruisers, lying at anchor – the Admiral Scheer, the Admiral Graf Spee and the Lützow. It is clear that they are in the harbor for a refit because two of the big guns of the Admiral Scheer in her forward turret were taken out – surely to receive a thorough overhaul. There are also a few destroyers.

While I am watching these big ships I conclude that they will be able to get the best out of any encounter with the British and French cruisers that I have seen. Their bigger guns can shoot further and they have better armour protection.

At the naval yard I also watch how the battleship, the Scharnhorst, is nearing completion.

Wilhelmshaven, Friday, 16 July 1937

It's Friday morning and I inquire from my father-in-law's secretary if he is available. He is. I immediately come to the point of my visit:

"Vati, yesterday I visited the Embassy in Berlin. To renew the validity of my passport. They wanted to know what I am doing in Germany."

"What did you tell them?"

"I answered that I came here to study maritime technology. I didn't disclose that I became an officer in the Kriegsmarine in the meantime. And now they want proof that I am still studying maritime technology. They have kept my passport and promised to send it by registered post as soon as I can provide proof that I am still a student. What do I do now?"

"Verdammt! That is a sorry, sad, stupid, and sticky state of affairs, a decent overdose of bad weather and calamities. Strictly speaking, you were still a student of nautical science while you were being trained as a submarine officer. But that is something that that minor official at the Embassy doesn't need to know."

"Can you perhaps help? You were, after all, the Direktor of the Seefahrtschule?"

"Perhaps we can still perform a piece of magic or mischief. Let me think."

"Is it possible for you to write a letter stating that I was a student at the Seefahrtschule since January 1933?"

"Perhaps I ought to conjure up such a letter by writing something and signing it. Yes, that's what has to happen. Fortunately, I still have my stamps from the time when I was Direktor, as well as enough letterheads of the Seefahrtschule containing my name as Direktor. I couldn't leave those for my successor because my name appears on those things. Right-oh, I will write a letter, dated the day before you and your class mates received your diplomas – stamped and dated and signed. And then I add today's date stamp somewhere so that it must appear as if you are still at the Seefahrtschule. It will be a grave sin if you were to be kicked out of the country. What will become of Cornelia?"

"Thank you very much for your help!"

"It will also be a sin to produce such a letter. It's actually fraud. But I don't believe the Embassy will in any way distrust my letter. In this case, we must choose the lesser of two evils – either you get kicked out or I commit a tiny little bit of fraud."

"I also believe that the Embassy won't question your letter."

"Right. I have the letter heads and the stamps at home. I will write the letter tonight. Fortunately, we have a type writer at home. And then you and Cornelia come to visit us tonight for dinner and afterwards I give you the letter so that you can post it at the post office tomorrow – with an accompanying note to explain everything. I suppose that you have given my home address in Bremen as your home address?"

"That's what I've done. Of course, I didn't dare to provide them with my address here at the naval base. I want to go directly now and see how the Marinelazarett looks as part of my exploration of Wilhelmshaven and try and locate Cornelia. We won't have to prepare dinner tonight."

"I will phone your mother-in-law and request her to prepare for both of you. Johannes is also due. And then you two stay the night with us. Now that you are married, I revoke my previous prohibition of prohibiting you to take a single step into Cornelia's room, even with only one foot."

"How about the rest of my body?"

"Yes, that as well."

Dinner at my parents-in-law is quite pleasant. It is also nice to see Johannes again. He is also a second watch officer on a submarine that is due to leave on a training voyage on Monday, the

U-39. I announce that I have been informed that the U-30 is expected back in port on Monday.

After dinner, my father-in-law and I disappear into his study where he magically creates the required document. After having completed this task, he informs me as follows:

"I have drawn your personnel file in the office of Fregattenkapitän Scheer. As administrative officer in the office of the Harbor Captain I am entitled to do so. I noticed that your place of birth was given as Swakopmund and that you were born there in 1912, in the previous Deutsch-Südwestafrika. You are, therefore, automatically deemed to be a German citizen. There is no sign that you grew up in Walvis Bay. You may simply apply for a German passport with your Kriegsmarine 'Personalausweis' (identity document)."

"Then I have, strictly speaking, dual citizenship without the two countries being aware of the fact?"

"Precisely. Put that South African passport of yours away in a very secure place because if the 'Gestapo' (Geheime Staatspolizei or Secret State Police) catches you with it – especially if you are having trips on German warships – your fate will be sealed. But keep that South African passport, just in case you have to leave the country in a hurry. One never knows."

Wilhelmshaven, Monday, 19 July 1937

Together with a number of other officers I wait on the jetty just after daybreak where U-30 is in the process of docking. Although it is the middle of summer a thick fog descended upon the sea, but it will surely disappear when the sun appears. It is, accordingly, rather cool. Kapitän zur See Karl Dönitz, the commanding officer of the submarine branch, is also present. He initiates a conversation with me after I have been introduced to him by Fregattenkapitän Werner Scheer. He congratulates me with the fact that I was the top student at the training base of Neustadt in Holstein.

It impresses met that the man is on top of the movements of his officers. It is told that Napoleon Bonaparte and Alexander the Great knew the names of all the officers in their armies.

It takes a while before the Kommandant of the submarine, Kapitänleutnant Hans Cohausz, steps ashore. He, first of all, converses with Dönitz and Scheer. It takes more or less half an hour before I am able to report to him. I salute him as I was taught during basic training and I mention that I am his new second watch officer.

"Herr Leutnant, it is still too early to get settled in the boat. We must first sort out the problems with the electrical system before we can be operational again. The chaps on the submarine tender could only effect temporary repairs."

"Herr Kapitänleutnant, please forgive me for sounding arrogant. But perhaps I can help. I am a trained electrical mechanic and I've obtained a diploma in nautical technology from the Seefahrtschule in Bremen."

"Fantastic! Get dressed in your overalls as son as possible and go and see what you can do. And after that, you talk to Leutnant Fritze Jost, your predecessor as second watch officer who is leaving for a more senior position. It will be worthwhile to hear from him what he did while with us."

He turns around and yells: "Jürgen! Please come here quickly."

Jürgen is, the same as me, a Leutnant zur See, and he approaches us.

"Please take this man to the machine cabin so that he can have a look at the batteries and the electrical systems. He is Leutnant zur See Strauss, our new second Wachoffizier. He is also a trained electrical engineer. Give him some time to get into his overalls and then you go and introduce him to the people who are working there inside."

I disappear to get dressed in my overalls. Those I have, fortunately, left in my luggage bag in Scheer's office complex.

Ten minutes later, I am back and Jürgen indicates to me that I must follow him and we descend into the submarine with a ladder. The electrical lights inside shine feebly and I find a team working and messing around with torches in the machine room while they do their best to look important. I am introduced and I ask the engineering officer, Oberleutnant zur See Franciscus Fipps, what's the matter.

"We cannot locate the problem. The damn dynamo doesn't charge the batteries. We have dismantled it and we could not find anything amiss."

"Have you inspected the condition of the batteries yet?"

"Those are new batteries. We had them installed two months ago."

I borrow a torch and I start to look at the batteries. "Perhaps we must make sure about the acid quality in these batteries," I suggest.

That is being done. With a flask of battery acid from each battery cell I hasten to a workshop at the shipwarf where the acid can be tested. Furtunately, I can be assisted immediately and the results show that the acid got mixed with sea water, somehow or other. No wonder that the batteries refused to be charged.

I return and announce what the result was. The battery acid is pumped out of the batteries and new battery acid is ordered. That is being done at the workshop and we get the assurance that it will be delivered on Wednesday. Hans Cohausz, who has joined us in the meantime, announces that we are to depart again on Thursday.

Cohausz gets me aside: "Look here, Herr Leutnant, here on my boat we are not very much worried about ranks and titles. We are friends with everybody. I am going to call you Stefan and you may address me as Hans – but only when when we are on board."

That fits my Afrikaner background very well because we are not so stiff and formal as these Germans.

Me: "Oekee, Hans. I like that. We may be more or less of the same age. Bu I have a concern of another type that I have to mention."

"Yes?"

"That sea water in the batteries – how do you think that may have happened?"

"By accidenr perhaps? Carelessness?"

"How about somebody doing it on purpose?"

His eyes open wide: "Do you suggest sabotage?"

"That's the only explanation."

"Look here. You are new on this boat. You can watch the crew members without any prejudice. It's your job henceforth to catch the saboteur – if there is one."

"There must be one."

Wilhelmshaven, Thursday, 12 August 1937

After a voyage of three weeks during which we performed various maneuvres, including stalking some freighters, we return to Wilhelmshaven.

U-30 is more or less a year old and a member of the VIIA class. It is a smallish boat with a tonnage of less than 700 tons. She may not dive deeper than 250 meters. There are two diesel engines for sailing on the surface and two electric motors that propell her under water. The crew is comprised of four officers and forty non-commissioned officers and seamen. There are five torpedo tubes of which one is at the stern and she has a load of eleven torpedoes. She can also carry a number of mines when fewer torpedoes are loaded. On the deck she is equipped with a 88 mm gun and a 20 mm gun to protect her against enemy aircraft.

The space inside is extremely cramped and it gets stuffy when the boat spends a long time under water without an opportunity to let in fresh air. Some of the men have to sleep in shifts, due to a lack of sleeping space. Some of them even have to sleep on top of the stored torpedoes.

There is a good team spirit because we are all dependent upon each other. The Kommandant has the final say because he has to take all the important decisions, which may impact upon life or death for us all.

My watches were usually twelve hours at a stretch and I spent that usually on the conning tower when we were sailing on the surface, or at the periscope if we haven't dived too deep. In my off-duty times, I often helped the engineering officer to inspect and service the electric motors and the batteries – for which I gained the gratitude of the Kommandant.

And now we are getting back to Wilhelmshaven after a voyage during which nothing of importance happened – except for the fact that there is a terrible stench on board. The whole crew developed stomach cramps and horrible diarrhoea the day before yesterday. The toilet system could not handle everything and we had to return to port a few days early.

Hans confides in me: "I think you are correct about a saboteur on board. This epidemic of tummy trouble did not happen by accident."

Me: "Somebody must have slipped something into our soup or stew while helping in the Kombüse."

"That's what I also think."

We report to the commander of the flotilla and I am surprised to find my father-in-law who is occupying that office.

"Gentlemen, you have certainly not heard the news, but the poor Fregattenkapitän Scheer had an accident and broke a leg. He is with sick leave at home – until whenever. I was seconded from the harbor captain's office until a new permanent commander can be appointed. After all, I was a submarine captain during the Great War and I, therefore, understand a few things about this job. What can I do for you, gentlemen?"

Our Kommandant: "We are only here to report that we are back and that we don't have anything of importance to report."

He doesn't mention the possibility of sabotage because we don't have any proof as yet."

North Sea, Sunday, 26 September 1937

We are patrolling the North Sea, off the coast of Denmark. I am in control of the boat at the moment and we are practising crash diving procedures. Suddenly, the steering goes dead and we are unable to change course.

I summon the engineering officer and we investigate. It seems that one of the cables connecting the rudder with the wheel in the control centre got snapped.

While the two engine room artificers are splicing the cable, the engineer calls me and the Kommandant to one side: "That cable did not snap suddenly. It was cut."

Me: "How?"

"It could only have been done with strong wire cutters."

Hans Cohausz: "Do you have such an instrument in your tool chest?"

The engineer: "Certainly."

Hans: "Is it still there?"

The engineer: "Let's have a look."

The three of us proceed to his tool chest and it transpires that the cable cutter is missing.

Me: "This is our chance to catch the saboteur. Hans, please give the order that all activity aboard has to stop and that every man stays where he is at this moment. The three of us have to search every nook and cranny to find the cable cutter and catch the culprit."

Without any comment, the Kommandant rushes to his intercom system and orders: "We are to stay on the surface and drift right where we are. The diesel engines are to be killed. Every crew member is to stay exactly at the spot where he is at this very moment. Nobody is to move more that two millimetres in any direction from his present posistion – not even if he wants to go to the toilet. You have my permission to wet your pants."

The crew members in the control centre look startled. The three of us start to look into any and every likely and unlikely spot where the cable cutters could have been hidden. After more than an hour, I find the tool inside the hammock of our "Sanitäter" (medical orderly).

I call the Kommandant and we start to interrogate the frightened man.

The Kommandant: "What did you put in our food last month to make us all sick?"

The medic: "I didn't do anything of the sort."

Me: "Bullshit. I've talked to our cook and he gave me the names of the guys who helped him on that particular day. Two torpedo men and you were his assistants on that day."

The Kommandant: "And how did you manage to pour sea water into the batteries?"

The young man's eyes grow wild and his jaw starts to quiver as he cannot control his sobs: "It wasn't sea water. It was my piss that I collected over a few days."

"Ah, thanks for that confession. Do you realise that we can lock you up and have you courtmartialled as soon as we return to port? You will be found guilthy of sabotage and you will be sentenced to hard labor in a concentration camp or a labor batallion somewhere."

Tears fill his eyes and he buries his head in both his hands.

Me: "Tell us why you did all these things. You did very dangerous things. We had to stop you before you sank this boat with all aboard. What drove you to these steps?"

The Kommandant: "If there are any mitigating circumstances, it might help us to make life a little bit easier for you. You are anyway in deep shit, as it is."

Silence.

After a minute I break the silnece: "Your family might also be in trouble, on account of you. Big trouble."

The guy looks up: "Really?"

The Kommandant: "Certainly, certainly. If you want to help them, you had better come clean. Tell us everything. What drove you to these dispicable steps?"

After some more silence, the young man sobs: "I had to take revenge on the bloody nasty Nazis for what the did to my family."

I prod him gently: "Tell us more. That will help us to onderstand."

"My dad was fired from his job in 1934 for being a communist. I was at university, studyng medicine and I wanted to become a doctor. But they threw me off the course because of my dad's political background. The only career that was left to me was that of a Sanitäter. I wanted to work in a civilian hospital, but I could only get free training in the Wehrmacht. And this is where I am now."

The Kommandant: "And then you wanted to take revenge on the system by sabotaging our boat?"

"That's right."

"The system will only crush you, as well as your family. I don't approve of everything I find in the system, but there is no choice – we have to work inside it. The best way to take revenge is by becoming the best Sanitäter you can possibly be. Patch up your wounded mates, treating your sick fellow crew members. You have a wonderful opportunity to make this miserable world a better place by doing your job properly and forgetting about politics."

Me: "That sound like very sound advice. Take revenge on the system, on these Nazis you despise, by being the best German you can be. How about that?"

"Can... can you perhaps for... forgive me for what I've done? I didn't think properly."

The Kommandant: "First of all, you will have to confess in front of the whole crew your sins and crimes. And then, everybody will know to watch you carefully. You won't get another chance to be naughty again. And if I'm satisfied with your remorse, I might just forget about what happened the last few weeks."

Wilhelmshaven, Saturday, 12 February 1938

It is a very sick crew that arrives at Wilhelmshaven after a sortie of only nine days. Kapitänleutnant Hans Cohausz is furious.

Directly after we have docked, the Kommandant calls the whole crew up onto the deck, even before the boat is handed over to the harbor personnel to be serviced: "Men, this sortie of ours was a waste of valuable time, expensive diesel, man-hours, good food and good liquor. I hoped to douse all of you with alcohol, but to no avail. This may never happen again that a sick crew member reports for duty before we sail.

"Obergefreiter Schäfer, you had better become a real Schäfer (shepherd) and look after a lot of silly stupid sheep, instead of becoming a U-Boat crew member. Come and stand here, next to me, and repeat out aloud after me: 'I am very sorry for infecting the whole crew with the flu!'"

Schäfer moves forward to a position next to the Kommandant and shouts as loud as his hoarse voice allows: "I am very sorry for infecting the whole crew with the flu! I promise never to do it again! Please forgive me."

The Kommandant: "Apology accepted. So, Schäfer, what happens when you again report for duty and you are sick?"

Schäfer: "I go to the sick bay and get a sick note that I cannot join my boat."

"Yes, that sounds sensible. Men, all of you heard. I can't tolerate sick seamen getting onto our U-Boat! Schäfer, more than thirty men got down with the flu and they were totally useless – all because of you. I have spoken with our flotilla commander and he ordered us to stay away from other U-Boat men for the next fortnight. All of you, go home and get better. Our next sortie will start on 28 February, but all of you – if you are healthy! – come back on the day before that so that we can get ready for our voyage. Verstanden?"

The whole crew: "Jawohl, Herr Oberleutnant!"

"Dismiss! Go back to your work stations and shut down everything, collect your gear and get away. I don't want to see another sick man ever again!"

Fortunately, I wasn't one of those who got the flu. Somehow or other, I stayed healthy. But it was a horrible time with more than half of the crew being useless. Our poor Sanitäter was one of those who got sick. The only medicine he could lay his hands on, was Schnapps. Of course, the sick men were so sick that they couldn't even enjoy getting inebriated. It only worsened their headaches and fever.

I'm glad for the extra number of days that I get to spend with Cornelia. Actually, I'm grateful for Schäfer's indiscretion. Flu germs can easily be passed on from one man to another within a closed space, such as a U-Boat's interior.

Atlantic Ocean. Tuesday, 21 June 1938

We left Wilhelmshaven three weeks ago on yet another training voyage. The hot summer sun bakes on our U-boat where she is sailing on the surface of the Atlantic Ocean, west of Portugal. It is stuffy, stiflingly humid and stale inside the sub, although all the hatches are open and the fans are working overtime to recycle the air.

It is my turn to do watch service on the conning tower and I'm glad for the fresh sea breeze as we sail along at no more than five knots. At first, I think that it is the hot sun and the sweat on my body that make me itch, but when I take my shirt off, I discover a bunch of lice all over my torso. I ask Obermaat (Petty Officer) Schmidt, who shares my watch, whether he's also suffering from a plague of lice.

He also takes his shirt off and he discovers these crawling insects on various spots of his belly and breast. He strips completely and discover more lice on various other spots. I follow his example. We both observe red warts on our bodies as these vermin have been feeding on our blood.

Me: "Where the hell did these crawling, swarming, wriggling, and irritating creatures come from?"

Schmidt: "Some or other fucking fool, who was infected. He must have smuggled them aboard. And these miniscule pests started breeding and multiplying and increasing in numbers. They must be all over the place inside by this time. They spread rapidly."

The Kommandant, Hans Cohausz, appears: "And who gave you two wise guys permission to start a nudist club here on my U-boat? Get into your clothes. Immediately. You might get blisters on your bodies from sun-burn. Yes, look at all those red blotches all over your bodies. Protect yourselves."

Me: "If I may give you some sound advice, you also ought to become a nudist. We are all infected with lice. Look here on my chest. I'm sure you must be itching all over your body."

"Stefan, you may be right. I do feel itchy all over. I only thought that it was due to the stuffy atmosphere inside."

Our Kommandant follows our example and gets rid of his clothes: "How did these creatures come aboard?"

Schmidt: "Some or other stupid sod. He must have carried them clandestinely on his miserable anatomy when we started this voyage."

The Kommandant calls over the voice pipe to the control room: "Send Kowalski, our Sanitäter, up here. I want to speak to him."

Kowalski appears two minutes later and his eyes pops out of his head as he sees the three of us on the conning tower, stark naked.

The Kommandant: "Kowalski, please remove your clothes."

"But why?"

"I want to see your body."

"Herr Kommandant, I'm not a fairy. I can't allow you to force me to perform indecent acts."

"Bullshit, Kowalski. Take off your shirt. And your pants. And your underwear. I don't have any designs on your body. I want to make sure whether you are also covered by lice, as we are."

The Sanitäter obliges very slowly, while he watches the three of us with suspicious glances.

Kowalski: "Herr Kommandant, you are totally correct. I also have this lice infection. Hell!"

"Oekee, you are the medical expert on board. What can we do to eradicate this epidemic?"

"Herr Kommandant, it might help if we all strip and rub our bodies with oil. Any oil. Olive oil, lubricating oil, sunflower oil, whatever. The lice won't like that and suffocate. Or we may use alcohol."

"Do you advise us all to get drunk?"

"No, no, Herr Kommandant. We don't drink it. We rub our bodies with alcohol. Unfortunately, we don't have medicinal alcohol on board, but we may use our stock of Schnapps."

"Out of the question. Our stock of Schnapps is far too valuable for that. I don't want a swarm of drunken lice all over my body. They might start fighting each other. Will soap and water help?"

"Yes, Herr Kommandant, yes. Fortunately, we have a stock of salt water soap."

"Go and fetch a bar, immediately. And bring a bucket and a rope along."

The Kommandant orders through the voice pipe: "Stop all the engines! We are going to drift on the current for a few hours."

Kowalski reappears with a bar of soap and a bucket with a rope.

It takes five minutes before the submarine is stationary. The four of us get down onto the deck. Each one pulls a bucket of sea water up from the Atlantic Ocean and pours the contents over his head and body. The soap is applied generously and we succeed in getting all the lice off our bodies. We rinse the soap and the lice off with more sea water.

The Kommandant: "At least, the four of us are now clean. What are we going to do with our clothes? All our garments must be swarming with these tiny little devils."

Kowalski: "We must wash them as well and drown the lice. I don't think they will love the salt water. We also have to shave off all our body hair. From top to bottom. These blooming bugs lay their eggs on a man's scalp and on other hairy spots."

The Kommandant roars though an open hatch: "Send me all the buckets we have on board. Immediately! With some ropes! And some shaving equipment!"

Three minutes later three more buckets and ropes are delivered to us. The seaman who delivers them, is also ordered to get rid of his clothes and he gets a shower. Thereafter, we wash our clothing in the buckets and make sure that we get rid of all the lice in every pocket and fold. We become bald and hairless all over our bodies.

The Kommandant roars through the hatch: "Bring me a long rope! The longest one on board!"

The rope is delivered a few minutes later. We fasten one end to the railing of the conning tower and the other end to a ring on the bow. We tie our clothes onto this rope by tying knots with the sleeves and legs around the rope.

The Kommandant: "It will take some time to get dry. Make sure that we don't damage the radio aerial."

He bellows down the hatch: "Send all the torpedo men up here!"

When the five torpedo men, under the command of a Feldwebel, appear, they start to laugh. One asks: "Are we all going for a swim?"

The Kommandant: "That's a good idea. Each of you has to get rid of your clothes and wash the lice off your bodies. Shave off all your body hair, all over. Thereafter, you jump into the ocean to rinse off the soap and then you sunbathe here on the deck until you are dry. In the meantime, you wash your clothes and let them dry on this long rope."

The Feldwebel: "Herr Kommandant, I am itching all over the place – als on places where I don't even have places. Thanks for this help!"

After the whole crew has received the same treatment and all the men are assembled on the deck with the same outfits with which they came into this world, the Kommandant addresses the assembly: "Now, who is that blinking silly soul who is responsible for the presence of all these millions of ugly, unpleasant, and unwelcome insects on U-30? Who smuggled them aboard?"

Silence.

"Oekee, that man seems to be dead. All right, if nobody confesses, then we are all going to spend the night here in the open air. We cannot dare to go back inside because the whole place is infected – our bedding, our utensils, our engines, everything."

Silence.

After five uncomfortable minutes, Hauptgefreiter Sapolski holds up his hand.

The Kommandant: "Yes? Are you the guilty guy?"

"No, Herr Kommandant. I think nobody will ever claim responsibility. He will be hated by everybody and that's why he stays silent. But you cannot punish us all by allowing us to get the flu or pneumonia or bronchitis of something if we have to spend the night here on the open deck. May I make a suggestion?"

"Yes, what is it?"

"I suggest that we wash our bedding, just as we washed our clothes. And then we fumigate and disinfect the interior of the U-30 while we sit here outside."

"And how on earth are we going to fumigate the place? Washing the hole submarine with our valuable stock of Schnapps?"

"No, Herr Kommandant. We ask the engineering officer to start the diesel engines and let the exhaust fumes into the interior of the submarine. After an hour or so, every little crawling specimen of this plague will be eradicated, eroded, evaporated, and extinguished. They will smother in these toxic fumes. Then we can shut off the engines and blow all the exhaust gasses out again."

The men start to applaud this little speech.

"Sapolski, you are a genius. You will be rewarded with a double tot of Schnapps tonight, after we have fixed this little problem."

Some more applause.

A passenger liner appears a few hundred meters from us on our starboard side. A German voice booms through a loudhailer: "Hallo, U-30! Do you need assistance? You seem to have some trouble. Nobody is answering your radio."

I notice that it is none other than the steamer of the Deutsche Ost-Afrika Linie, the Usambara, the ship on which I sailed to Europe five years ago. She is steaming south, to Africa. The passengers are crowding on the decks to watch these naked and bald seamen on a U-boat's deck – something they have never seen before.

The Kommandant: "Men, turn around and face away from that ship. I don't want the ladies on that ship to see too much of the proud and glorious Kriegsmarine. They might get funny ideas."

The naked Kommandant drops through the hatch to get to our radio, presumably to tell the captain of the Usambara of our little problem. The Usambara keeps on sailng further.

Eight hours later, at dusk, we deem it safe to get clothed again and enter the U-boat. The engines are started and we move again, relieved of all the unwanted passengers. We stay on the surface to allow some of the damp clothes and bedding on the rope to get dry during the night.

North Sea, Monday, 3 July 1939

U-30 is on her way back to Wilhelmshaven after a training sortie on the North Sea. I am doing watch service on the conning tower while we sail on the surface. A flight of Heinkel He-111 bombers fly overhead. Suddenly, one of the three aircraft looses height and it's clear that she has engine trouble. Her pilot manages to land on the sea, about a hundred metres from us, while the other two planes circle overhead.

Our new captain, Kapitänleutnant Fritz-Julius Lemp, calls me over the voice pipe: "We've received a distress call from some Luftwaffe (the German Air Force) planes flying overhead. One of their mates plunged into the sea. We must rescue the crew. I'll order four men to help you to launch the life raft."

As the Heinkel slowly sinks into the water, two crew members leave the cockpit through the upper hatch and slide down onto the port wing. Both have donned their life vests to stay afloat.

Just as the Heinkel is about to disappear beneath the waves, they jump into the water to get away. They have already noticed that a life raft has been launched from our U-boat and they wave in our direction.

A few minutes later, the life raft reaches them. I ask: "Hallo! Are there only the two of you?"

The Oberleutnant: "Yes, just the two of us."

They are being pulled from the water and given seats on the raft. The four crew members row back to the U-boat.

I introduce myself: "I'm Leutnant zur See Stefan Strauss, second watch officer of U-30. We are on our way back to Wilhelmhaven, where we can deliver you the day after tomorrow."

The senior officer introduces himself as Oberleutnant Karl Krause. He explains that their plane ran out of fuel, due to the negligence of the other officer, who piloted the Heinkel.

After the men have been taken aboard the U-30, they are welcommed by Fritz-Julius Lemp, and are given dry clothes and a mug of warm tea each. The U-boat dives again and I start chatting with the friendly Oberleutnant who was rescued. He asks: "I can't quite place your German accent. From which part of the country do you come from?'

"My folks live in Bremen, where I am married. And where do you come from? Your accent, also, doesn't sound familiar."

"My folks live in Berlin. That's where my wife is waiting for me."

"You certainly don't speak like the people in Berlin. If I may say so, your accent betrays some Afrikaans from South Africa."

He gulps and swallows.

"Aaah, I see, you've given yourself away."

I switch over to Afrikaans: "From which part of South Africa do you hail? If I may betray myself: I come from Walvis Bay. But keep that under wraps, because I'm not supposed to be a member of the Kriegsmarine with my South African passport."

Krause responds in Afrikaans: "Well, well. I grew up in the vicinity of Rustenburg in the Transvaal. But my parents are German. I also hold a South African passport and I'm also not supposed to be part of the Luftwaffe."

"Only my mother is German. My dad is Afrikaans."

I find it strange to speak Afrikaans again.

Atlantic Ocean, Sunday, 3 September 1939

The past two relatively peaceful years glided by. Cornelia became pregnant and our daughter Nicoletta was born two months ago. The Second U-boat Flotilla got a new commander in the person of Kapitänleutnant Hans Ibbeken. U-30's captain is still Kapitänleutnant Fritz-Julius Lemp.

In the meantime, I was promoted to first Wachoffizier, although I remain only a Leutnant zur See. We are on yet another training voyage on the Atlantic since 22 August and we have been spending our time mainly below the surface during the past two days.

Today, we sail again on the surface and the Kommandant addresses the crew over the public address system: "Männer (Men), Germany is yet again in a state of war. We only now made radio contact with OKM and heard the youngest news. Our soldiers invaded Poland the day before yesterday and they have already logged important victories. Great Brittain and France declared war against us, yet again. This is, therefore, not a training exercise anymore.

"We are now on an operational voyage and we have been ordered to attack enemy targets."

My first thought is: "We will spend much more time at sea now. There will be much less time to spend with Cornelia and little

Nicoletta. How often will we be able to see each other? This war may tear us apart in a cruel way."

The news about the start of the war doesn't come as a surprise because we often heard reports and rumours of war during the past months. I realised that Hitler simply wanted to continue with the Great War of 1914 to 1918 in an effort to revenge the humiliation and losses of the defeat of 1918. If I wanted to leave Germany, it became impossible now. I am a crew member of a German warship and we will only return to Wilhelmshaven in a few weeks' time. And then all the borders will certainly be sealed.

I find myself in a somewhat precarious position. The Germans regard me as a fellow German, while South Africa – who will certainly also declare war against Germany – regards me as a South African. After all, I renewed my South African passport two years ago. That causes me, technically, to be a traitor against my country because I am actively aiding and helping my country's enemies. It won't do, though, to become worried about this state of affairs at this time. For me the most important objective is that I and my family survive the war, it doesn't matter how.

It is my shift on the conning tower while we are sailing in an easterly direction, more than 250 nautical miles west from

Scotland. On the horizon, I spot a big ship steaming in our direction and I call Fritz-Julius Lemp. He gives the ship one look through his binoculars and orders that we dive to just below the surface.

Lemp takes his position at the periscope and he orders that we sail forwards to get nearer to the big ship. It transpires that she is a big British passenger liner and Lemp mumbles: "I'm sure that I can see guns on her deck. This is, therefore, a warship of the enemy."

I also get a turn to look through the periscope and we consult Lloyd's shipping register. It is the passeneger liner SS Athenia of about 13 500 tonnes. The ship steams without a whisper of a suspicion onwards, in a northerly position from us. Lemp manoevres the submarine so that her bow is pointing in the direction of the ship. He orders: "Torpedo tube number one: ready!"

The boatswain in charge of the torpedo tubes reports that the torpedo is loaded and ready to be fired. Lemp presses a button that serves as a trigger and we feel how the torpedo leaves the boat and causes a little bit of turbulence in the process. It takes about a minute before we hear and feel an explosion.

Lemp calls out: "Bull's eye! That ship is going to sink rapidly."

I also get a chance to watch through the periscope and I see how the ship keels over to one side and how the lifeboats are being launched. I remark: "I believe those guys were on their way from Liverpool to North America. Probably Canada."

After Lemp has made sure that the ship had disappeared beneath the waves he gives the order that we dive deeper and return to Germany. We maintain radio silence because we don't want to betray our presence to the enemy.

Later, at dinner, every crew member receives a tot of Schnapps to celebrate the sinking of our first victim.

While I try to fall asleep on my bunk, I cannot but think about all the people on the sunken ship. Did all of them get onto the life boats? Did any of them drown? How much did they lose? I can remembe when we almost got shipwrecked on one of my father's trawlers and how afraid I was. These poor mariners who have lost their ship must have felt much worse. Will they be rescued by other passing ships?

But I also tell myself: "This is what you have been trained to do. You chose the career of an officer in the U-boat branch. This will happen again. And again. After all, we are at war. Our enemies won't cry when they harm us. You are doing your bit to keep Cornelia and the rest of your family safe."

These thoughts keep me awake, despite the tot of Schnapps.

Atlantic Ocean, Monday, 11 September 1939

It is a week since we have sunk our first ship. It happens that we encounter the British freighter Blairlogie of 4 400 tonnes today. We follow the same routine as with the Athenia and we use a single torpedo to send this ship to a watery grave. We still maintain radio silence so that the Royal Navy or the Roayl Air Force cannot locate us.

Atlantic Ocean, Thursday, 14 September 1939

It is during my watch at the periscope, shortly after one o'clock, that I observe the smoke of a ship sailing in the direction of the British Isles. Lemp gives the order to surface and to allow the ship to overtake us.

We discover that she is the Fanad Head – another British freighter of 5 200 tons. Our "Funker" (radio operator) warns that the ship is broadcasting distress calls. Lemp orders that a shot from our 88 millimeter gun be fired across her bows and the captain of the Fanad Head is persuaded to stop. About forty people scramble to the lifeboats and they leave the ship.

Lemp: "Strauss, you are to take posession of that ship and plunder her supplies. And, thereafter, you scuttle her. I don't want to waste a valuable torpedo."

Me: "I will need a crew of five men to assist me."

Lemp orders that the U-30 be taken to a position directly next to the freighter so that the prize crew can get aboard. I call for five volunteers to help me and we scale the hull of the ship with ropes hanging from grapples that we threw onto the railings of the deck.

While my volunteers are ransacking the ship in search of portable supplies, such as food and liquor, I go to the bridge to confiscate any available documents, including the log book of the ship. Just as my men announce that they have found everything they could lay their hands on, I hear an aircraft approaching us.

One of the crew members cries out: "It is a Skua! She is coming to bomb us!"

Me: "She must have been launched from an aircraft carrier, somewhere near us!"

We watch helplessly as the Skua launches a bomb with the U-30 as target. Fortunately, the pilot of the aircraft aims badly and the bomb explodes a distance away from our U-boat in the sea and the shrapnel of the bomb damages the Skua, setting her on fire and forcing her to ditch in the ocean. The two crew members jump out and swim in the direction of the Fanad Head. I order that a rope be lowered to help the men aboard. They are extremely thankful to be rescued, albeit by the Germans. Three of my men on the captured ship are wounded by the shrapnel.

I suddenly find we are stranded upon the Fanad Head as the U-30 crash dives to hide from any other possible aerial attacks.

Ten minutes after the first Skua has attacked us, another one appears. The pilot drops his bomb on the wreck of the first Skua.

One of my men laughs: "Those stupid Brits thought that they hit our submarine!" We all laugh while the second Skua flies off.

I notice that the U-30 has surfaced again, apparently to take me and my men off before more aircraft arrive. The second Skua turns around to come back and strafes the U-30 with machine gun fire. The U-30 dives again.

I gather that Lemp decided that it was safe to surface again after the second Skua has left the scene. He shouts to me that we have the leave the Fanad Head as fast as possible, before any more attacks are made.

While we prepare to slide back onto the deck of our U-boat, with much of the provisions we have secured, a third Skua appears. Her attack is a repetition of the first attack. The pilot drops his bomb prematurely and the explosion in the water causes the Skua to crash into the sea. Only the pilot manages to escape and he is rescued by my men who are still on the freighter.

U-30, eventually, manages to get alongside the Fanad Head again and I and the prize crew rush back aboard. Our captured airmen come with us, because I warned them that the U-30 will certainly torpedo the freighter.

Shortly afterwards, a British biplane, a Swordfish, arrives and opens with machine gun fire on our U-boat. We all hastily get below and Lemp orders yet another dive.

We hear how other aircraft drop depth charges and bombs into the water in an effort to sink us. The operator of our hydrophones (microphones that can register sound under water) also reports the machine noises of three warships. We manage to dive deep enough not to suffer any damage.

Our almost fruitless foray to the Fanad Head – except for the documents I have secured, as well as a few bottles of rum and brandy – together with our maneuvers to evade the attacks from the air, took a number of hours and Lemp is only ready after six o'clock to send a torpedo to the Fanad Head. She sinks.

The sinking of the freighter causes renewed attacks by the warships. Lemp announces that he has spotted an aircraft carrier through his periscope. He launches a torpedo in her direction, but misses as she turns her bow in our direction. We manage to survive the renewed attacks and get away.

We still maintain radio silence.

Reykjavik, Tuesday, 19 September 1939

U-30 reaches Reykjavík in Iceland, a neutral port. We leave one of our seriously injured crew members in the care of a medical facility in the harbor and we manage to rescue the crew members of an interned German freighter.

Lemp orders that we return to Wilhelmshaven where the U-30 has to be inspected for any possible damage, due to the repeated attacks we suffered. The captured airmen and the rescued German seamen also have to be taken to Germany. Life becomes difficult with all the extra bodies aboard.

We still maintain radio silence.

Wilhelmshaven, Wednesday, 27 September 1939

The Kommandant broke radio silence yesterday when we were a day's voyage away from Wilhelmshaven and we were sailing though the Skagerrak. He signalled our three victories to the commander of the Second U-Boat Flotilla, together with the request that OKM be informed.

And now we are busy docking in Wilhelmshaven. The commander of the flotilla, Kapitänleutnant Hans Ibbeken, awaits us on the quay. When Lemp and I get off the boat to step onto a solid surface – in a hurry to take a shower and get into clean clothes after we have completed all the landing formailities – Ibbeken indicates that we should follow him immediately.

In his office we encounter Karl Dönitz. He was promoted to "Konteradmiral" (Rear Admiral) since we have last seen him. He is furious:

"Do you wise guys realise into which international mess you have dumped us? How did the Devil inspire you to torpedo a passenger liner full of civilians? America demanded an explanation because a dozen American citizens have drowned. America is, as you surely know, a neutral country and we cannot afford to make them angry."

Lemp: "It seemed to me that she ship was armed and she was, therefore, a warship. I also believe she was a troop ship."

Dönitz: "You must have watched better. Our Minister of Foreign Affairs assured the American government that it could not have been one of our U-boats because we were unaware of any such craft in that vicinity. And now you confess openly over the radio that you were complicit in this crime!"

Lemp: "I am truly sorry. It was a mistake I made in good faith. I really thought I saw guns on the ship."

Dönitz: "In any case, your boat has achieved the distinction of being the first to torpedo a ship of the enemy. That happened only a few hours after Great Brittain declared war against us. Your patrol was actually a great success because you sank three ships. Fortunately, you signalled your successes to us via a secret code and I doubt if the enemy could decipher it – that is, if they happened to have intercepted it by chance."

Lemp: "Thank you very much, Herr Admiral."

Dönitz: "And now it is necessary that we erase the tracks of your serious mistake. Fetch your log book and then we perform some magic upon it so that nobody will be able to allege afterwards that you sent a number of civilians – neutrals, to wit! –

to a watery grave. We won't court martial you because then the whole story will be revealed in public. And that is something we don't want. Keep going on in this fashion and one of these days you may be awarded an Iron Cross, First Class."

The little voice in my head starts: "That admiral wants all of us to hide the truth. The trouble is that the truth has the habit of coming out in the end."

We also tell Dönitz about our scrap with the Fanad Head and the three Skuas, two of which shot themselves down. He likes the bit about the Skuas and remarks: "If the Brits continue along those lines, they will remove themselves from the war in no time. We need not shoot a single shot. However, it was rather foolish of you to try and capture a ship, the way you did it. It could easily have ended in a tragedy. I will issue a standing order that no U-boat captain is to try to capture an enemy ship. The risk is too great."

Lemp also tells of our scrap with the aircraft carrier.

Dönitz: "I know. It was the Ark Royal. Winston Churchill announced to the whole world that she had survived an attack by a U-boat. So, that was you lot who almost did it."

We return to our U-boat and hand our prisoners over to men who take them away in a truck. They are probably the first inmates of a prisoner of war camp for men of the Royal Navy.

Wilhelmshaven, Friday, 8 December 1939

After we were grounded for three months because the OKM did not quite know what to do with us, we received the order yesterday to depart tomorrow and perform a patrol along the coast of Denmark up to the Norwegian coast.

During the past three months it was highly pleasant to fall asleep next to a cousin of the Queen of Fairyland every night. After Cornelia had given birth to little Nicoletta she only grew prettier and prettier in my eyes. By this time, Cornelia is a fully qualified nurse and she still works at the Marinelazarett in Wilhelmshaven. Mother-in-law Nicoletta cares every day for her granddaughter who is her namesake. She always travels with her husband, who has an official motor car at his disposal. She gets off at our apartment in Wilhelmshaven and at night they return home together.

I regard myself to be very lucky for having had all this time with the love of my life. Front-line soldiers will, perhaps, get home leave every two years. I know, though, that this blissful state of affairs cannot endure. We will be torn apart again and again by this war.

Our submarine got a thorough service and I helped to oversee the work that was done on all the mechanical and electrical components, together with our engineering officer.

Father-in-Law Achim's uncle, count Hermann von Czapiewski, died with his family last year in a flying accident. Hitler had appointed him as ambassador to America and on their flight thither the accident happened. His youngest son, Friedrich, somebody whom I never had the pleasure of meeting, died along with the rest of the family. He was supposed to inherit the title, as well as the estate in the east of the country. Father-in-law Achim's father, Dietrich, the only brother of the late count, accordingly, became the heir.

And this morning we find ourselves next to the tomb of Dietrich in the cemetry of Breslau. He died of a heart attack at the age of 66. My father-in-law is now, accordingly, Korvettenkapitän Joachim Graf von Czapiewski. Johannes must inherit the title and the estate along the border with Poland after his death.

The position of the estate, adjacent to Poland, explains the Polish-sounding family name of von Czapiewski.

Wilhelmshaven, Monday, 18 December 1939

After a patrol of only eight days, during which nothing of importance happened, we return to Wilhelmshaven – except for the fact that I was able to watch the Norwegian town of Kristiansand from the sea, the place where Cornelia and I spent a spot of honeymoon.

Because it became clear that there were no enemy ships to be found in the area we had traversed, we return to Wilhelmshaven on this Monday night with the hope of spending a carefree Christmas with our families.

Exactly at the time while we are docking, I hear a number of aircraft approaching from the west. There is a crescent moon in the sky of which the light is reflected upon a few clouds and it is possible to see the intruders. I rapidly conclude that they cannot be aircraft of our Luftwaffe because the anti-aircraft guns in our base start shooting at them.

The battalion ack-ack guns forming part of the harbor protection let loose with everything at their disposal. Searchlights catch some aircraft in their beams. The warships in the port join in and their guns start rumbling and growling. The Kommandant sounds the alarm and the crews of our two guns who are already on the deck jump into action. The covers of the guns are hastily removed and we also start shooting at the aircraft. They look like Wellington bombers of the Royal Air Force. One after the other tumbles to the earth and the crew of our 88 millimeter gun cheer when they shoot one airplane's wing to pieces and she crashes down.

The battle takes only a few minutes and the remaining planes flee after they have dropped their bombs on us. A few fighters of the Luftwaffe appear on the scene and they shoot two more bombers down.

18 December 1939

The trucks of the fire brigade are rapidly deployed to find out whether there are any fires to extinguish.

Wilhelmshaven, Tuesday, 19 December 1939

A post mortem is being held in the headquarters of our flotilla. It appears that 22 Brittish birds of prey laid their toxic eggs on our base, that twelve of them were shot down and that only minimal damage was caused.

Korvettenkapitän Ibbeken congratulates the gunners of the U-30's 88 millimeter gun – with the endearing nickname of "Acht-Acht" (Eight-Eight) – with the aircraft they have shot down. About fifteen crew members of the aircraft that were shot down managed to get out with their parachutes and were captured.

Later that night, Cornelia lies in my arms: "The war has started three months ago but we only really saw something of it yesterday. Four men of the poor captured English aircraft crews were seriously wounded and I had to bandage one of them. I think he will lose a foot. Another one I saw has lost an eye."

"That is what you were trained for – to nurse sick and wounded people, regardless of whether they are friends or foes. It doesn't matter."

"Why can't the nations live in peace with one another? Why must they throw bombs at each other or sink their ships? It's actually horrible."

"Yes, you have a valid point. But we also have the right to shoot back if they attack us. Remember, I am part of the Wehrmacht – our country's defence force. The Führer has reminded us quite often that the British Tommies and the French Frogs have declared war against us – not the other way. But, I must declare: I don't enjoy killing people."

Atlantic Ocean, Thursday, 28 Desember 1939

My hope to spend Christmas with my family was dashed when we sailed again from Wilhelmshaven on 23 December. We made good progress and today we are south of Ireland after we have navigated north of Scotland around the British Isles.

Our second Wachoffizier, Leutnant zur See Ferdinand Frenzl, is doing duty on the conning tower this morning and he sounds the alarm. Our Kommandant and I join him immediately and through our binoculars we spy a trawler at a distance. We creep carefully under water in that direction and we recognise the anti-submarine trawler HMS Barbara Robertson. We read the name on her bow. Just when it seems that the Brits have noticed us – according to the Kommandant who watches the trawler through the periscope – the order is given to launch a torpedo from tube number one.

The trawler sinks within five minutes.

Later during the day, it is my turn to keep watch on the conning tower. From the south I see the smoke of a number of ships sailing towards us and Lemp comes to help me to observe them. We gather that it is a task force of the Royal Navy, consisting of two battleships and a few smaller craft.

Before the Brits can see us, we hastily get submerged and we wait for the task force steaming in our direction. Half-an-hour later they are almost upon us and Lemp announces that he is seeing the HMS Barham and the HMS Repulse through the periscope. He launches four torpedoes from all four tubes at the bow in the direction of the battleships. We don't hear anything.

Lemp: "We missed!"

The crew members in and around the control room groan.

We hastily depart before any destroyers can detect us. There is no time to reload the torpedo tubes at the bow, but we still have a torpedo in the tube at the stern and that is sent off while we move away. We wait in silence and hear an explosion two minutes later.

Lemp: "We must have hit the Barham!"

A few crew members give applause by clapping their hands.

Lemp dares to peek through his periscope again much later. He reports that the Barham hasn't sunk but that she was, nevertheless, badly damaged and would be out of service for some time.

I cannot but agree with Tante Stockhausen who said that a relatively inexpensive submarine is able to give a battleship a knock-out blow.

Atlantic Ocean, Thursday, 11 January 1940

Fritz-Julius Lemp announces that the time has come to return home. Our stocks of fuel and drinking water are getting depleted. We still have a few sea mines that have to be planted somewhere and Lemp decides to lay them in the busy sea lane between the Scottish island of Islay and the most northern point of Ireland. Vessels coming from America or somewhere else on their way to Glasgow have to sail through that point.

We succeed in performing this task unobserved during the night and we return via the north of Scotland to Wilhelmshaven.

Wilhelmshaven, Wednesday, 17 January 1940

Our submarine docked again in Wilhelmshaven. After the crew has handed the boat to the harbor personnel to be serviced, Korvettenkapitän Ibbeken orders us not to proceed to our homes.

After we all got the opportunity to wash and put on clean clothing, the crew members of U-30 fall into ranks for a parade. We are very proud of our captain, Fritz-Julius Lemp, because the Knight's Cross to the Iron Cross is being handed to him personally by Admiral Dönitz. The admiral announces that our sea mines caused three British freighters to sink along the western coast of Scotland. A total of more than 18 000 tons got sunk. That, together with the damage inflicted upon the Barham, justify the Knight's Cross. Lemp wears the decoration with pride while wearing his white cap as a sign that he is a ship's captain.

Wilhelmshaven, Saturday, 4 May 1940

The U-30 returns on this lovely Spring morning to Wilhelmshaven. After our scrap with the Barham we have undertaken two more patrols – both times along the coast of Norway and in the North Sea.

While we sailed around fruitlessly without encountering a single enemy ship, much happened elsewhere. German forces overwhelmed Denmark within hours on the 9th of April and they are at the moment in the process of subdueing Norway. The Brits and the French are still trying to stem the tide in Norway but is doesn't seem as if they are achieving anything.

After Lemp and I have handed the boat over to the harbor personnel and most of the crew members went on leave to their homes, we go to report at the headquarters of our flotilla. There I receive a signal from the BdU ("Befehlshaber der U-Bote" – Commander: U-boats), Admiral Dönitz. I am to be promoted to Oberleunant zur See with effect from 1 May and appointed as commander of U-57. The home port of this submarine is in Kiel and I must report there as soon as possible.

After Lemp and I have concluded all formalities at the headquarters and I have received the congratulations from Korvettenkapitän Ibbeken, I go hastily to father-in-law Achim's office at the department of the Harbor Captain. He is somewhat surprised to see me and before we can start a conversation I push the signal into his hand.

He gets up and comes to give me a hug to congratulate me.

"Stefan, you know certainly as well as I do that the U-57 is a much smaller boat than the U-30. Although she has a later number than the U-30 because she was commissioned on a later date, she is actually an olderr type of U-boat. A Type IIC."

"I know. Johannes and I were trained on that type. She is only half as big as the U-30 and has only three torpedo tubes. She cannot dive as deep and her range is also less."

"But you have been promoted, nevertheless. And you have gotten your own boat, even if it is an outdated model. But I believe that you will achieve much. It's Saturday today. You and your family are to visit us tomorrow and then we are going to celebrate your promotion properly."

Kiel, Monday, 13 May 1940

The war only really started in all its fury two days before yesterday when German forces invaded Holland, Belgium, Luxemburg and France. It is being described as a "Blitzkrieg" (lighning war) because our men advance so rapidly that the enemy forces get no chance to dig in somewhere and defend themselves. All they can do is to flee as fast as possible away from our armour and artillery. It is clear that the German generals don't want a repetition of the Great War where the Germans and the Allies glared at each other from their trenches a number of years and attacked each other from time to time – without making any mentionalble progress.

I arrive shortly before lunch by train in Kiel and I have to find my way all by myself to the naval base. Allthough I am far away from the action in the west, I hope to do something in this regard at sea one of these days. At the naval base I report at the headquarters of the First U-Boat Flotilla where Korvettenkapitän Hans Eckermann is the commander.

He takes me immediately to the spot where U-57 is moored and I meet the first watch officer who takes care of the boat for the time being, Leutnant zur See Ludwig Lämpel. The crew is comprised of three officers and 22 other ratings.

Kiel, Thursday, 11 July 1940

After two extremely frustrating months in Kiel, U-57 at last gets the opportunity to sail away. There were so many defects in the boat that all her mechanical and electrical components had to be dismantled and reassembled from scratch.

The campaign to invade Norway was completed a month ago and I am ordered to take the U-57 to Bergen in Norway. I am told that the Kriegsmarine has established bases in all the Norwegian ports and that Grand Admiral Hermann Böhm was appointed as commander-in-chief of all German maritime forces in Norway.

Bergen, Monday, 15 July 1940

The war in France came to an end three weeks ago when an armistace with the French was signed. German forces occupy the northern half of France and the south is administered by a regime that is favorably inclined towards Germany. The British task force fled with their tails between their legs back to England – actually, only the remnant because thousands of them had been captured or had fallen.

The U-57 left Kiel a few days ago with the object of reaching the Norwegian port of Bergen today. I visited the place in July 1933 with the von Czapiewski family and I can still more or less remember how the place looks. I was able to take two days' leave before our departure to pay my darling Cornelia and precious Nicoletta a flying visit.

And today we sail up the Kjors Fjord – fortunatly under water. Suddenly, the man at the hydrophones says that he can hear the electric motors of another submarine.

Me: "It must be one of ours. I can't imagine that the Brits will dare to come messing here."

Four minutes later, the man at the hydrophone calls out: "Torpedo!"

Me: "Dive! Dive! Get down to at least thirty meters! Machine room, full revolutions!"

Because the U-57 is relatively small and very manouvreable we are able to descend rapidly. The fjord is fortunately deep enough. The man at the hydrophone announces twice more that he could hear torpedoes being launched. He adds: "They fly over us. Harmless."

Me: "I don't think they can really fly through the air. They remain in the water, but not deep enough to catch us. That stupid Brit just wasted three valuable torpedoes."

After it became clear that the Brit started to move away, I order that we reach pericope depth. I give the order that we turn around to face the enemy submarine. I order that a torpedo tube be readied and I fire a torpedo in the direction of our foe whose periscope is to be seen above the surface. After two stressful minutes we hear an explosion. We have a hit!

The man at the hydrophone: "I can still hear the motors of that submarine. She is running away from us."

My first watch officer: "We also wasted a valuable torpedo by blasting a rock in the fjord."

After it became clear that the British submarine got away, I suddenly start to tremble. Today was the first opportunity where I faced danger in my capacity as submarine Commandant. My thorough training immediately kicked in and I took the correct decisions without thinking. Everything is now behind us and I discover that I am shaken.

We reach Bergen without any further mishaps.

Atlantic Ocean, Wednesday, 17 July 1940

We lingered at Bergen only one night to replenish our stocks of fuel, dinking water and food. We sailed out again yesterday afternoon, in a westerly direction, to the deep sea.

And today we managed to sink two ships: a British freighter and ta Swedish ship. It was actually a mistake to attack the Swedish ship because Sweden is a neutral country and Germany is quite dependent upon Swedish iron ore, steel and other products. I had no choice but to stop this ship because she was on a straight course to a port in Scotland, certainly with a cargo to support the British war effort.

About an hour after I have ended the voyage of this ship, I suddenly realise that I must be responsible for the deaths of an unknown number of seamen. I don't like this idea in the least, but I have no choice – this is, after all, the task for which I was trained. But – I must agree with Cornelia that war is horrible. Her lovely face intrudes upon my consciousness and I wish that she could be with me and embrace me. When will I have an opportunity to see her again? That is, if I survive this mission.

The little voice inside becomes active: "Yes, Stefan Strauss, you freely made the choice to join the Kriegsmarine and become a submariner. You cannot undo that and you will just have to carry on. But it's also your duty to keep the enemy away from your family. But it's never a pleasure to make other people drown in the sea."

Atlantic Ocean, Saturday, 3 August 1940

We have passed the Orkney Islands and sailed along the west coast of Scotland in the direction of Ireland. While we are staying under water, the man at the hydrophone informs me that he hears the engines of a ship. I investigate with the periscope and I discover another Swedish ship of 2 200 tons, and it is clear that she is on her way to a port in Northern Ireland.

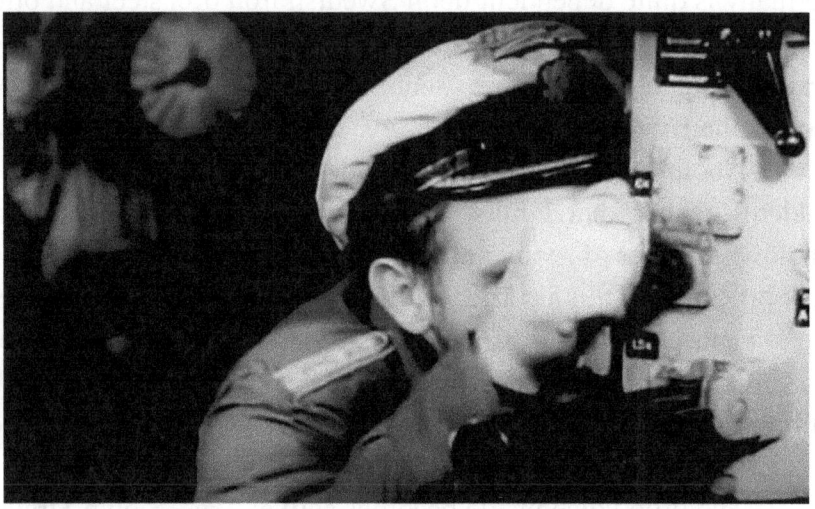

I order that torpedo tube number one must be brought to readiness, but suddenly I am reminded of the fact that I am again planning to end the lives of a number of people – people who have never harmed me, but also people I cannot allow to carry on with whatever they are doing. I get the shakes, but I succeed, nevertheless, in launching the torpedo.

The freighter sinks three minutes after my torpedo has exploded against her hull and caused a big hole to appear.

I wonder how many sailors drowned this time or were shot into eternity due to the explosion of the torpedo. I decide that I will lose my sanity if I think too often about these things. That night, I allow all the crew members to enjoy a tot of Schnapps. I allow myself three tots to put me to sleep. My last thoughts before I drift away deal with Cornelia whose job is quite the opposite of mine. She nurses wounded and sick people to health, while I kill and wound people. Horrible!

Lorient, Wednesday, 7 August 1940

After the surrender of France all the French ports are at the disposal of the Kriegsmarine. We enter the harbor at Lorient, from now on our home port.

Lorient is hopelessly too far away from Wilhelmshaven that I can slip away for a weekend to reach my family. I will have to keep contact with Cornelia by means of mail, although I am not allowed to inform her about my movements.

Atlantic Ocean, Saturday, 24 August 1940

Today is due to become a very busy day. We find ourselves about 25 sea miles north of the most northerly spot in Ireland, Malin Head. Within two ticks we send two British freighters with a combined tonnage of more than 16 000 tons to a oceanic sepulchre. I pray a silent prayer that their loved ones must stay safe, even if I have shortened the lives of a number of these seamen.

Before these ships disappeared under the waves they managed to send out emergency signals by radio. Within an hour we hear the engines of at least three British warships – possibly destroyers or frigates, or perhaps also an anti-submarine trawler. They start dropping depth charges in an effor to hit us but we are by this time already far away from the spot where the last ship has sunk and we escape without a scratch.

Shortly after dark we hear the engines of yet another freighter and I discover in the feeble light of a crescent moon a ship of 5 700 tons. One torpedo suffices to remove her from the surface of the ocean.

Later that night, while retiring into my miniscule cabin, I think that today was certainly the busiest day in my career until now. Three ships in one day! And we survided an attack by three warships! The tot of Schnapps that I dispensed to my crew members at dinner was well-earned. Hopefully, the Schnapps will help me to forget all the miseries that I have caused a bunch of people today – people I have never encountered in my life and who have never wronged me personally.

How am I going to survive this crazy war and preserve my sanity?

Atlantic Ocean, Sunday, 25 August 1940

As if the adventures of yesterday weren't enough, we again blow a ship sky-high tonight: a British freighter of 7 500 tons. She disappears within ten minutes.

After this encounter we have to returen home because our store of torpedoes is getting low. It happens, though, that we encounter mechanical problems and I receive a signal that we have to return to a German port. Lorient doesn't have the necessary repair facilities yet.

I hope that I will get a good period of rest after all the excitement and stress and insecurity of the recent past.

Hamburg, Tuesday, 3 September 1940

The most successful voyage of U-57 ends disastrously. We sink to the bottom.

We sailed along the river Elbe towards the biggest German port city, Hamburg, to have repairs done. Halfway between the Elbe estuary and Hamburg a stinking small Norwegian freighter, the Nora, collides with us and knocks a hole in our hull. Water of the river streams rapidly into the interior and there is only enough time to order the crew to grab their life jackets and diving equipment.

Suddenly, I am grateful for the fact that I can swim fairly well and that I have done a diving course at Neustadt in Holstein. Fortunately, the river isn't very deep and most of our men succeed in jumping into the river before the submarine disappears under the water and they swim to the river bank. I remain standing on the deck and I call into the open hatch whether anybody was still trapped inside before I also swim away.

After the last man has reached the northern river shore at a place called Brunsbüttel, I order the men to get into a long line so that I can count them. There are nineteen of us. Six men are missing – they either drowned of were killed by the crash.

The Nora succeeds in getting stranded on the opposite bank of the Elbe. The captain, fortunately, decides to fire emergency flares and to request help on his radio. We have to wait more than two hours before a tug turns up to pick us up. Fortunately, it is still late Summer and nobody of us get frozen in our wet clothing.

I was able to grab the boat's logbook and put it into a watertight bag before I left the submarine as the last man and swam ashore. All my personal belongings are gone, including my South African passport. I suspect that to be the case with all those of us who survived.

Bremen, Friday, 6 September 1940

Today, three days after the accident, I arrive in Bremen during the evening. I hurry to the home of father-in-law Achim. He and mother-in-law Nicoletta are very surprised to see me.

After I have given a summary of what had happened, my father-in-law takes me in his official staff vehicle, a "Kübelwagen" (litteraly: a 'bucket wagon' – a military vehicle built on the chasis of a Volkswagen Beetle) to Wilhelmshaven and my family.

Along the way I tell him in more particulars: "After the tug unloaded us in Hamburg at the port, we were taken by truck to the Marinelazarett where a team of doctors and nurses examined us thoroughly. Two of my men were rather seriously injured, but the rest were unscathed – only shocked. We spent the night in hospital. Because I struggled to fall asleep a nurse gave me a sleeping pill so that I could get some rest.

"The following day the rest of the crew got sick leave and they departed by train to wherever. Only me and my first watch officer had to stay behind and provide statements. I handed in the submarine's logbook.

"And yesterday a board of inquiry was convened. We went to the accident scene to have a look at the wreck of U-57 where she lies in the water and the Nora where she is stranded on the southern river bank. There was unanimity that the captain of the Nora was negligent, if not guilty of malevolent damage to state property. He was dismissed from his position and I suspect that he disappeard into some or other concentration camp. And here I am now."

"How long do you have sick leave?"

"Hell knows. They will probably have to look for another U-boat for me. In the meantime they will try to salvage the U-57. She cannot remain for ever there in the river. She is just an accident waiting to happen when a ship should sail over that spot during low tide and even only strikes her obliquely."

"But in the meantime, you can recuperate from your shock in the arms of my daughter."

"May I politely remind you: It happens that I am legally married to your daughter…"

Later my father-in-law says: "I have concentrated so much on your story that I have totally forgotten to tell you the news."

"What is it?"

"Johannes was also promoted to Oberleutnant zur See and he is to receive his first command of a submarine soon. And in the meantime I became a Fregattenkapitän. For the time being, I am to stay in Wilhelmshaven but it may happen that I get transferred to Norway or France. Or even Holland. Most probably Norway, because I speak the language after having lived there four years after the previous war."

"That's wonderful. Actually, fantastic."

"What is so wonderful and fantastic? My transfer?"

"No, the promotions."

After a while my father-in-law remarks: "Did I see correctly? Are you wearing an Iron Cross there on your chest?"

"Yes. First Class. It was given to me yesterday due to the work that I have performed on the U-57."

"Please, tell me more?"

6 September 1940

I tell everything as well as I can remember. With the U-57, I and my crew have sent seven ships to the bottom of the sea and the BdU has decided on account of the logbook that I had handed in at Hamburg that I deserve this decoration."

Bremen, Saturday, 21 December 1940

I get the feeling that the OKM has forgotten me. I am sitting at home for the last three months and I enjoy every moment with my little daughter. She is one-and-a-half years old and she can already walk a few steps. Before my home-coming, my mother-in-law initially used to look after her when Cornelia went to work, but later Cornelia took her along to her workplace where she could be cared for at a day care centre at the Marinelazarett.

Nowadays, I am staying home and I have taken on the role of houseman, while earning a salary. I took over the housekeeping to make life easier for my working wife.

Cornelia and I have just fallen asleep after a bout of love making when the sirens of our town start to howl. We jump out of bed, grab our gowns, blankets and Nicoletta and flee to the nearest bomb shelter. It appears shortly afterwards that Wilhelmshaven is not the target of the air raid, but the harbor at Bremen.

Bremen, Saturday, 4 January 1941

The attack on the docks at Bremen didn't cause much damage. After that, we could enjoy a pleasant Christmas with Cornelia's parents. Johannes could not join us because his U-boat is somewhere on the North Sea. Franz has home leave. He is a Fähnrich zur See at the Submarine School at Mürwik and he expects to complete his course during the middle of the year and to receive the rank of Leutnant zur See.

Since New Year's Day, we constantly live in fear. During the past four nights there was an attack every night by the bombers of the Royal Air Force on Bremen and environment. That meant that we had to flee to the bomb shelter every night, which disrupted our sleeping patterns drastically.

Father-in-law Achim delivers a signal to me this afternoon. I have to report to the ship yard at Kiel one of these days, as soon as the new submarine U-199 is launched. I must supervise as first captain of the boat the installation of all equipment and accompany the boat on her trial voyages. After that, the flotilla commander and I have to accept the boat on behalf of the Kriegsmarine before she can be commissioned and deployed operationally.

Kiel, Monday, 10 February 1941

Today is my first working day since September. I arrive at Kiel just before lunch and I report to the new commander of the First U-Boat Flotillla. He is Kapitänleutnant Heinz Buchholz, an experienced U-boat captain.

Buchholz is glad to see me: "Wellcome! Ah, I see that you already have the Iron Cross, First Class. I only have the Iron Cross, Second Class. In a certain sense, I am jealous of you because I spend my days in an office while I would rather sail somewhere on the sea. Perhaps, I might apply later on to take over the command of a U-boat."

Buchholz takes me to the spot where U-199 is to be launched this afternoon without much of a ceremony: "From now on, she is yours. Good luck!"

"Thanks."

"Please take note: our flotilla is being moved to Brest on the north western corner of France, one of these days. At the end of May."

Kiel, Friday, 21 March 1941

A period of only six weeks elapsed between the launching of the U-199 and her commissioning by the Kriegsmarine. During this time, all the equipment inside and outside was installed and a trial run of ten days was completed yesterday. As future captain, I had to supervise and observe and inspect and approve everything – especially with my knowledge of nautical engineering.

In the meantime, my crew members arrived piecemeal and they were accommodated temporarily in the barracks at the base. I greeted everyone of them and had a separate conversation with each one to get to know them better. I found that more than half of the previous crew members of U-57 were assigned to U-199.

And today, the full complement takes on the first training voyage on and beneath the Baltic. There are four officers and forty-five other ratings. The U-199 is the newest example of a Class VIIC submarine – an improved version of Class VIIA, of which U-30 was an example. Dozens of Class VIIC's were already built and it appears to be a very successful design.

Bergen, Wednesday, 21 May 1941

We docked in Bergen shortly to have a few minor repairs attended to and to replenish our stocks after we had completed our initial training on the Baltic. And this morning we sail out again for a further training trip on the Atlantic Ocean where the sea will be much rougher.

Becauase we are only embarking on a training trip and everybody is not yet familiar with all the routines and equipment, we were ordered to avoid any contact with enemy ships. It is necessary that our training should be of top quality because it might mean the difference between success and disaster. We carry a few torpedoes, though, but just in case we have to defend ourselves.

Just before we reach the open sea, we see a breathtaking sight: two gigantic warships of the Kriegsmarine entering the fjord to dock at Bergen. It is our newest battleship, the Bismarck, and the heavy cruiser, Prinz Eugen. They are accompanied by three destroyers.

We sail along in the direction of Iceland in the northern Atlantic Ocean.

Atlantic Ocean, Saturday, 24 May 1941

It is shortly before six-o-clock in the morning, local time. We are south of Iceland. Because the sun has already risen, we have dived again after having travelled on the surface during the night to charge our batteries with the diesel engines.

My second watch officer comes to me in my miniscule cabin where I succeeded in getting a few hours of sleep: "The man at the hydrophone reports that he detects the engines of big ships. You must come and listen."

I jump out of my bunk and go to listen. It is really clear that there must be two big ships directly south of us. I order that the periscope be raised and I look around. My eyes almost cannot believe what I am seeing – it's the Bismarck and the Prinz Eugen appearing on the horizon, travelling in a south westerly direction. There is also smoke behind the horizon, south of the German ships – probably enemy ships.

The man at the hydrophone: "There are loud gun shots, to our south."

That must be the smoke I can see on the southern horizon. That can only be battleships of the Royal Navy, shooting at the Bismarck and the Prinz Eugen.

Exactly at 05:57, the Bismarck starts to shoot back. I can clearly see how the flames erupt from the giant gun barrels and I take a photo through my periscope. Because the distance is great I am not confident that the photo will come out clear. I comment throughout the event over the intercom system to keep my men informed.

Four minutes later, exactly at 06:01, we feel a huge explosion. It is louder than any salvo fired by the Bismarck. On the horizon, far to the south of the Bismarck, I see a flash and a column of smoke shooting into the air.

I report: "Men, the Bismarck has just blown a British ship to pieces! I cannot say which ship it was, but it certainly was a big ship. It's too far. Perhaps a batteleship or a cruiser. All of you have felt the shock."

I take a photo of the column of smoke through the periscope and we dive again into deeper waters. The man at the hydrophone: "The two bigs ships sail away in an easterly direction."

24 May 1941

Directly afterwards, I make an entry into our log book about everything that I have observed.

Trondheim, Friday, 6 June 1941

During the fortnight after we have seen the Bismarch in action, we sailed around on and inside an empty ocean and practised all sorts of maneuvres. I feel confident that the men on my boat – the personnel in the machine room, the torpedo crew, the gunners, the radio operators, the navigators, the coxswains, the operators of the hydrophones, the chef, the medic and my officers – all know exactly what is expected of them in any situation.

And today, on this Friday morning, we enter the harbor at Trondheim in central Norway. It is currently the headquarters of the 24th U-Boat Flotilla. After I have completed all the formalities and left the boat in the hands of the harbor personnel, I hastily go to the headquarters of the flotilla where I encounter the commander of the flotilla, Korvettenkapitän Hannes Weingärtner.

After I have reported to him about our trip, I ask if there is somebody who could develop the photographs on my camera. He promises to pay attention to my request. I return to the spot where the U-199 is moored.

Later, during the after-noon, I get a signal via one of our signalmen who is still doing duty. I must report immediately, toge-ther with Weingärtner, at the "Admiral der Norwegischen Nordküste" (admiral of the Norwegian Northern Coast), Rear Admiral August Thiele.

After we have saluted each other, Weingärtner and I are invited to take a seat oppoite the admiral in his office.

Thiele: "Herr Oberleutnant, thank you very much for these photos (and he indicates some photos lying on his desk). Do you realise that you have observed a historic moment and gathered photographic evidence of the event? "

Me: "I believe so, Herr Admiral."

Thiele: "I believe that you are not familiar with the tragic aftermath of this great sea battle?"

"Herr Admiral, I and my crew were out of touch with the world, untill this morning."

"This photo, containing the cloud of smoke on the horizon, shows that the Bismarck hit the HMS Hood, a British battleship, on a strategic spot – probably her ammunition store or something of the sort. That caused the ship to explode and she disappeard within minutes beneath the waves. The other ship that you can see on this photo is another British battleship, the HMS Prince of Wales."

"Did the Bismarck also hit her?"

"Not really. Only superficial damage. The Prince of Wales also caused some minor damage on the Bismarck and Admiral Lütjens, the commander of the German task force, ordered that the two ships under his command return to Norway. After the position of the Bismarck became known, the British sent all sorts of other naval units to track her down. A torpedo aircraft damaged her sterring and then she started sailing in circles. Instead of being sunk by the enemy or even being captured, it was decided that the crew themselves would scuttle the Bismarck and send her to the bottom of the sea. That happened a few days after the destruction of the Hood."

"I believe it was an unfortunate lucky shot when the steering of the Bismarck was damaged. Otherwise, she could have reached safety and be repaired."

"Precisely. And now, Herr Oberleutnant, as soon as your boat has been serviced, you venture out and return to Kiel, your home base. Heil!"

Trondheim, Monday, 9 June 1941

Me and my crew, therefore, sail out again with the U-199, back to Kiel.

We are still on the surface in the Trondheim Fjord, far away from the open sea, when a huge explosion rocks the U-boat. We immediately start to sink. My first thought is that it must have been a sea mine that the Brits have dropped at this spot.

Although I am deeply shocked, my thorough training immediately kicks in and I call over the intercom system that is still functioning: "Life jackets! Diving apparatus! Abandon the boat!"

Fortunately, the U-199 sinks rather slowly and we succeed in opening the hatches to the deck and the men start jumping into the water. As captain, it is my duty to make sure that everybody has reached safety before I can leave the boat. I call into the hatch in the conning tower and the hatch on the foredeck for the last time to hear if somebody was still inside. There is no time to launch the lifeboats.

When I receive no reply, I jump – just in time because the water is already sloshing over the deck. Because the deck is wet I slip and fall. A sharp pain shoots through my left leg, but I succeed in falling into the water. Our engineering officer sees that I'm not able to swim and he grabs me by my collar and pulls me away from the sinking boat – before I am sucked into the depths together with the disappearing vessel.

Fortuantely, the island of Munkholmen is not too far away and all the men who got out swim in that direction while their life jackets help them to stay afloat. I discover that my left leg is broken, but our engineer tows me to the beach of the island.

Fortunately, there is an anti-aircraft battery of the Kriegsmarine stationed on the island and the gunners help us as fast as possible from the water. I can only use my right leg and two men come to my aid so that I can hold onto their shoulders on both sides while we are moving through the gate of the wall surrounding the buildings on the inside.

The commander of the battery, Kapitänleutnant Bernd Bolte, comes to greet me immediately and he assures me that he has already given the command that we be taken back to Trondheim. He has only one patrol boat and she will have to make at least four trips to get everybody ashore – except if the harbor captain also sends a boat to fetch us.

It seems that the island Munkholmen contains a small medieval castle and convent. The anti-aircraft guns are positioned outside out of respect for the old buildings, although the gunners of the battery utilise the old buildings as sleeping quarters and stores.

It transpires that we have three wounded men. Four men didn't make it and we assume that they lost their lives when the explosion shattered the bow.

The three casualties are loaded as soon as possible onto the island's boat, together with the two Sanitäter of the U-199 and the battery, respectively, to look after us.

Trondheim, Tuesday, 10 June 1941

When I wake up, I think that I am still dreaming because I am addressed in Afrikaans: "Hey! Are you awake? How do you feel?"

I open my eyes wide and I feel around me. I feel sheets and blankets. A friendly face appears next to my bed. I realise that I'm in a military hospital.

The friendly face speaks again: "Stefan, do you remember me? David Scholtz. We sailed together on the Usambara many years ago en route to Europe."

"Yes, crikey! David, is it really you? What the blazes are you doing here?"

"Is asked that question first. How in hell did you land here, you bloody, blooming, blasted Nazi?"

"Got injured. I believe I have broken my bloody leg. That's how."

"Yes, of course you did. And I have fixed it with a splint after I have inserted a piece of steel with screws, because you were injured seriously. But how is it that you are sailing around in a fucking U-boat? In Norway, of all places?"

"It's because I am helping in the war against Engeland."

"And then you got injured and landed upon my operating table."

"Oh, yes! If I remember correctly you studied medicine in Berlin. Are you the quack who patched me up?"

"Yes, that's me. And – I'm not an ordinary quack. I'm a qualified specialist surgeon and that is why I was called to work on your ugly broken leg. I specialise on knees and hips. Your leg broke just below the knee. It broke horribly bad. I see on your admittance form that your Santäter completed on your behalf that you have the job of submarine captain and that your rank is Oberleutnant zur See. How the Devil did you get into all this? If I

208

remember correctly, you wanted to study nautical engineering in Bremen and return to South West afterwards."

"That's right. And after I've obtained my diploma I joined the Kriegsmarine. But I fell in love in the meantime – the daughter of the Direktor of the Seefahrtschule and that's why I didn't return to South West. We got married and I have a beautul little daughter. But – what in thunder's name are you doing in Norway in a military hospital, of all places?"

"The same as you – fell in love and got married. And just before I completed my studies the war broke out and trapped me over here. I was given a choice: either join the Waffen-SS or admittance to a concentration camp."

"And then you chose the SS? Do you also guard concentration camps?"

"No, stupid. I am with the Waffen-SS, a fighting unit. I am a medical officer with an artillery regiment and we are sitting around, waiting for better days. In the meantime, I help here at the Lazarett to stay busy because my division must help to protect Trondheim and it seems as if everybody is healthy and strong – except for the men who sometimes get hangovers or get blisters or their private parts due to overuse."

"Well, well. When can I get out of here?"

"Take it easy. I am going to book you off for two months. And then you fly home and get some rest there."

"To South West?"

"What do you think, you imbecile? To your home in Germany, to your wife and your child! Where else?"

"Oh."

Afterwards I think that this was the first opportunity I had in many years that I spoke and heard Afrikaans. Fortunately, I haven't lost it yet.

Trondheim, Tuesday, 17 June 1941

This morning, I am loaded into an ambulance plane, a Junkers Ju-52. En route to Hamburg. From there, I will be taken by ambulance to Bremen where I can recuperate at home. I have convinced David Scholtz that it will be best to be cared for by my own wife. She is, after all, a qualified nurse.

Bremen, Monday, 23 June 1941

We heard disturbing news on the radio today, namely that Germany is again in a state of war against Soviet Russia since yesterday. According to the youngest news bulletins, the German Army and the Luftwaffe are making remarkable progress and thousands of Russian soldiers surrendered or were shot dead.

I discuss this news with my family and all of us agree that Hitler started something that he won't be able to finish. Russia is so vast and has so many people that we will never be able to occupy the whole country or to shoot all soldiers or capture them. Napoleon received a good hiding when he invaded Russia in 1812 and that will also be our fate. The icy Russian winter weather caused Napoleon's army to get frozen and that will also happen to our men.

I have a strong suspicion that the SS division of David Scholtz waited in Trondheim to fight the Russians in Finland.

Brest, Saturday, 23 August 1941

My recovery progressed at a reasonable pace and the 'Stabsarzt' (staff surgeon) at the Marinelazarett in Wilhelmshaven, Cornelia's boss, removed the plaster cast from my leg, but he ordained that I stay another month at home to recuperate fully.

Nevertheless, I was hastily deployed to the U-202 as Kommandant because the Kriegsmarine needs all trained officers urgently. Too many submarines have been sunk by the Royal Navy and the Royal Air Force to allow somebody like me to sit around at home, playing with my toes. The captain of U-202 suffered a nervous breakdown and was sent to a sanatorium. I was, therefore, appointed on short notice to take his place. The crew of the boat is already well trained and I only have to take over.

Cornelia took leave of me with tears in her eyes: "When will we be able to have a normal married life? It's always so difficult to say 'farewell', not knowing whether you will ever come back."

"That's the fate of all the wives of mariners, unfortunately."
I fought back the tears in my own eyes.

And today, my first operational voyage on the U-202 comes to a close. Nothing of importance happened and and we reach the harbor of Brest.

After completion of all the docking formailities, I send an "Unteroffizier" (petty officer) to fetch the mail for our crew members. There are letters for me from Cornelia and from my father-in-law.

Both write that yet another air raid on Wilhelmshaven by the Royal Air Force took place on 8 August – in other words, a fortnight ago. Only a single bomb hit a significant target. Apart from that, all of them are still in good health. No news was received from Johannes for a long time.

I don't like this news.

I also don't feel safe here in Brest because it's an important German naval base and, therefore, a taunting target for air raids. The battleship Gneisenau lies here in a dry dock and the cruiser Prinz Eugen is also moored here. We are within easy reach from British air bases.

Brest, Sunday, 24 August 1941

We are scarcely a day in Brest or the Royal Air Force sends a few dozen heavy bombers during the evening in our direction to sow chaos and to disturb our sleep.

Our ack-ack batteries shoot with all they have at their disposal. The guns of the ships bark, rumble, say "boom" and throw red flames into the air. The gunners of U-202 also do their bit. A few Messerschmitt fighters of the Luftwaffe pounce upon the bombers, but three of them are shot down by the machine gunners of the bombers.

Because the anti-aircraft fire is so dense, the British bombers don't venture low enough to unload their bombs accurately onto their targets. Quite a number of the bombs fall in the vicinity of the Scharnhorst but she doesn't receive a direct hit. A few buildings, though, get damaged. A few British bombers are being shot to pieces and they tumble down to earth.

I decide that Brest is not a healthy environment for me and my crew and we would prefer to be on the open sea – although it would have been much better to be at home with Cornelia and little Nicoletta.

Brest, Wednesday, 17 September 1941

U-202 moors alongside the quay in Brest today after I have completed my second operational voyage with her. We have reason to feel satisfied because we have sent two British ships to an aquatic grave on 11 September. We encountered both of them in the vicinity of Greenland and Iceland.

The BdU initiated a new tactic in response to the convoy system that Great Brittain had introduced. Since it soon became apparent that ships sailing on their own are easy targets for the U-boats, they are being organised in convoys. Such a convoy, often containing between thirty and fifty freighters and tankers, are being protected by a number of warships – often a cruiser, one or more destroyers, frigates or anti-submarine trawlers.

The reponse of the BdU was to organise the U-boats in "Rudeln" (wolf packs). As soon as a submarine or a big bomber of the Luftwaffe becomes aware of a convoy, the position and direction of the convoy is immediately signalled to the BdU. All available U-boats are then ordered to await or stalk the convoy and often a great slaughter occurred on a certain day – despite the presence of warships that could not chase all the submarines at the same time.

U-202 took part in two such wolf packs between 17 and 27 August and again between 27 August and 11 September and found a victim on both occasions. My crew members feel proud to serve on a successful submarine, but the responsibility to ensure the safety of my men, to take all the decisions and also to send torpedoes to unwary ships give me sleepless nights. Every time when I peer through the periscope to ascertain how I can hit an enemy ship, something growls and grumbles in my stomach. It feels like battery acid that is bubbling up inside me. It is much worse than that day when I asked my father-in-law's permission to visit his daughter.

Brest, Thursday, 13 November 1941

My third operational voyage with the U-202, which ends today, was also successful. On 3 November, we torpedoed and sank two British freighters near the coast of Newfoundland with a combined tonnage of 8 600 tons.

During this patrol, which started on 16 October, we took part in two more wolf pack operations, namely from 20 October to 1 November and again from 1 November to 5 November.

By this time, I have lost count of the tonnage that I have sent to the ocean floor. I cannot even calculate how many mariners must have died due to my efforts. My insomnia gets worse. When will I share in these peoples' fate? When will Cornelia become a widow and little Nicoletta an orphan?

Brest, Thursday, 11 December 1941

Together with a number of other submarine officers, I and my three officers from the U-202 are sitting in a saloon near the harbor of Brest during the evening. We are waiting for our U-boat to be serviced for yet another operation. Some of the men drink French wine while I and my men prefer German beer. We submariners feel superior to other naval officers in the base and we annexed this bar more or less as our stamping ground and other officers prefer to avoid it because they rapidly get the message that they are not welcome in our vicinity.

The radio in the bar is on and we hear the news that Hitler has declared war against the United States of America. That follows the news that the Japannese attacked the American naval base at Pearl Harbor, Hawaii, with aeroplanes from aircraft carriers and that they have sunk or damaged a few ships. That was to prevent the American Navy from interfering in Japan's campaign to attack and conquor Singapore, Indonesia and the Philippines.

The men take note of the news of the declaration of war with equinamity. It does not seem as if one of them is in any way excited about the fact that America is now also our enemy.

One of the men, who has allowed too much French wine to disappear through his throat, sighs: "We lost the previous war after the 'Amis' (Americans) started interfering during 1917 – on the side of the English. The same thing will happen again. How the devil does Hitler think that our soldiers must be able to occupy the whole of Russia and America? They are the biggest countries in the world. It's loony. It's insane. It's mad. It's foolish. It's stupid. Shit!"

Somebody helps him: "The Japs are going to give the Americans hell. Just wait."

Another man sighs: "The Japs don't have the capacity to wage a long war and the Americans will throttle them – just as will happen with us."

Another guy grumbles: "You must be careful what you say. The Gestapo might hear what you are saying. They don't work gently with their guests."

The first man: "Ach, them! They will have to swim or run on water if they want to come and catch me because one of these days I will again be in the middle of the ocean (and he demonstrates with his right hand how his submarine dives beneath the waves)."

I tell my first watch officer: "The lot of us are suffering from shell shock by this time. In the most severe degree. We live in constant danger – here in this fucking base with the bombs raining upon us like confetti at a wedding and on the sea where bombers and destroyers chase and hunt us. It's no wonder these guys booze so much."

He only grumbles something inaudible.

Me: "And how long is this shitlike war supposed to continue? It has already gone on for more than two years, two long years   …"

Brest, Saturday, 27 December 1941

Any hope that we may have had to spend Christmas on land – or even in Germany – was dashed when we suffered diesel engine problems in the Bay of Biscay, two days' travel from Brest. We could, therefore, not charge our batteries. We struggled for four days to restart the diesel engines. We came to the conclusion that there were impurities in the diesel fuel that we took on in Brest – probably due to sabotage by the French harbor workers. During the day we stayed under water, without using the last bit of power left in our batteries, and at night we drifted on the surface.

We reach the port of Brest, therefore, only two days after Christmas – after a fruitless voyage since 13 December up to the coast of Marocco in North Africa. We have nothing to show for the trip.

There was, though, a narrow escape when a British bomber spotted us near the coast of Portugal and fired at us with her machine guns. We wanted to shoot back, but our 37 millimeter gun misfired and one of the barrels of the 20 millimeter double barrel gun exploded. The bomber also threw a depth charge in our direction. It bounced on our deck with a loud bang and fell into the water, without exploding.

Fortunately, we suffered no damage because we could dive reasonably hastily when our gunners gave up their efforts. In order to dive as rapidly as possible I ordered all the off-duty men to scramble to the front so that the boat's point of balance could be adjusted and her bows pointing down.

After all the landing formailitie were completed and I reported to the flotilla commander, I receive the order that my whole crew must get dressed in their parade uniforms and get in line for a parade – me included.

This we do.

The 'Marinebefehls-haber Westfrankreich' (the naval commander, Western France), Vizeadmiral Eugen Lindau, takes the salute. I am called to step forward and a citation is read. According to that, I am to receive the Knight's Cross to the Iron Cross because I have sunk eleven enemy ships with my three submarines and for the excellent leadership that I have displayed.

Secretly, I think that my so-called good leadership is nothing but the obedience to standing orders and my thorough training that kicked in every time we got into difficult situations. I certainly don't feel like a courageous leader because I often get the shakes and need a tot of Schnapps to fall asleep.

In addition, I and all the members of my crew receive the golden U-Boat badge, which has to be worn on the left breast. It is awarded to seamen who participated in at least two submarine operations.

Bremen, Wednesday, 31 December 1941

A miracle happened: I am home for Silvester. Because the U-202 needs much repair work, including the replacement of her guns, she will be out of action for quite some time. As Kommandant, I am supposed to supervise the repairs, but I was able to get leave for a few days and I travelled with the train through France and western Germany to reach Bremen.

I find my family at the home of my parents-in-law in Bremen. The atmosphere is sombre because the Royal Air Force attacked Wilhelmshaven again two nights ago and caused much damage. My family is, fortunately, unscathed. Johannes and Franz can't be here because both of them are officers on U-boats messing around somewhere on the Atlantic Ocean, trying to pounce on prey.

My family is, though, very proud of me where I wear my Knight's Cross and U-Boat Badge with pride.

Father-in-law Achim: "It's a shame that you can't send a photo of yourself with these shiny trinkets on your jacket to your parents in far-away South West."

31 December 1941

Me: "I want to have a photo taken of me and present it personally to Tante Stockhausen."

Atlantic Ocean, Saturday, 14 March 1942

At last! We are again sailing around since 1 March after the U-202 was trapped in Brest with problems for two months. These problems are, though, now something of the past and I and my courageous crew departed with great relief from Brest because we don't like the place. There was every so often an air raid from England.

From Brest, we sailed to the west of Ireland and now we find ourselves to the west of Scotland. We haven't received any signals to join a wolf pack yet and we have to scout the Atlantic Ocean on our own.

On the open ocean we are also prone to air raids. Because we want to sail to the coast of North America we stay as much as possible on the surface to preserve our batteries. My second watch officer and one of the petty officers are keeping watch on the conning tower. They suddenly sound the alarm because they hear aircraft engines at a distance. There isn't enough time to dive and I order the gunners to jump out as fast as possible to get the two guns ready. That is something they have practised often and they are ready when three twin-engined fighters attack us from the west with the sun behind them.

Before our men can start to shoot, the machine gun bullets rain upon us. It's a miracle that nobody is wounded and most of the bullet seem to hit the water harmlessly. Just as the planes fly past us at a reasonable low altitude, our twin 20 millimeter gun at the back of the conning tower manages to hit the last plane. Smoke appears at the engine on the starboard side and it is clear that the pilot suddenly lost control and the plane crashes into the sea. The remaining two disappear in a westerly direction after they have made a wide turn – directly back to Canada.

The "Hauptgefreiter" (able seaman) in command of the gun calls out: "Those were blasted Bristol Blenheims!"

His mate announces: "Look, there are two parachutes!"

In the meantime, I have also appeared on the conning tower and I order: "We must capture those two aircraft men. Full speed to the east!"

I give this order in spite of standing orders from the BdU that U-boats are not to rescue drowning enemy seamen of airmen. I tell myself: "Strauss, to hell with that standing order! I can't leave these two poor sodden souls in the middle of the ocean."

We find the two men a quarter of an hour later in the water. In the meantime I have investigated the damage to our submarine and it seems that the conning tower received a few holes. We will be able to close those holes temporarily with wooden plugs, which will swell out when becoming wet under water.

The two soaked aircraft men are only too grateful to be rescued. Because I am more or less the only man aboard who can speak a passable English, it is my task to interrogate them after they were taken inside. It happens to be the pilot and the navigator. Their radio operator/rear gunner didn't make it.

I tell them: "Both of you are going to be our guests from now on. We will certainly find a spot on board where you can be held in safety. We are not going to sail back to France or wherever just for your sake and you guys will have to sail along with us. You must pray every day that we are not going be subjected to target practice by a warship or a bomber because then you will drown, together with us!"

The teeth of the leader, Flying Officer Chester Cromwell of the Royal Canadian Air Force, are chattering from the cold and the shock. He only nods his head up and down. Both are very grateful for the mug of hot tea each one gets from our medic.

Me: "There is still lots of time to chat."

I give the order that we dive as soon as possible after the holes to the conning tower have beem plugged and sealed and we sail in a south easterly direction because the other two Blemheims have certainly reported our position.

Atlantic Ocean, Sunday, 22 March 1942

A full three weeks after we have left Brest we find our first victim, a British cargo ship of 8 800 tons, south west from the coast of Nova Scotia. Somehow or other she succeeds in staying afloat, although our torpedo must have hurt her. She is faster than we are and she escapes.

I tell myself: "Lucky buggers. Your wives and children will be grateful that you got away, although your ship will be useless for some time."

Western Atlantic Ocean, Wednesday, 1 April 1942

Our second victim on this sortie is a British freighter of 5 300 tons. We bury her under the waves with one torpedo, about 500 sea miles north of Bermuda.

About an hour after having torpedoed this ship, the chap at the hydrophone reports that he hears another ship's engines: "She travels fast. It must be a destroyer or something similar."

I dare to lift the periscope for a few seconds above the surface and I see an American destroyer that is steaming more or less in our direction. We seek the depths with as little noise as possible. It seems as if the crew members of the American ship are either asleep or poorly trained because they give no sign of being aware of our presence. They simply carry on to sail along and disappear. I gather they came for us after we had sunk the freighter.

Afterwards I want to kick myself – even with six consecutive kicks – because I would have been able to add this warship to our list of victims. I was too cautious and thereby this chance slipped through my fingers. I feel sorry for the crews of freighters and tankers but I have little sympathy with the men on warships because they hunt us with the object of destroying us.

I promise my crew that we will all get a tot of Schnapps toninght. Our two guests will also receive a tot each due to my kindheartedness and generosity. They have already picked up a few German expressions.

Trondheim, Monday, 27 April 1942

We reach the harbor of Trondheim today after the longest voyage that I have undertaken until now – 58 days. It is considerably nearer to Trondheim in Norway than to Brest from the spot near Iceland where we were unsuccessfully hunting for prey. Our fuel stocks are too low that we can reach France.

We are thankful to get rid of our Canadian prisoners of war and they are taken away on a lorry – perhaps to some or other camp. I am ordered to write a special report about the two of them because they told me much about their training and their base in Nova Scotia.

Of course, these two wanted to know where I acquired my excellent English. Naturally, I did not disclose that I grew up in South West Africa and I simply explained that I learnt it at school.

After I had given the U-202 to the harbor personnel to replenish our stocks of fuel, food and water, I take a walk to get some exercise. To be cooped up in a stuffy and overcrowded submarine for almost two months is rather uncomfortable. I amble past the administrative offices. A door suddenly flies open and a man who evidently did not expect me almost bumps into me.

I grumble: "Shit, man! Can't you look where you're going! Dammit!"

He calls out: "Stefan, is this really you?"

It's my father-in-law, Achim. We get hold of each other and we are extremely glad to see each other.

"Vati, what are you ding here?"

"I work here, of course. I am a member of the Kriegsmarine and we are here at a naval base, after all. They sent me here because I can speak Norwegian."

"Since when?"

"The beginning of last month. Come in. I was on my way out but that can wait. Sit down." After attempting a feeble and crooked smile, together with a frown on his forehead, he continues: "Stefan, I almost don't know how I must give you the news. I have bad news. Very bad."

"Yes, what is it?" My stomach turns inside me and my heart starts beating faster. The drops of sweat run down my spine where I suddenly sit upright to listen better. It is as if a few spark plugs suddenly start firing inside my brain.

"Last Saturday there was a heavy aerial assault on Bremen. Again. Much damage was done. Many civilians did not survive."

The tears in his eyes cause him to take out a handkerchief and he cannot talk any further. I wait for him to continue with a horrible feeling inside my insides. I also feel dizzy and I get a funny taste in my mouth as if battery acid was being pushed up into my throat.

After a while he says: "I am sorry, but our family did not make it. Cornelia had the weekend off and she visited her mother with little Nicoletta. They… they were part of the casualties. I… I'm sorry. They couldn't make it to an air raid shelter, unfortunately. They were caught at home while the bombs rained down."

It feels as if I am paralyzed. I cannot move or use my vocal cords and I can only sit and swallow. I simply sit and stare at my father-in-law. The news is too sudden for me to believe – and yet, I must believe it, even if it too difficult.

Me: "Could you attend the funeral?"

"No. There was no opportunity to get away from here. It's just not possible to grant compassionate leave to all the men who lose loved ones. There are just too many civilian casualties. And, anyway, there were no bodies to bury. The authorities informed me that our home was completely flattened by a powerful bomb. After that, the place also burned down. They were completely incinerated before the firebrigade eventually turned up. There were too many other fires to attend to."

27 April 1942

"So, there isn't even a grave where I can place flowers?"

"No."

Atlantic Ocean, Thursday, 30 April 1942

The U-202 sails back to Brest. I act like a somnambulist and my crew members understand that I have suffered a serious loss. A number of them have also lost family members on account of the bombing raids on German cities, but no one has, as yet, lost a life partner or a child as I did. I wonder how my dad-in-law Achim can survive in his office because he has lost a life partner, a daughter and a grandchild.

Sleep eludes me whenever I lie down to rest. There are so many things I still wanted to tell my darling wife. There are so many things about her that I still wanted to discover. Both of us hoped to spend our days together after the war but those hopes are dashed. My future looks like one big, gaping, dark, empty cavity. I can't imagine myself latching onto another woman ever again in my life. My relationship with Cornelia was so special, so extraordinary, so unique, that I cannot think that anything like that can ever happen to me again.

Atlantic Ocean, Thursday, 25 June 1942

The past two months went by as if in a dream. The war didn't stop and I had to continue running along, regardless. The U-202 departed on 27 May for yet another voyage – again to North America. Four saboteurs were put ashore during the night of 12 June in the vicinity of New York. They were very uncommunicative during the voyage and I couldn't find out precisely what their instructions were, except to cause harm to the United States of America and to create chaos. They told me, though, that they are involved with something called Operation Pastorius.

It was very remarkable that a woman of the German Secret Service, the Abwehr, delivered these men to the U-202. She heard how I swore in Afrikaans and sy informed me that she is married to a South African. Her husband is Karl Krause whom we rescued with the U-30 in July 1939 when his airplane fell into the sea. I wonder whether I will ever see him again.

Two ships disappeared beneuth the waves with the help of our torpedoes off the east coast of America. While I was helping to remove these ships from the ocean I told myself repeatedly: "This is for Cornelia, this is for Nicoletta, this is for my mother-in-law."

I don't like the embittered human being that I have become – a man who suddenly enjoys sending the crew members of ships to wet graves. That is not how I was in the past.

Trondheim, Thursday, 1 October 1942

My new U-boat, U-212, is a sister boat of U-202. I was sent to Kiel in August to take over the command after the previous captain had been promoted and moved on.

I receive orders to join the Thirteenth U-Boat Flotilla in Trondheim – to my joy. This is a new flotilla that is to take up accomodation in Dora-1, an impreganble bunker of steel and concrete and in which a dozen submarines can be serviced, safe from Allied bombers.

I hope that father-in-law Achim is still stationed in Trondheim. Although he is, strictly speaking, no longer my father-in-law because I am no longer marrid to his daughter, I find it impossible to think of him as anything else than my father-in-law.

The U-212 enters the harbor of Trondheim slowly to await directions how to dock inside Dora-1.

A pilot boat sails in front of us to indicate the place where we are to dock.

Trondheim, Monday, 1 February 1943

I get the feeling that this new year started slightly better than last year since I may call myself a Kapitänleutnant from the beginning of February. Perhaps I may become commander of a flotilla some or other time with the result that I will not anymore have to spend my time inside a floating coffin, a U-boat.

I am not the only person to be promoted today. The BdU, admiral Dönitz, is promoted to "Großadmiral" (Admiral of the Fleet) and he becomes commander-in-chief of the Kriegsmarine in the place of Großadmiral Erich Räder who has retired. The new chief of the submarine fleet is Konteradmiral Eberhardt Godt.

We are losing more and more submarines. Shortly before New Year's Day, I heard from father-in-law Achim that Johannes' U-boat was supposed to have arrived three weeks ago at Trondheim, but has not yet shown up. His last radio message was received four weeks ago and he and his crew are being regarded as missing in action.

This news does nothing to improve my horrible state of mind. I cannot but address myself: "Kapitänleutnant Strauss, when will it be your turn?"

Near Iceland, Sunday, 2 May 1943

It is a clear spring night, about an hour before daybreak. We are sailing east of Iceland, in the Denmark Strait, near the spot where the HMS Hood was blown up by the Bismarck. We sailed from Trondheim a week ago and we are part of a wolfpack, waiting for a reported convoy on its way to Russia from America.

I keep watch on the conning tower and I scour the horison in the feeble light of a crescent moon with my binoculars. The Unteroffizier manning rhe hydrophones reports through the voice pipe: "Engine noises to the west. A whole crowd of them."

A quarter of an hour later I scout the smoke of some ships steaming in our direction. I give the order to dive to periscope depth. Just as first light appears I watch an American destroyer coming our way. She will pass less than one hundred metres in front of us. I wait for her with all my torpedo tubes ready.

While staying stationary with as little noise as possible so as to stay undetected, I allow the destroyer to pass in front of my boat. A torpedo is launched from tube number one. I am confident that I cannot miss. However, we hear no explosion.

The man at the hydrophone reports: "I heard the torpedo striking the hull of that ship. No explosion."

I carefully swing the bow of my U-boat to face the destroyer again and I launch another torpedo from tube number two. The same result.

All of a sudden, the destoyer changes course and starts chasing us. Her "asdic", an apparatus that sends sound waves through the water in an effort to locate us, starts to make "ping" noises that we can hear clearly. We dive as we hear depth charges detonating behind us.

We dive as deep as our hull can stand the water pressure and we stay there for two very tense hours before ascending carefully again. Instead of being the hunters, we became the quarry

– not a nice situation to endure. During this time, we heard two far-away explosions as other members of the wolf pack achieve hits.

Through the pericope, I notice that the convoy has disappeared. We are lucky to have escaped.

I am perplexed, yet also furious, and I ask my first watch offer, Leutnant Hugo von Helmstedt, whether he has any explanation for the fact that our torpedoes malfunctioned.

"Let's go and inpect our remaining torpedoes. Perhaps something is wrong with the whole batch that we loaded in Trondheim."

"Nice idea."

Together with the Feldwebel in charge of the torpedo tubes, we inspect all our torpedoes. The Feldwebel discovers the problem – one of our torpedoes isn't fitted with a detonator that causes the load of explosives to detonate as soon as something is struck. We inspect the rest of our torpedoes and all of them lack detonators.

"What do you think?" Hugo asks.

"Sabotage. No doubt about it. Somebody doesn't want us to sink enemy ships and clandestinely removed those detonators before they were given to us."

"But who would so such a stupid thing?"

"There are enough traitors and saboteurs, people who have no love for the Nazis. It could be anybody along the line, anywhere between the manufacturers and the dock workers. We will have to send an urgent message in code to Trondheim to warn them about this sorry, sad, stupid state of affairs."

"Can we continue with this sortie without any usefull torpedoes?"

"Of course not. We return immediately. Lots of bloody time wasted."

Half an hour later I talk to my first watch officer again: "It suddenly strikes me that we may perhaps have a saboteur on board.

Do look around to see if he perhaps hid the detonators somewhere."

"Do you really think so?"

"I have had such a trouble maker on board in the past."

I catch myself that I am seething with fury – directed against the saboteur, the Allied bombers who killed my family and the Allied navies, which sank Johannes' U-boat. I retire to my miniscule cabin and I tell the crew members in the control room: "Don't disturb me. I don't want to be messed with."

Barents Sea, Thursday, 5 August 1943

More than a whole year has elapsed since U-212 could record any successes. The Brits and the Americans deployed more and more destroyers and frigates together with their convoys to Russia. These ships are fitted with radar with which a submarine's periscope can be located from a distance of a few nautical miles.

Bombers with radar patrol the Atlantic Ocean from Nova Scotia, Iceland and the north of Scotland and it became increasingly dangerous for U-boats to dare to attack convoys.

During the past year, U-212 took part in three wolf packs, which could only achieve limited success. The "good times" of 1939 to 1942 seem to have passed and it appears as if the Allies are winning the battle against the U-boats on the Atlantic.

Today, we get some luck. We succeed in blowing a small Russian vessel of only 80 tons from the ocean. This happened in the vicinity of Spitzbergen, the most northerly group of Islands belonging to Norway but which was occupied by the Allies. The explosion, though, drew the attention of an American cruiser, which steamed at full speed in our direction. Fortunately, the ice mass of the Arctic, a heap of ice floating on the water, was nearby and we could hide under the ice cap where the cruiser's instruments couldn't locate us.

We stayed under the ice for more than a day where we lay immobile and we nearly froze solid in the icy waters. Afterwards, I thanked my men for enduring this hardship without a murmur. They are rewarded with a tot of Schnapps each.

Norwegian Sea, Tuesday, 10 August 1943

A few days after my first success with U-212, we sail in a southerly direction to reach Trondheim again. A Catalina flying boat of the American Air Force that must have taken off from somewhere in Scotland, spots us where we are still on the surface, shortly after daybreak. U-549, that accompanies us, dives instantly but I decide to fight. After all, I have a personal war to wage against the Royal Air Force and the American Air Force.

Our gunners do their best to shoot the plane down but without success, although her hull must surely have received a fair number of holes. Perhaps that will make her sink when she gets back onto the surface of the water. The machine gun fire directed in our direction hits me in my left foot where I'm standing on the conning tower from where I watch the action. Two of our gunners are being wounded, respectively in a shoulder and a right hand. The U-212 herself does not receive any mentionable damage.

Our Sanitäter does his best to patch up all the wounds but he declares that we need better medical assistence. I give the order that we return to Trondheim at a steady speed.

Trondheim, Saturday, 14 August 1943

Our Sanitäter gave me a strong pain shot, otherwise I would not have made it. I stand on the conning tower while the U-212 is docking at her position inside Dora-1, although I have requested my first watch officer to handle the maneuvre. It was a rather difficult operation because it is already dark.

After we had docked, two medics came with a stretcher to take me off the submarine. The two other wounded chaps are able to walk on their own. My first watch officer must handle the remaining formalities.

Trondheim, Sunday, 15 August 1943

A part of my left foot is being amputated in the military hospital in Trondheim. The wound is too severe and the bones crushed to suchan extent that the wound can just be sewn up. The three smaller toes and part of the foot behind them have to be removed. Fortunately, I keep my big toe and his companion.

Father-in-law Achim visits me afterwards: "Stefan, with only one-and-a-half feet it won't do to sail around as Kommandant of a U-boat anymore. As soon as you have healed sufficiently you are to get a new posting."

"Will it be on land?"

"Yes and no. They need a new commander for a flotilla Speedboats or S-boats at Bodø, about 250 kilometers north from here. I understand that the Brits call these boats E-Boats. I don't know why. Anyway, the present commander is to be promoted one of these days to somewhere else. The boats mostly stay in the harbor and they only venture out when their services are needed somewhere."

"Must I accompany them?"

"That will be necessary. These S-boats, as you must have seen in the past, have a low profile. It won't be necessary to climb ladders all the time as in a U-boat. You may even sit on a stool on the bridge and control the flotilla from there."

"Sounds oekee. But in the meantime the Arzt arranged for me to get sick leave. He says there is a sanatorium here in Trondheim where wounded and sick naval officers can recuperate."

Bodø, Tuesday, 28 September 1943

During the few weeks at the sanatorium, during which I had to learn how to walk with half a port side foot, Cornelia often visited me at night. I had the most wonderful dreams where I made love to her and had emotional conversations with her. I expressed my ecstatic joy that she was, after all, able to cheat death and returned to me. There was, though, one unpleasant conversation when I expressed my anger and disappointment because she had abandoned me.

After such a dream, I always woke up again feeling despondent, tired and worn out.

I arrived at the naval base in Bodø last week. It is not a large base and the most important unit here is the Eighth S-Boat Flotilla. There is a harbor captain who also controls the anti-aircraft batteries, workshops, store rooms and administrative offices.

Bodø is a small harbor town on the Saltfjord. There is quite a large number of Wehrmacht personnel because there is also an airfield housing two squadrons of the Luftwaffe – fighters and reconannaisance aircraft, together with an anti-aircraft battery and a workshop unit. Seaplanes often land on the waters of the fjord. A POW camp is situated next to the air field. It will be difficult for enemy forces to attack the naval base because there are a few dozen small islands just outside the fjord, which makes navigation hazardous. There are also mine fields that ought to frighten off any enemy from the sea.

There is a dearth of living space for officers and I am quartered in with the family of Fredrik Freiberg. The name suggests that the father, a teacher, must have had German forebears. There is, in addition, Missus Ruth Freiberg and their daughters Hedda and Hilde. The last-named is a widow; her husband was a lieutenant in the Norwegian Army and he fell during the German invasion in 1940. Hedda has a boyfriend who is a prisoner of war of the Wehrmacht.

It is quite understandable that these people would not feel very positive about the Germans, but they just have to accept me against their will.

Their home is built of wood – as are most houses in Norway – and it is reasonably large and I get the guest room to occupy. Fortunately, they do not have to provide me with meals, because I eat at the officers' mess at the base. Food is, in any case, in short supply due to the war because the Wehrmacht often confiscates the food supplies of the Norwegians. It is also not possible to catch fish – the staple of the Norwegians – as in the past because the Kriegsmarine is afraid that the fishing trawlers would escape to Scotland. The few trawlers that are allowed to catch fish do so with armed guards aboard.

The fast attack craft – there are seven of them – are speedboats armed with torpedoes. There are two torpedo tubes athwart the bow and two anti-aircraft guns. Near the stern, a 40 millimeter gun is fixed and near the bow a twin 20 millimeter gun is placed. The boats can achieve 40 knots and each one carries four torpedoes. There is also a tender, a small freighter that can take provisions and spare parts to the boats at sea, if necessary.

The skippers of the seven boats are pleasant guys and they understand that I cannot be as agile as they are since I only have seven toes. They cannot but notice my decorations and they treat me with respect.

The day before yesterday was the first opportunity I had of venturing out with with the whole flotilla. We had received a report of a convoy on its way back from Russia after having unloaded valuable equipment and stores to the Russian armed forces. Although the ships are sailing back empty they are a valuable prey because every empty cargo ship that is being sunk, cannot carry any more freight to Murmansk on Russia's northern coast.

And today, shortly after daybreak, we encounter the convoy, about 170 natical miles (more than 300 kilometers) north west from our base. I order that we attack as fast as possible and to retreat immediateky afterwards before we can be targeted. The two destroyers and two frigates escorting the convoy must, surely, have picked us up with their radar and they shoot in our direction. With our high speed, we are able to get into range of the convoy unscathed. All of us launch our torpedoes in the direction of the convoy and we retreat again. We hear two explosions and it seems as if a freighter and a frigate had it. It is impossible to tell which boats' torpedoes did the damage and the success is being notched up as a success of the whole flotilla.

At a safe distance we reload our torpedo tubes for another attack. One destroyer receives a direct hit.

Bodø, Monday, 4 October 1943

Shortly after breakfast, I hear strange aircraft approaching. The sirens at the air base start screeching and screaming and shouting. Very shortly after that, the air field and the harbor are being attacked by eight blue American light dive bombers. The anti-aircraft batteries start shooting and most of the crews of my S-boats succeed in firing as well.

Two of the eight Americans are hit and fall from the sky. The crew of one plane succeeds in escaping with their parachutes. The other one breaks up in pieces while colliding with Mother Earth.

The attack ends after a few minutes with the remaining aircraft flying away. I gather that they must have come from an Americam aircraft carrier.

The harbor captain orders all available men to inspect the damage. It appears that four small German freighters were damaged, one of which was sunk. They were all taking on iron ore that had been transported by train from Sweden. That means that German steel furnaces might experience a slight lack of iron ore and that not quite enough steel may be produced to build new tanks and U-boats.

4 October 1943

Because the attack came so unexpectedly not all the crews of my boats reacted immediately. One boat, of which the crew members were on board when the attack happened, got seriously damaged. A bomb hit the boat and four men were killed and three were wounded badly. The boat, itself, sank and we have only six boats left.

Bodø, Friday, 29 October 1943

Shortly after breakfast, I call the skippers of my flotilla's fast attack craft to a meeting: "Men, a signal has reached me three minutes ago. One of our reconnaisance planes has seen a convoy en route to Russia. According to the photos taken, there are more than fifty freighters. They are being escorted by a few warships, including a light cruiser. Get your men ready. We sail in thirty minutes' time. See to it that you have enough fuel and ammo for your guns. Fortunately, we have already made sure last week that the torpedos are loaded."

The men get going and I sound the siren to call all the crew members to report to their boats.

We succeed in sailing half-an-hour later. I sit in the first boat on the bridge. We navigate carefully between the small islands and mine fields outside the fjord before reaching the open sea.

Suddenly, I hear an explosion. The boat directly behind me is blown out of the water. The coxswain next to me exclaims: "It's a torpedo! A blooming British submarine stalked us!"

Over the radio I order: "Full spead forward! Get away as fast as possible before another one is hit!"

The other boats shoot past me and I order my boat to return to search for survivors. We succeed in getting the whole crew alive out of the sea, except for the two men in the engine room. The men are shocked, drenched and a few are hurt.

On the radio I give the order that the rest of the flotilla must wait five nautical miles from the coast until I return. I must take the injured men of the sunken torpedoed boat to our sick bay.

Suddenly I hear another hard bang, more or less three hundred meters from us. Pieces of a submarine are thrown into the air.

The coxawain remarks drily: "That's the bloody shits who have blown our mates out of the sea. Now they have reaped their just reward by being caught by one of our mines."

I give the order that we sail in the direction of the explosion. Maybe there are survivors. We find six men struggling in the water. They are the only survivors of the submarine's crew. They are helped aboard and I turn around with my overloaded S-boat to have the injured men attended to.

Two hours later I rejoin the rest of my flotilla and we move north in an effort to intercept the convoy.

Bodø, Saturday, 30 October 1943

We succeed in taking two feighters out and to damage a destroyer before we hastily retreat – in spite of the fact that my flotilla was reduced to five craft. We turn around to attack a second time with our second loads of torpedoes and we hit a tanker.

Bodø, Sunday, 31 October 1943

When we are still twenty nautical miles from our base, my coxswain calls out: "Our fuel tank is empty! We forgot to top up before we sailed out a second time."

The only remedy is that one of the other boats has to tow us and take us back.

Bodø, Tuesday, 15 February 1944

The Eighth S-Boat Flotilla receives four more boats of a more advanced design and there are nine boats now. I am simultaneously promoted to Korvettenkapitän – slightly more than a year after my previous promotion.

In the meantime, I and the Freiberg family became good friends. I surreptitiously took food from the officers' mess to prevent these poor folks from starving and to compensate them for the involuntary lodging that they had to provide me with. Although I suspect that they have connections to the Norwegian underground resistance, I don't interrogate them in this regard because that might force them to tell lies. On the other hand, I naturally don't inform them about the plans and movements of my S-boats.

With the Freiberg family I usually speak German, but as time went on I picked up quite a bit of Norwegian and I can conduct a simple conversation in this language. When they discovered that I wasn't a "real" German, but actually a native of South West Africa and Afrikaans-speaking to wit, they opened up to me and treated me with kindness.

The Freiberg family are simple, yet educated, country folk. They grow their own vegetables in their garden and the two girls are fit and strong from all the diggings and harvesting. It is also the girls' task to chop wood to keep the cooking fire burning. All of them are qualified teachers and each one has a university diploma.

They are also a musical family. Father Fredrik plays the piano and the guitar, Mother Ruth plas the cello, Hedda plays the violin and Hilde plays the clarinet. I am treated to a musical concert at least twice a week when they form an ensamble to play classical music and folk tunes, while they also sing. They even taught me the words of a few Norwegian songs.

During these concerts I got a good look at Hilde and decided that this atractive blonde Viking girl will make a good wife for a lucky man and a good mother for that man's kids.

Both girls like to tease me by declaring that the Wehrmacht did a very bad job of conquoring Norway. Countries like Denmark, Holland, Belgium and Luxemburg fell within hours when they were invaded. France fell within six weeks, but it took the Germans more than two months to subdue the Norwegians, although Germany's population is more than ten times that of Norway.

Hilde has a wicked sense of humour. One day she told me: "When we see a blue airplane flying, we know it's an American plane. When a green plane flies over us, we recognise it as British. When there are no airplanes flying, we know it's the Luftwaffe."

She also told me that when the Wehrmacht crossed the border to invade Poland in 1939, the British Prime Minister sent an urgent telegraph to Hitler, asking him why his troops crossed the border. Hitler promptly replied: "To get to the other side."

It is clear to me that the German occupation of Norway causes much hardship and suffering and I can understand that the Norwegian Resistance tries to thwart the German occupationary forces and to sabotage infrastructure to impede the movement of troops and supplies as much as possible. The result is that German armoured vehicles often rumble past the Freiberg home to remind the local population that the Germans are in control here.

Since the attack by the American planes, my S-boats undertook three fruiless excursions – each time due to faulty information about the position and course of convoys to and from Russia. I hope that our reinforcements will help us to achieve more success.

Bodø, Monday, 30 October 1944

Last week, I was informed that I am to be transferred from 1 November 1944 to Kristiansand in southern Norway and that I must assume command of the flotilla harbor protection craft there.

It is with a heavy heart that I say good-bye to the crew members of my boats. Since the beginning of the year, when we received reinforcements, I undertook six more sorties with them. On three occasions we attacked a convoy en route to Russia and every time we sent two freighters down into the icy depths of the Arctic Sea.

All the crew members of my fast attack craft have received the golden S-Boat Badge – me included. I wear it with pride directly next to my U-Boat Badge. The design is basically the same, except that a U-boat is replaced by a S-boat.

Of course, I didn't inform the Freiberg family earlier of my departure. While I am packing my bags this morning I mention that I am going to leave them during the day. Hilde, who is two years younger than me – helps me to pack. She has tears in her eyes.

"Stefan, you cannot leave me now. It's not right that you go away."

"Why do you say this?"

"I am expecting your child."

"Are you sure?"

"Absolutely sure."

"All right, my girl. I couldn't help it, but you conquored my heart. As you well know – I am a widower. My wife and child were hit by a bomb two years ago. In your arms, I found solace. I wish I could have taken you along with me but that is, of course, not possible. I'm very sorry."

"But what must I do? Everybody knows that Germany is losing the war. The Allies have already liberated large parts of France. The Russians have driven the Germans almost totally from Russia and it is only a matter of time before they surround Berlin. If you leave Norway after having lost the war, my people will never forgive me for bearing the child of a German officer. I will be regarded as a traitor."

"I know. I know. I wish I could do something about this state of affairs. But I promise you that I will come back to fetch you, as soon as I am able to return after the war has ended. I agree that it is impossible for Germany to win the war. It is only a matter of time before everything in Germany will come crashing down. But I promise that I will return for you. Will you wait for me?"

"Yes, I will. What must I call our child?"

"If it is a boy you may call him after my father: Septimus. If it is a girl, you may call her after your mother."

"Septimus is Latin for seventh. Your father was probably the seventh generation from your first South African ancestor. This little one (and she points at her stomach) will be the ninth generation. He cannot, therefore, be called Septimus."

"All right. Let us name him after a very good friend of mine who has found his end at sea: Johannes. Do your folks know that you are in the family way?"

"No. They never suspected our nocturnal adventures."

"You won't be able to hold it secret for ever. But I promise that I will come back to collect you and the baby."

"All right. Please hold me for a last time before you go away and disappear."

Kristiansand, Wednesday, 1 November 1944

The journey to Kristiansand was rather difficult. Because partisans have blown up the rail track between Bodø and Mo i Rana I was intitially forced to travel by truck. At Mo I Rana, yesterday, I caught a train, which took me to Oslo. There I slept at the Kriegsmarine headquarters and this morning I took the train to Kristiansand where I arrived this afternoon.

During my journey, I involunatrily thought about Hilde. My affair with her came unexpectedly and we both just slided into a physical relationship. I didn't really court her as I courted Cornelia – there was no opportunity for that. It just happened naturally that we were drawn to each other.

I cannot but help to compare the two women in my life. Cornelia was this boysterous, lively, joyful and playful extrovert. Hilde is this serious, mature and quiet introvert. They could not have been different. I had an immediate crush on Cornelia when I first met her. My love for Hilde grew with time. Initially, she crept to my room at night just for a chat. We found that we liked each other and, eventually, the inevitable happened: she ended up inside my bed. We both had this urgent need for physical contact and everything that comes with that. We made love every other night.

When I reach Kristiansand I go the harbor captain's office to report. The clerk behind the desk next to the harbor captain's office asks me to wait a while because the Herr Kapitän zur See is busy. After an uncormfortable half-an-hour the door of the harbor captain's office opens at last and an Oberleutnant zur See leaves with a very worried look on his face.

My first thought is that the harbor captain must be a very difficult man who insults and scolds everytbody, left and right. The clerk announces that I may step inside and I move forward with heavy feet.

In the doorway to the inside office I stand at attention and salute, while I stare straight ahead and call our: "Herr Kapitän, Korvettenkapitän Strauss reports for duty!"

A gruff voice barks: "Come in and sit down, you cheap piece of stinking seaweed."

I fall on my back – or that is how it feels. Behind the desk, father-in-law Achim von Czapiewski is seated with four golden stripes on his sleeves. He is the harbor captain!

Father-in-law Achim leaves his seat behind the desk and grabs me. I cannot stop smiling. And suddenly I understand how I got this posting to Kristiansand – my ex-father-in-law must have pulled a few strings!

Coffee is being ordered and we start conversing. It appears that Franz has been promoted to Kapitänleutnant and he is the local submarine commander. Kristiansand doesn't have an own submarine flotilla, but it often happens that U-boats arrive her for repairs and the replenishment of fuel and other stocks. Franz's team has to handle that.

My father-in-law: "Tonight, the three of us are to dine together in the officers' mess. Then you and Franz can swop yarns. There is also accomodation for you in the officers' barracks."

"Thanks a lot. I look forward to see Franz again. But I will also have to get familiar with my flotilla. How do I get there?"

"I will take you. You control a flotilla of seven armed trawlers. It's a special design and the most of them have been built in Sweden. Only the civilian version And afterwards they were equipped with armaments in Wilhelmshaven – guns and depth charges. Radar as well."

"I am curious to see them. As you know, I have grown up with trawlers. Hopefully, these trawlers are better than my father's trawlers."

"I'm sure they are."

We stroll down to the harbor and there I see three of the trawlers anchored in the water.

Me: "I want to sail out on one of them tomorrow."

"Two or three of them are continuously on the sea outside the harbor – seeking enemy submarines or airplanes. And in due course, I will show you all the installations here in Kristiansand. I am actually more than just a harbor captain. My title is 'Kommandant der Seeverteidiging, Kristiansand-Süd' (Commander of the Coastal Defence, Kristiansand South). I am called, in short, the 'Seekommandant'.

"Perhaps I will get promoted before the end of the war. My predecessor in this position was a Konteradmiral and perhaps I am to become one as well."

Kristiansand, Thursday, 2 November 1944

The seven skippers of the armed trawlers sit in my office. The office is in a temporary wooden building because Kristiansand has been attacked by enemy bombers in the past and some of the buildings were damaged – also the headquarters building of the flotilla of harbor defence craft.

Two of skippers have the rank of Oberleutnant zur See and the rest are only a Leutnant zur See. They are still young men – conscripts who sat at school only a few years ago. They address me with great respect due to the fact that I can sport a Knight's Cross, as well as the badges for U-boats and S-boats on my uniform jacket. I arrange with Hans Huckebein, the eldest of the group, that I am to be taken on an excursion with his trawler this afternoon.

"I would very much like to sail regularly with you men, but I am afraid that my office duties will suffer if I do that often. I love the sea, though, and I will sometimes join one of you. Please take into consideration that I am almost an invalid because I have lost a part of my port side foot. I cannot ascend a ladder so easily to reach the bridge of a trawler."

The men assure me that they understand.

I question the men about their boats that are officially known as "Kriegsfischkutter" (armed fishing trawlers). It transpires that such a trawler displaces a mere 110 tons and carries a crew of 18 men of which two are officers. They are rather slow and can only do nine knots. They are armed with a 37 millimeter gun on the foredeck and a 20 millimeter double-barelled gun just behind the bridge. They are equipped with a number of depth charges for use against submarines. They have hydrophones to detect the machine noises of submarines under water and radar to detect approaching ships and aircraft.

I ask if somebody can supply me with the construction plans for these boats and I am informed that these plans are being kept somewhere in a drawer in my office. I decide silently that I must find them and inspect them with my knowledge of nautical engineering.

After the meeting, I am taken to one of the trawlers and we sail out so that I can get the feeling of the boat.

I ask if I can handle the wheel and it feels familiar – quite a bit like one of my Dad's trawlers.

Kristiansand, Friday, 3 November 1944

My father-in-law orders his adjutant to accompany me so that I can observe all the sections under his command and get on top of things over here. It is also important for me to visit all the spots where Cornelia and I held our honeymoon, many years ago. It will be a nostalgic trip.

Cornelia paid me another visit in my dreams last night. I conclude that I must be a bigamist at heart because I love two women at the same time, although one of them isn't alive anymore. I miss both Cornelia and Hilde rather terribly and I am terribly tired of this war.

At and around the harbor office, there are various sections: a weather office, a sick bay, an administrative office, a radar station, an intelligence section, a department to service U-boats, a vehicle park, fuel tanks and storage rooms. There is also a flotilla minesweepers, a battalion with 88 millimeter ach-ack guns and a battalion with six batteries of coastal artillery.

I ask to see these batteries and we drive to each one of them. It appears that some of these batteries were inherited from the defeated Norwegian armed forces, but newer ones were added by the Kriegsmarine. The battery with the heaviest guns have the callibre of 380 millimeters – the same calibre as the main armamanet of the Bismarck and her sister ship, the Tirpitz. Other guns have callibres of 210 and 150 millimeters. Every battery has machine gun nests at its disposal, just in case they are attacked directly.

When I visit my father-in-law again later during the afternoon, he says: "Welcome to Fortress Norway. It's actually a military secret, but the Norwegian coast line is being guarded by more or less 650 000 men. It is no wonder that the Allies haven't tried to invade the country."

Kristiansand, Tuesday, 14 November 1944

This morning, I wake up with the ugliest belly pain imaginable. I feel nauseous and dizzy in my head and I conclude that this cannot be the result of my emotional turmoil. It must be something else. I struggle to get into my uniform and I stumble along to the sick bay.

I tell the "Sanitäter-Feldwebel" (medical chief petty officer): "I am as sick as a dog."

"Herr Korvettenkapitän, do you want me to take you to the vet?"

"Are you stupid or only silly? Or totally deranged and loony?"

"Vets know how to deal with dogs and their illnesses."

"I'm not a dog with rabies or something. Shit, I need a human doctor, for heaven's sake!"

The Sanitäter-Feldwebel takes my fever, feels my pulse, looks at my tongue and organises an ambulance to take me to the military hospital.

At the hospital, the Stabsarzt doing duty isn't quite sure what is the matter with me. "Herr Korvettenkapitän, there is more than one possibility. It may be a tumour – or an ordinary appendix. Perhaps also something toxic or a bad allergic reaction. We will have to examine you under anesthesia. I will ask the SS-surgeon, who arrived here a few days ago on his way to Denmark, to come and help as well."

"Do anything. Just help me to get rid of this pain."

Later that day I wake up in a bed, although I am not sure whether I am really awake or not because somebody is speaking Afrikaans to me. It may also be a dream.

"Isn't this that bloody guy from South West again? By Jove, what are you doing here, my friend? Last time I saw you, you were a big shot on a submarine."

I open my eyes and I decide that I am not dreaming. The friendly face of David Scholtz appears above me.

Me: "I ought rather to ask you what you are doing here. Last time I saw you were in Trondheim with a bunch of SS butchers."

"Don't insult my division! We are elite troops, mountain troops, if you want to know, and we were shooting the shit out of the Russians. That is what we were doing before the fucking Finns decided to throw in the towel and chased us away. Now we are back again."

"Are you the quack who worked on me?"

"Don't insult me, you idiot! I'm not an ordinary quack! That is something that I made clear to you three years ago. I'm a specialist surgeon."

"OK. What did you do to me?"

"Ever heard of appendices? We butchered yours out. It was rotten and it could have killed you – just as effectively as a Russian or a British bomb. Only slower."

"Thanks, man."

"When you are better you are going to visit me. And then we can gossip at leasure about these Germans. These stiff Nazis give me a cramp in the bottom."

"More or less the same here. Tell me, what do you hear from your brother Willie? Does he also fight the Russians?"

"No, he has a civvie job. Research or something of the sort. Busy with some or other wonder weapon, I suppose."

"I also work with wonder weapons."

"Oh, yes?"

"Yes, I wonder every day what the poor conscripts of my flotilla will be able to achieve when the enemy really strikes. The poor sods were only halfway trained and then let loose."

"Yes, one can only wonder. We are supposed to receive reinforcements one of these days in Denmark, but I also wonder where they will come from."

"You mentioned last time that you married a German girl – the same as me."

"She was hit by an American bomb last June in Berlin."

"Sorry, man. My wife and little daughter were also blown up by a British bomb, two years ago in Bremen."

"Therefore, both of us are widowers."

"Yes, I'm officially one. But in the meantime I have made a Norwegian girl pregnant. I miss her quite a bit. But I will only be able to take her away from here after the war."

"Only if you don't kick the bucket or buy a one-way ticket to the mortuary. You naughty boy!"

"This bloody appendix is certainly the punishment for my sins. But – I will struggle to kick the bucket because I only have one-and-a-half feet."

It's rather strange to have a conversation in Afrikaans again.

Just before David leaves, my father-in-law and Franz arrive to visit me. I introduce "Oberstabsarzt" (medical officer with the rank of a Major) David Scholtz to Kapitän zur See Joachim Graf von Czapiewski.

My father-in-law: "Thanks for fixing this man. He isn't too bad, except for the fact hat he has the habit of making women pregnant."

David gives a sly smile: "That's something I can cure with a small operation."

Me: "Hey! You leave my male instruments alone! Do you get that?"

Kristiansand, Sunday, 19 November 1944

Yesterday, Saturday, David Scholtz visited me for the last time in hospital and discharged me. I am certainly not yet fit for active service and he has given me another fortnight to regain my strength. The medic in our sick bay must remove the stitches ten days from now. He also asked me whether I would like to attend a religious service as his guest today – something I could not refuse.

After breakfast at the officers' mess, David comes to fetch me. The chaplain of the artillery regiment to which David is attached, leads the service in the open air. It seems as if the whole regiment has turned up voluntarily for the service. The chaplain, a Catholic priest, says mass and delivers a short but inspiring sermon. David, and I, who are staunch Protestants, do not take mass but we find the rest of the service uplifting.

David: "That priest is a wonderful man. He has withstood all the hardships with the men and he proved to be a capable medic who helped me in the operating tent. That's why these men have the greatest respect for him and attend his services willingly. I think he qualifies for sainthood."

After the service, David invites me to have lunch with him and his officers in their temporary lodgings where they were housed before they will be taken over the Skagerrak to Denmark in a few day's time. Because the men would certainly never see me after this I deem it safe to divulge that I am actually a compatriot of their medical officer who hails from South Africa. We sit next to the Catholic priest and David assures me that they are best friends, although they support different brands of Christianity.

After lunch, David and I go to sit outside on a rock where we can watch the harbor. David produces a bottle of vodka: "I have kept this for a special occasion, like today. I carried it all the way from Finland where a Russian officer in my medical tent presented this to me out of gratitude that I had saved his life."

"And now you want to share it with me?"

"Yes, and then we can talk nonsense while none of these stupid, slow-witted, simple-minded Nazis can understand what we are telling each other. We are going to empty this one litre bottle while we are conversing in our mother tongue, Afrikaans."

"Marvelous. It seems as if you don't have a high regard for the Nazis."

"Let's each take a swig from this bottle to accentuate that profound conclusion of yours."

Both of us take a mounth full of this fire water and I get tears in my eyes. I wonder what half-a-bottle of this strong stuff will do to me, but I cannot insult my new friend by refusing to drink with him.

We start gossiping about the Nazis. We both agree that Hitler is a fool, a megalomanic idiot. It is actually a pity that those generals didn't take him out last July. By this time there is no chance whatsoever that Germany can win this war.

We drink another generous toast to accentuate another profound insight.

David: "We were told that the Russians are barbarians and that Stalin is a full cousin of Satan himself."

Me: "And I have been taught that Churchill is a drunkard and that Roosevelt is a secret criminal Jew."

"And yet, I have found that the Russians are just ordinary folk who speak a strange language and who love this stuff (and he holds the bottle up in the air). I have operated on quite a number of wounded Russian prisoners and they have the same feelings and aspirations as we have."

"And I had lengthy conversations with two Canadian airmen whom we captured after having shot down their plane in the Atlantic. I found them to be very decent guys. If we weren't waging war against them, I could even have befriended them."

"Let's drink on that piece of deep wisdom!"

David: "And yet, I hate the Americans and the British. The Brits allowed thousands of our women and children to die in their concentration camps during the South African War. And an American bomb killed my dear wife and my brother's wife."

Me: "My Dad fought in the South African War against the Brits. Since he was an inhabitant of the Cape Colony he was a subject of Her Majesty, Queen Victoria. He was a member of the commando of Commandant Golding that operated in the mountains, south of the Karoo town of Fraserburg. They didn't know that peace was declared on 31 May 1902 and a few days later they ambushed and killed a few British soldiers on patrol in the mountains. He was sentenced to death in absentia for being a murderer and a so-called traitor and he and a few friends fled to German South West Africa where the Brits couldn't touch them. That's where he met my German mother. During the previous war, he helped the Germans in South West against the troops of Louis Botha and Jannie Smuts when they invaded the country."

"So, your folks were always anti-British. Was it an American or a British bomb that killed your family?"

"It was a bomber of the Royal Air Force. It's called 'Royal' because these guys are supposed to be loyal to His fucking Royal Majesty, King George."

"This information makes us almost blood brothers. Here, take another mouth full."

I do so and David follows my example.

David: "Now that you mentioned the king, I can remember something we kids sometimes sang. It goes like this:

> 'God save the King
> With a bottle of paraffin.
> Out came a flame
> And away with the King!'"

I start laughing out loudly at this hilarious rhyme and I hold my belly with the operation wound. We both swallow another mouth full of fire water. After that, I say: "I can also remember a silly rhyme from long ago. Here it is:

'King George flies in his airy,
The people see his canary.
The canary can't fly
And hides behind the King's fly.'"

David rocks to and fro as he laughs almost his head off: "Wonderful! How does the King's canary look like? Any idea?"

We fall silent again.

Me: "Do you have to give the Nazi salute often?"

David: "Unfortunately, yes. But I try to sidestep it as often as I can. We are, after all, a SS unit and we are supposed to be the vanguard of the Nazi Party."

"While I was serving on U-boats and other naval craft, we dispensed with that nonsense. But here, at this headquarters, it is expected of us to salute the photo of Hitler whenever we pass it and call out, 'Heil Hitler!'"

"Do you really do it?"

"Not really. Every time one of us has to raise his right arm at forty-five degrees, we mutter: 'So hoch die Scheiße!' (the pile of shit is this high!)"

"Ha-ha! I like that! Let's swallow some more of this stuff!"

The silence descends again.

Me: "Tell me about your wife, please? What type of person was she?"

David starts explaining how beautiful she was, about her wonderful family and then he starts crying. I pat him on his shoulder and the sobs subside somewhat.

David: "How did you and your wife get to know each other?"

I waited for this question and I start telling him how we met and what happened after that. I take out her photo to show to David and suddenly the tears start running down my cheeks.

David pats me on the back and he takes out a photo of his wife. We both agree that we had married beautiful and wonderful girls.

None of us can talk any further and we finish off the last few drops in the bottle.

David: "How in hell are we ever to get back home after this fucking war?"

Me: "Heaven knows. You must ask that priest pal of yours to pray for a miracle. I need two miracles, actually."

"How?"

"I fell for this young Norwegian widow in Bodø, as I told you the other day. I made her pregnant. I dare not contact her from here and that priest of yours must pray for a miracle that I can reach her after the war again and marry her."

"You definitely need a miracle for that. Perhaps my friend the priest can use his contacts in heaven to recruit a flock or a platoon or a squadron of angels – or whatever a bunch of these creatures is caled – to come to your assistance with this girl."

Both of us remain sitting on the rock, watching the harbor and feeling very sorry for ourselves.

Kristiansand, Monday, 23 April 1945

David Scholtz and his SS division have left a long time ago and I feel trapped here in Kristiansand. Really bad things are happening in Germany. The Russians have cut Berlin off from the outside world and hemmed in the Führer over there. Vienna in Austria was taken by the Russians and the Amercans are running circles around our men in southern Germany.

The sirens in our base suddenly start to scream. That means only one thing: an air raid! All the administrative staff dive into bomb shelters. I run as well as I can to reach the nearest trawler. I jump on board, just before she moves away from the jetty.

I yell: "Get out of the harbor. Otherwise we will be a target. Load the guns immediately!"

Two minutes later a swarm of American bombers come flying along and they download a few tons of bombs. Our anti-aircraft people were, fortunately, ready and they get a flying start with their guns. My armed trawlers also shoot with everything they have. We all know that we cannot depend on the Luftwaffe at this stage of the war anymore to stop these bombers because there are almost no fighters left. The firing tempo of our gunners is high enough to force ten of the more or less forty bombers out of the sky.

I have to stop the gunners on my trawlers when they start shooting at the men who glide down to earth with their parachutes: "No! We're not murderers!! Stop!"

It, nevertheless, happens that a few of the parachutists are hit by other guns. I can understand that the men are furious and they want to take revenge.

The battle is over after a few minutes when the last Americans disappear behind the horizon – minus the bombs they have left with us.

I get back onto solid land and I help to gauge how much damage was caused. Two minesweepers, two submarines and one trawler were sunk. A few buildings are in flames. Fire fighting teams start with their work. Many bombs did not cause any damage and only blasted big holes in the dirt.

That evening I chat with father-in-law Achim and Franz somewhere outside so that we cannot be overheard: "There is absolutely no chance that Germany can still win this war. The Yanks and the Brits bomb us at will. Almost the whole of Germany is already occupied by the Allies. What is going to happen to us, here in Norway?"

My father-in-law: "The attention of the Allies is almost totally focused on Germany itself. The only naval bases we still have are those at Flensburg and Kiel, apart from these here in Norway. It's only a matter of time before we will have to capitulate."

Me: "And then?"

My father-in-law: "Camps for prisoners of war."

Franz: "Let's steal a U-boat and flee somewhere."

My father-in-law: "Are you serious? Really serious?"

Kristiansand, Tuesday, 24 April 1945

The air raid of yesterday caused the deaths of a number of men. Members of the crew of my armed trawler that was sunk are among those who have fallen. A big funeral service is being held in the open air, just outside the base. There is absolutely no possibility that the remains of these men can be repatriated to their home towns in Germany.

Although only a few men form the guard of honor for the ceremony, a spirit of despondency, pessimism and dark depression pervades the whole base – worse than in the past. The despair also takes hold of me. How will I survive when the bombs start falling again? How on earth will I ever be able to fulfil my promise to Hilde to fetch her after the war?

Kristiansand, Monday, 30 April 1945

We listen to a radio broadcast. Admiral of the Fleet Dönitz announces that the Führer has fallen in Berlin and that he has been appointed as the successor of the Führer. His headquarters in Flensburg at the Marineschule Mürwik is temporarily the administrative centre of Germany – or those parts of the country remaining under German control.

Some time later, father-in-law Achim calls me and Franz and we go outside where nobody can overhear our conversation.

My father-in-law: "I received two identical signals this morning. They were delivered by Luftwaffe couriers in their planes. There were two of them to make sure that at least one of them reaches me."

Me: "Why by plane? Why not by radio?"

My father-in-law: "There is reason to believe that the Brits are able to decypher the codes of our radio messages."

Franz: "That sounds serious."

My father-in-law: "You're dead right. It's horribly serious."

Me: "And how does it concern the two of us (and I point to myself and Franz)?"

My father-in-law: "Quite a bit. Really very much, actually. Here, I have orders that I must collect a crew of ten men who must depart on a secret mission with one of these brand new Type XXI U-boats. No later than tomorrow. Stefan, you must send three of your trawlers immediately to Skagen in Denmark where they have to meet three trucks at the harbor. A number of boxes and trunks have to be loaded there and brought back here."

Me: "What do these boxes and trunks contain?"

My father-in-law: "That's something I will tell you later. Those boxes and trunks must then be loaded onto this Type XXI submarine and then we have to depart tomorrow night after dark.

To a secret destination. Franz, am I right in stating that we currently have three of those super submarines in port?"

Franz: "Dead right."

My father-in-law: "Get one of them ready so that we can get away with her tomorrow night. In the biggest secrecy. Get enough diesel, water and victuals."

Franz: "How many torpedoes must we take on?"

My father-in-law: "Not a single one. The war is almost over and we are not going out to sink British or American ships. We simply have to take a secret cargo somewhere."

Me: "I'm going to take all six remaining trawlers to Skagen and spread the cargo over all six. Then our chances of getting those crates and trunks over here will be so much better. One never knows when we will be attacked from the air again."

Franz: "Or strike a mine…"

My father-in-law: "Sounds good."

Me: "Do you now how heavy all these trunks and boxes are?"

My father-in-law: "I was given to understand, more than three tons."

Me: "Then every trawler will carry about half-a-ton each. That may work well."

I lead my flottila two hours later across the Skagerrak to Skagen.

Kristiansand, Wednesday, 2 May 1945

The crew members of the three class XXI U-boats in our harbor are assembled on our parade field and father-in-law Achim addresses them:

"Men, I know that your limbs are itching to get a go and sow havoc amongst the fleets of the Allies. Unfortunately, your training has not yet been completed and we cannot send you out as yet. I need, though, seven men to participate in a secret project, seven men who have experience of these wonderful boats. I am looking for men who don't have families left in Germany – men whose parents, wives, children, brothers and sisters are all dead. Will those of you please come and stand here on my left side?"

Of the about 120 men who assembled, only thirty shift to his left side. He dismisses the rest.

He addresses the remaining men: "Guys, I really need only seven men. It may become a dangerous mission and we must travel to somewhere far away. Nobody knows when we will be able to return to Germany, if ever. Those of you who don't feel like participating, may also dismiss."

Fifteen men remain.

"I already have two officers (and he points at me and Franz). I need two coxswains. Are there any coxswains here?"

Two men step forward and father-in-law lets them go to his right.

"I need two men who understand the engine room of a Class XXI."

Three men step forward, one of them a Leutnant zur See.

"Who of you has the least years of service?"

The Leutnant zur See lifts his hand. He is excused.

"We must have two men who can man the hydrophone."

Two men lift their hands and they join the other chosen ones.

"And I want a Sanitäter who can also man the galley."

One man joins the group.

"Thank you, you other men. I will need you tonight to help us load a number of of chests and trunks and boxes into our U-boat. Please report to the quay directly after dinner. At the Type XXI U-Boat, which is moored directly next to the quay. The seven men who are sailing with us must bring their luggage along. All your personal belongings. Also civilian clothing. I need your full names, please. Please be ready to have your photographs taken in civilian clothing."

My father-in-law later approaches me: "All Seekommandants and harbor captains received an urgent signal today. The Gestapo is looking for a certain Oberleutnant zur See Strauss of the submarine branch. They retrieved his South African passport from the wreck of the U-57 near Hamburg. It took a long time before they could connect the name on the passport with the name of a specific submarine officer. He is now being charged with espionage."

"Did you answer them?"

"Are you mad?"

Kristiansand, Friday, 4 May 1945

It took a bit longer than we thought to store all the cases and trunks inside the submarine. At Skagen, it was relatively simple to divide the cargo between the six trawlers. The spaces inside the submarine are, though, very cramped and it took time to climb down a ladder with a box or a crate of 20 kilograms and to dump it somewhere. My father-in-law supervised the process of storage to make sure that the weight was distributed evenly.

We counted more or less 170 chests and trunks. At twenty kilograms per item it amounts to 3.4 metric tons. Actually, it is only the contents that are supposed to weigh twenty kilograms, but when the weight of the chest or the trunk is added, then every item easily weighs 23 kilograms.

It is only shortly after daybreak before we can sail away and disappear under the waves shortly afterwards.

The men who have previously served on this type of U-boat assure me that she can remain under water for long periods of time. If she sails just under the surface she can "breathe" through a snorkel so that the diesel engines can still propell her. Her batteries have a much, much longer endurance than those of the Class VIIC with which I am familiar. This type of boat also moves almost totally silently and cannot be detected by the enemy. This is, without doubt, the most modern type of submarine in the world. If we had them a year earlier, the outcome of the war could have been different.

But these super boats only started coming from the production lines during 1945 – too late to influence the course of the war. Our particular boat, U-3531, has received her number, but hasn't been commissioned into the Kriegsmarine yet since her crew had to receive intensive training after she had been been delivered by die Marinewerft in Wilhelmshaven.

Franz declares: "If we had twelve of these boats in June last year along the French coast, we could have stopped the invasion of Normandy in its tracks. And then the Yanks and the Tommys would have had to beg for peace because their invasion fleet would have been resting on the ocean bed. They would not have been able to start another invasion."

Father-in-law Achim: "And then we could have withdrawn our forces from France to face the Russians and we could have pinned them down in the Ukraine or Poland. Stalin would not have had the strength to dislodge us – especially because he would no longer have received all those massive amounts of supplies from the Americans. That would have ended the war with Germany the occupier of large parts of Europe."

Me: "You say – just twelve of these U-boats?"

Franz: "Only twelve of these super boats. The Allies don't have anything like this and we could have sunk their aircraft carriers, cruisers, destroyers, freighters and landing craft by the dozen. The invasion would have been a disaster."

Me: "And then it would not have been necessary for all those generals to try to blow Hitler up last July."

Father-in-law Achim: "Yes, yes. It's easy to speculate now. Unfortunately, it didn't happen that way. We've already lost this bloody war and nothing can change that."

Father-in-law Achim calls a meeting in the control room: "Men, the time has come that I tell you more. You are surely curious about the cargo we are carrying You have seen the dozens and dozens of trunks and boxes and crates that we have stored all over the boat. It's gold, heaps of gold, more than three tons of gold. It's a large part of the gold with which the Reichsbank planned to pay for the war.

"Let me tell you a secret. The Reich was on the brink of bancruptcy by the time the war broke out in 1939. All the tanks, guns, trucks, airplanes and warships that were being built for the Wehrmacht had to be paid for in money, heaps of money. That is one of the reasons why so many junior officers had to perform the work of more senior officers during the war and never got the promotions they deserved because there wasn't enough money to remunerate them properly. There was simply no more money available to the Reich.

"We traded with countries like Switzerland, Sweden, Spain and Portugal and they, of course, expected to be paid for the products they sold to us. We only had gold to pay them. When we overran Poland, Denmark, Norway, Belgium, Holland and France, special units confiscated as much gold as they could lay their hands on. That helped to pay for the continuation of the war. Our cargo is part of our stocks that were left at the end of the war. We must now take it to South America where a team of scientists is supposed to complete the planned super weapons that we have been promised so that we can revenge ourselves on our enemies for all the damage they have done to our cities. You are all men who have lost your families. They were killed by American, British or Russian bombs. The day of reckoning is coming.

"I have a strong suspicion that other U-boats also departed with gold and key personnel. The people who want to have the gold smuggled to South America would certainly have seen to it that not everything was transported in a single submarine.

"How do you feel about our project? Do you agree that we are tasked with a very important mission? What do you say?"

The men started to appload spontaneously and it is clear that they feel enthusiastic about our project.

My father-in-law continues: "We are sailing to South America, to Montevideo. There, a freighter will come to offload our cargo and take it further. And then we are to scuttle this submarine after we have also been transferred to the freighter. These two officers (and he points to Franz and me) are simultaneously our radio operators and signallers. They must broadcast our precise coordinates on a daily basis at midnight, Greenwich Mean Time, on a certain frequency so that our friends in Spain, Portual and Argentina can keep track of our progress.

"I am in overall control of this project. Korvettenkapitän Strauss is captain of the boat and the Kapitänleutnant is the first watch officer.

"Somebody fabricated forged Swiss passports for each one of us before we departed from Kristiansand. You keep your own names, but you are supposed to be neutral Swiss citizens from now on. With those passports you will be able to survive anywhere in the world. I will distribute your passports in due course.

"This boat has all the comforts we need, but I would like to ask you to all sleep in the same space so that we do not have to live all over the boat. Let's use the space directly in front of the control room. We even have enough water so that you may enjoy a brief shower every second day."

While we are sailing submerged on this secret mission, I cannot help but to wonder how I will ever be able to reach Hilde again. I have dreamt about her often during the last few weeks, while Cornelia paid me fewer and fewer nocturnal visits. Our destination is very, very far from Norway. It is probable that we will get stuck somewhere in South America. It's anybody's guess how long that wil take. I fight back the tears when I think back on the beautiful nights we spent together in Hilde's parents' home while all the others were asleep.

English Channel, Monday, 7 May 1945

Our passage with U-3531 through the North Sea and the English Channel proceeded uneventfully. Our hydrophones picked up the sounds of various vessels, but all of them were far away as we sailed at a steady ten knots.

After three day at sea, we see the beam of the lighthouse on the Lizard Peninsula in Cornwall through the periscope. It is the most southerly spot in Great Britain. This must be the first time that this lighthouse has been switched on since the start of the war and we all agree that the war must have ended without us knowing anything about it.

With my father-in-law' s permission I order the boat to break surface so that we can have radio contact with Germany. We listen to the news broadcast at 05:00, informing us that Generaloberst Alfred Jodl, chief of Staff of the Wehrmacht, has signed a deed of surrender to the Western Allies a few hours earlier at Reims in France.

Father-in-law Achim: "That means that the Royal Navy won't chase and hunt us anymore. We are no longer in danger if we sail on the surface."

Franz: "But it' s better that nobody knows that we are here because they will order us to surrender at the nearest base of the Royal Navy, which is at Devonport, near Plymouth, just north east from us here."

An hour later we listen to the news again. Hitler's successor, Großadmiral Karl Dönitz, announces that he doesn't approve of Jodl's signature and he orders the Wehrmacht to continue the fight, especially against the Russians.

I sigh: "Are we still at war, or not? I know the German Forces in Italy and Austria have already surrendered, but others are still shooting at the enemy. What will the Royal Navy do with us if they discover us?"

Father-in-law Achim: "Stay careful. Don't let them discover us, as Franz has reminded us."

We continue at periscope depth, just to make sure that we observe what is going on on the surface, although our hydrophones will also warn us of any shipping in our vicinity.

Sunrise occurs at 0745 local time. The man at the hydrophone: "I can hear the engine noises of three or more big ships to our rear."

I swing the periskope to our rear and I observe something in the light of the rising sun that would have made the heart of any submariner bounce with joy: four fat, juicy, enticing, and delicious targets are coming our way! The leading ship is an aircraft carrier and she is followed by a cruiser and two destroyers. It is clear that they don't expect any units of the Kriegsmarine to be operational anymore because they are not steaming in battle formation. For that, the two destoyers would have taken the lead to detect any possible U-boats in advance and protect the bigger units against attacks from below the surface.

Father-in-law Achim also takes a peek through the periscope: "Those Limeys are either asleep or badly trained. They don't seem to notice us. What on earth are they doing at sea?"

Me: "They're probably on their way to the Pacific. Remember, the Japs are still fighting."

Franz: "While we don't know whether the Wehrmacht has surrendered or not, we may just as well do our Jap friends a favor by sinking these ships. They evidently left the naval base of Devonport at Plymouth two hours ago."

Me: "How? We don't have a single torpedo."

Franz: "I almost forgot. Sorry. So, we can't do anything to help our Jap allies?"

Me: "I we had any torpedoes, we could have caused a serious blow to the Royal Navy right at this moment. Those guys won't ever know what hit them because we are undetectable."

The task force of the Royal Navy overtakes us while I watch them through the periscope. In these uncertain times it's better to stay extremely careful. Suddenly the two destroyers turn to port and sail directly in our direction.

Me: "Crash dive! Crash dive!"

I order the coxwain to steer directly to a position underneath the aircraft carrier and to stay there. The destroyers will never expect such a maneuvre and the engine noises of the aircraft carrier and cruiser will completely blot out the little noise we make.

When we are about a hundred metres from the aircraft carrier, we hear depth charges exploding somewhere behind us.

Father-in-law Achim: "Stefan, that was brilliant of you to do the unexpected. They are bombing us blind in the futile hope of causing some damage. It's clear that they don't want to take chances because they don't know whether Germany has really surrendered, or not."

Me: "Should they discover us underneath the aircraft carrier, they wouldn't dare to bomb us. This carrier will be our shield."

The aircraft carrier is doing a steady eighteen knots and we keep up with her for more than an hour.

As we enter the Bay of Biscay, I give the order: "Slow down to five knots. Dive to maximum depth."

The man at the hydrophone: "Those two destroyers have given up the hunt and they have fallen in behind the bigger units."

I give the periscope console a loving pat: "Yes, U-3531 is the most wonderful vessel that I have ever sailed in. Without doubt. We were in a position to achieve one of the most glorious maritime victories of this war if we had any torpedoes. But, on the other hand, we are not supposed to fight anymore and give our position away."

Father-in-law Achim: "It's a pity that this episode will never be reported in any history of the war at sea. We all would have qualified for the Knight's Cross with Oak Leaves and Diamonds!"

Our Sanitäter who is also in command of the galley quips: "We can always bomb them with the rotten eggs that we were given before we left Kristiansand."

Me: "Nice idea. That will produce a big stink."

Two hours later we continue our voyage southwards and we listen to the BBC news at eleven o' clock. It is announced that Generalfeldmarschall Wilhelm Keitel will sign a deed of surrender to all the Allies in Berlin tomorrow. Hostilities are to end today.

Atlantic Ocean, Friday, 18 May 1945

The German Wehrmacht has capitulated more than a week ago and the war has ended. Germany was beaten for a second time, fully, catastrophically, and humiliatingly. Our submarine is, though, the only element of the Kriegsmarine that is still operational – as far as we know. By this time, we are more or less between the bulge of West Africa and Brazil, in the middle of the Atlantic Ocean.

I ask my companions whether any of them has crossed the Equator in the past. It seems I am the only one who did. I suggest that we invite old Father Neptune aboard to initiate all the novices in this regard as tradition requires, but nobody knows how to do that.

Our medic: "On which radio frequency can we contact him?"

Me: "That's for us two Funkers to find out."

Franz: "I'm sure that old Father Neptune won't like to visit pirates, like us. I propose that we slip over the Equator without notifying him."

Father-in-law Achim takes Franz and me to the empty torpedo room where we can talk in private: "Men, we are supposed to take all this gold to South America so that the war can be continued clandestinely. I was also informed, in confidence, just before we departed, that Adolf Hitler did not commit suicide as everybody thinks. No, he got away with one of these super submarines from Trondheim to Argentina after having escaped from Berlin with his wife. The corpse that the Russians have found and identified as their bodies, are actually those of somebody else. Those bodies was burnt to such an extent that a positive identification was, anyway, impossible.

"In any case, during the past few days I have been thinking a lot, really a lot. Are we doing the right thing by continuing the war? Must we really take this gold to South America so that a gang of mad, insane, deluded, and demented Nazis can unleash some more misery on this world? I don't think so."

Me: "That is also how I have been feeling since we left. It is an open secret that a large part of the gold that we are transporting comes from people who died in concentration camps – their wedding rings and other jewelry, as well as the gold in their teeth. We are really indebted to these victims of the SS butchers to make sure that this gold does not fall into the hands of the remaining crazy and corrupt Nazis."

Franz: "I agree. I have already talked to some of the men and they aren't so enthusiastic about our project anymore."

My father-in-law: "Right, men. Then we bedevil the people who want to use the gold. We disappear with the loot."

Me: "Do you mean that we take it for ourselves?"

My father-in-law: "We divide it between us ten crew members."

Me: "And how is each one of us going to drag more than a dozen boxes filled with gold through the world?"

My father-in-law: "Simple. We sell the gold and divide the money."

Franz: "But where?"

My father-in-lawe: "Stefan, am I correct if I say that you hail from Walvis Bay? Your folks are surely still living there?"

Me: "I don't know if they are still alive. I haven't had any news from them since the start of the war. But I'm sure they are still there."

My father-in-law: "I think we sail to Walvis Bay. Your father has, after all, a fleet of fishing trawlers? He can help us to transport the gold onto dry land and then we scuttle the submarine in the deep sea. What do you think of that?"

Me: "Yes… It might just work. And then all of us can just disappear into South West. There are thousands of Germans and we will easily be swallowed by the masses – with our Swiss passports and all."

My father-in-law: "Then we stop broadcasting our position by radio from tonight onwards. The people who are listening must come to the conclusion that something happened to us and that we sank, or something."

Franz: "It will even be more convincing if we broadcast a 'May Day' right now and provide a false position. Then they will believe that we all got drowned and that the gold is just gone – somewhere between the fishes and octopusses on the bottom of the great wide ocean."

Me: "And for old Father Neptune to take care of it all."

My father-in-law: "Nice plan."

Walvis Bay, Monday, 4 June 1945

It's late on a Monday night as we reach the vicinity of Walvis Bay. My father-in-law has, in the meantime, explained the situation to the other seven members of the crew and there was unanimity that we take the Nazi gold for ourselves. It is stolen gold that, strictly speaking, doesn't belong to anybody. It's almost as if we have found the gold somewhere by chance and just picked it up. Therefore, it ought not to be a sin or a crime to divide it between us. It would rather have been an unforgivable sin to hand it over to the crazy and deranged. and insane and psychopathic Nazis.

It will, therefore, be necessary that we more or less disappear from the face of the earth and certainly not to reappear somewhere in South America in the midst of the fugitive Nazis. Walvis Bay is actually the only logical alternative Everybody agreed with that.

My father-in-law also explained that we will be very dependent on the help of my father and Onkel Helmut because we will need their boats to transport the gold secretly onto dry land. We can't just sail with our U-boat into Walvis Bay harbor and unload the crates and boxes there. My folks must be properly compensated for their aid. All of us find that in order.

Even before we can see the lights of Walvis Bay I can smell the place. I stand watch on the conning tower, together with my father-in-law. A warm wind is blowing from the east and we get the smell of the fish processing plant.

Me: "There is no better sign that we are sailing directly towards our destination. This smell is, as it were, the trade mark of Walvis Bay."

My father-in-law: "It's already late and it will take some time before we see the lights of Walvis Bay. The crescent moon rises only after midnight. That will certainly not be the right time to put you ashore."

"It certainly won't do to go and wake up my parents so late at night. Let's wait here on the ocean and then I can creep to my parents' home tomorrow night, just after dark."

"Where must we put you ashore?"

"It won't do somewhere in the bay or the harbor, of course. There will be too much activity and the U-boat musn't be seen. Rather a distance away from the entrance to the bay, at Long Beach. From there, it will be about five kilometers to the town, but I will manage that in the dark. I have, though, an ugly problem."

"What's that?"

"I will have to go on my own to visit my parents. I am the only one in our bunch who can speak Afrikaans and who knows the place. But I will have to remain invisible because many people still know me from the time before my departure to Germany, twelve years ago. I am sure that my parents told everybody that I joined the Kriegsmarine of Nazi Germany in thirty-six. They were very proud of me at the time. There will certainly be people who will report me to the Police if they see me. And then my parents will also be in deep shit and dung and problems."

"Because they will regard you as a traitor?"

"Exactly. After all, I helped the enemies of South Africa, although my parents thought it was fantastic that I became an officer in the Kriegsmarine. The rest of us are unknown in these parts and all of you can easily move around in the town and the rest of the country with your Swiss passports at a later stage. I cannot dare to show my pale face during daylight here, or in Swakopmund."

"All right. Then we wait till tomorrow evening early to move you onto dry land. Before the moon rises."

Walvis Bay, Tuesday, 5 June 1945

Franz and one of the other men take me with the submarine's life raft to the shore. It is agreed that I will light with a torch in the direction of the submarine just after dark tomorrow night to signal with Morse code what is going on.

The U-boat has moved nearer to the coast and she is waiting on the surface for the life boat to return after having offloaded me. It is the plan to wait there under the surface until tomorrow night when I will signal them.

I planned my moves during the day and prepared myself on how I was to approach my parents. The moment I was dumped on the soft sand of Long Beach it suddenly felt as if my legs turned into jelly or maize porridge. My batteries suddenly lost all charge and all my fuses got burnt out. I wonder if I haven't taken too much on myself – especially since I am struggling with only a part of my left foot.

I easily find the road just beyond the beach connecting Walvis Bay with Swakopmund. Fortunately, there is not much traffic and I have to move way from the road on a few occasions to stay invisible when I see vehicle lights approaching. It takes the whole of two hours before I reach my parent's home.

My folks are still awake and I look through the kitchen window. I see my mother washing the dishes. I look through the window of the living room and I see my father talking to Onkel Helmut where they sit. Simon is also there, but he is busy with something else.

I carefully knock on the front door. I think: "What will happen if I cause one of my parents is to get a heart attack if they see me so unexpectedly?" Before I can run away the door opens and Simon is standing there. It seems as if he has seen a ghost. His eyes blink rapidly and his mouth hangs open.

My Dad calls: "Simon, who's there?"

Simon remains dumb.

My Dad calls again: "Tell me, who's there?"

Simon succeeds in speaking: "Somebody who has been raised from the dead."

He pulls me into the house and closes the door behind me.

My father yells while getting to his feet from his chair: "Stefan, Stefan, my son! Is it really you?"

Onkel Helmut also gets up and he looks too amazed to say anything.

Simon grabs my hand and starts to shake it up and down.

My Mom, with her apron on, comes from the kitchen and gives a loud sob: "My child! My child! Where did you come from? We have long ago given up hope that you are still alive. If you were captured by the English the Red Cross would have informed us of that. But we never heard anything and we just accepted that you… are not around anymore."

My Dad adds: "We heard through the news how the Royal Navy and the American Navy reaped amongst the German U-boats and we could not believe that you survived the carnage. Mommy, this man is surely dying from hunger. Is there anything for him to eat?"

I get a chance to speak for the first time: "No, I'm not dead – only somewhat wounded. I'm also not really hungry. Only thirsty because I walked a long way to get here."

Simon: "All the way from Germany? You must be joking."

Onkel Helmut comes to hug me and the tears run over his cheeks. Thereafter, it's my mother's turn to press me to her heart. My father does the same.

Me: "Can we please close the curtains? Nobody must see me here. Only you may know that I'm here."

Simon: "Here are enough people who would regard you as a traitor because you helped the Nazis. All those who previously sympathised with the Nazis keep their beaks tightly shut nowadays – too afraid to say anything."

All of us hurry to close the curtains. I sit down. My Mom brings me a glass of drinking water, which I swallow eagerly.

My Dad: "How the blazes did you get here? Swam or walked from Germany? How did it happen that you are not being held in a prisoner of war camp?"

Simon: "You seem to be healthy and strong. What did you do during the war?"

My Mom: "What happened to our daughter-in-law? Cornelia? Is she still alive?"

Onkel Helmut: "Have you, perhaps, stolen a submarine to flee and to get here?"

Me: "You make me totally dizzy with all your questions. I will tell my whole story to you if you give me time. But, first of all, I would like to know: do you still have your fishing trawlers?"

My Dad: "That's a bloody stupid question to ask at this moment. We want to know: how the hell did you get here? How are you doing?"

Simon: "Yes, we have seven trawlers at the moment. Two of the boats that you have known from the past perished, but we replaced them with three new ones."

Me: "OK. Wonderful. I and my friends need those boats urgently. Can we borrow one or two of them for a little while?"

Onkel Helmut: "Why in hell do you need them? Who are your bloody friends?"

Me: "I and my chums want to get some gold that we swiped from the Nazis onto dry land."

Simon: "Your chums?"

My Dad: "Gold? How the devil did you obtain that?"

My Mom: "My son, are you delirious? Do you have fever?"

Onkel Helmut: "Must we get you to a doctor?"

Me: "Whoa, whoa, all of you. Give me a chance to speak. It's a long story, but I'm going to tell only the most salient points now."

My Dad: "Let's give the man a chance. He looks normal enough to me, although – his story up to this point confuses me totally. Are you sure that you're not drunk, or something?"

I hold up my hands and everybody looks attentively to me: "I and my chums departed from Norway a few days before the end of the war with one of the most modern submarines of the Kriegsmarine. We are ten men. Our assignment was to smuggle three tons of gold to South America. Many Nazis have fled there and there they want to continue with the development of secret weapons to take revenge on the Americans, the British, and the Russians after they have lost the war. Halfway there we all decided that we don't want to help the Nazis anymore and then we disappeared with the three tons of gold. That gold is still on our submarine. Here somewhere at sea. You have to help us with your fishing trawlers to get the gold, packed into boxes and crates, onto dry land. And then we divide the gold. The other men all have forged Swiss passports with which they can disappear – probably into the German community here in South West."

Silence.

Everybody's mouth is hanging open. I also don't know how to continue. Suddenly, I start to sob and I dry my tears with my sleave.

My Mom gets to my side and grabs me tight while the tears are rolling.

Onkel Helmut growls something about "shell shock".

My mother: "Give him a break. I'm sure the man has gone through hell."

Silence for a few minutes.

My mother hands me the kitchen cloth she is holding and I wipe my face – wet eyes and a running nose. I sigh: "Thanks that you didn't chase me away. Thanks for being concerned about my welfare. It is so – I litteraly went though hell. Two of the submarines of which I was the commander were sunk and it is a miracle that I escaped alive from those wrecks. They shot at us. They threw boms at us – too many to mention. I was wounded. It may be shell shock that is catching me now, now that I am back with my own people."

Onkel Helmut: "Stop just there. I must run home and go and fetch your aunt. She'll never forgive me if I forget about her at such an important moment."

He disappears.

My mother: "Even if you say that you're not hungry I am going to make you a ham sandwich – ham and tomato, with 'Senf' (mustard). This is the first opportunity in twelve years that you will get something to eat from your mother's hand. You may not say 'no'"."

Me: "Okay. Do it."

My mother disappears and I, my father and my brother remain in the living room. Simon plays with his fingers and my father stares at me, as if he cannot believe his own eyes.

While I am sitting with the last half of my sandwich, Tante Gertrud storms into the house and grabs me. The remains of the sandwich fall from my hand onto the carpet, but I leave it where it is. I hold tightly onto my dear aunt and we stand motionless for two minutes. She releases me when she has to dry the tears from her eyes and I hand her my kitchen cloth.

My Dad: "Right, all of us are here. Please tell us all that you have experienced throughout the war. I believe that you are tired and then we go to bed. The crews of the fishing trawlers can cope tomorrow without us because we are going to talk some more."

My Mom: "We are all curious. But if there are things that are too painful to discuss, then we will understand."

Me: "It's okay, Mutti. I think you have the right to know what happened with the lost son."

And then I start with a summary of my war career – the U-boats on which I served, the ships that I sank, the loss of my family, my broken leg, my maimed foot (which I show them, after having taken my shoe off), my redeployment to the S-boat flotilla, my transfer to Kristiansand where I encountered my ex-father-in-law and ex-brother-in-law and how we started our trip with the super submarine.

Onkel Helmut: "Received any medals and decorations?"

Me: "The Iron Cross, First Class, the Knight's Cross to the Iron Cross, the Submarine Badge and the S-Boat Badge."

Onkel Helmut: "My father only got the Iron Cross, Second Class. Gee whiz, you have much to be proud of."

Me: "I also have the deaths of hundreds of people on my conscience. I know – it was war. It was a case of either them, or me. I defended my adopted fatherland. But there are dozens and dozens of widows and orphans whose husbands and fathers are gone as a result of my so-called heroics."

The others fall silent – perhaps out of respect for the dead or perhaps because they simply don't know how to react.

Me: "Another thing that bothers me, is that I made a young Norwegian widow pregnant. You are going to become grandfather and grandmother one of these days, that is, if it hasn't happened already. I had no choice but to leave her over there. I promised to go and fetch her after the war and that's what I am going to do after this. That is, after we have got rid of the gold."

My mom: "Stefan, that's not how we brought you up. Shame on you! Making an innocent girl pregnant."

Me: "She wasn't so innocent anymore. She's a young widow. Her husband fell when the Wehrmacht invaded Norway. I promised to go and fetch her after the war and I intend keeping my promise. I must confess: I love that girl very much and I am sure that you will find her to be a very acceptable daughter-in-law."

Tante Gertrud: "Good for you. Yes, keep your promise."

Me: "But only after we've dealt with the gold."

Simon: "And how do you plan to do that?"

Me: "Your fishing trawlers are going to help us to fetch it from the submarine. And then we sell the stuff and divide the money. You will also get your share."

Simon: "Not so fast. To whom are you, perhaps, going to sell your gold?"

Me: "Jewellers, banks, rich people."

Simon: "Not so fast. No bank and no jeweller will dare to touch your gold. In their eyes it's stolen property. They will most probably demand that it be given to the British or the Americans as war loot."

I fall silent and after a few seconds I say: "Perhaps you're right."

Onkel Helmut: "Something else: if you look around for buyers of your gold all over the place the news will reach the Nazis in South America, sooner or later. They will want to take revenge because you cheated and bedevilled them."

Me: "Perhaps you are also right."

Simon: "I have, though, a proposal. Just tomorrow, you and I go and chat with our bank manager, here in Walvis. You disguise yourself with sun glasses that I can lend you. And then we inquire from him how we can sell a few pieces of gold. He must, of course, never know that you have three tons of the stuff."

Me: "Sounds all right."

My Mom: "It is getting bed-time. Stefan, I am going to get your old bedroom in order. We used it all these years as a store room. I will have to shift the goodies to one side and put clean bedding on your old bed. Simon, please come and help your mother."

Walvis Bay, Wednesday, 6 June 1945

After a good night's rest in my old bed during which I dreamt of Cornelia and a hearty breakfast prepared by my own mother, Simon and I stroll to the local branch of Volkskas Limited. We arrive two minutes before opening time and we are the fist clients who ask to speak to the bank manager.

The manager, Mr Bennie Beyleveld: "And how can I help you gentlemen? Do you want to apply for a loan?"

Simon, as the eldest, does the talking: "No, Sir. We need your expert knowledge and advice. My friend here (and he points at me) inherited a bit of gold from a distant family member – a bar of gold and a number of coins. Would the bank perhaps be interested in buying that from him?"

"Only if he has a certificate to prove his ownership. But we can only handle limited amounts. Golden coins can easily be stolen and it is always a risk to leave them lying around. No shop will accept them as payment, anyway. Shops only accept pounds, shillings and pence, or cheques. Also, we do not like to store something like that in our vault because it may easily disappear."

"What is your advice for us? How can we get rid of the gold and convert it into hard cash?"

"I don't want to be nasty, but you won't get help anywhere in the whole of South Africa or in South West. Why don't you try Portuguese West Africa? I know the Portuguese are less finnicky about these sort of things. If you are able to travel there, go and look in Lobito, or even better, Luanda. The Portuguese have several banks and I think that you will succeed there."

Back at home we discuss this state of affairs.

Onkel Helmut: "It seems to me that the only solution is that you sail with your submarine to the vicinity of Luanda. We two can take two of our trawlers and sail with you there. If you find two or three banks that are willing to buy your gold we can transport the boxes and crates with the trawlers. And then we hire a lorry or two to take everything to the particular banks. That is, if they are willing to exchange the gold for money."

Me: "I don't know if our guys will be able to do anything with Portuguese money. If those Portuguese banks can give us dollars or pounds it will help a lot."

My Dad: "Are those boxes and crates marked? Is it written on the outside what is inside?"

Me: "No, they are unmarked."

My Dad: "Excellent. It will, therefore, be easy to lug that gold around without anybody knowing what it really is – except when we open those trunks in the vaults of the banks and have the gold weighed."

Me: "As I have already told you I must return to the submarine tonight. I am sure that the men will agree with the plan to sail to Luanda. That's where we will scuttle the submarine, except if we return here afterwards. And then you sail with your trawlers more or less together with us untill we reach Luanda to help us there."

My Dad: "Excellent."

My Mom: "Please keep very clear from the Police. One never knows."

Simon: "Perhaps we should actually ask them to guard us with all these treasures!"

Luanda, Monday, 18 Junee 1945

We arrived yesterday, on the Sunday, in Luanda. Simon asked me whether he could travel with us in the submarine to this spot. He was curious to experience a German U-boat from the inside. My father and Onkel Helmut have each taken a trawler here and each brought four crew members along – after they had visited the submarine and I introduced them to my father-in-law, Joachim Graf von Czapiewski, and my brother-in-law, Franz. Fortunately, they could easily converse with each other in German.

The voyage proceeded rather slowly because the trawlers can only move at eight knots and we needed twelve full days to get here.

On our way here, my father and Onkel Helmut briefly stopped in Lobito to obtain a fishing license. With that they can fish legally in Angolan waters without being chased away. The plan is to catch a load of fish en route and to take a part of that to the fish market in Luanda. For that, they have to hire a lorry somewhere to transport the fish and later the gold.

While they went into Lobito our submarine hid somewhere along the coast and we caught some fish to supplement our food stocks.

A few men even ventured onto dry land to take a stroll on the beach.

And now the submarine lies off Luanda. We plan to smuggle the gold into the city during the night when the customs office in the harbor is closed and the boxes with gold can be taken into the city under a layer of fish – just in case somebody wanted to inspect the lorry.

We wondered whether we should have taken a Portuguese interpreter along but my Dad assured us that the bank officials in Luanda would certainly know some English – if not even German.

It is fairly easy to hire a lorry – a rather old, pre-war model – and at the fish market everything proceeds smoothly. With the proceeds of the sale of the fish we can buy fuel for the lorry and even retain some cash.

We drive into the city to look for a bank. En route we pass a post office and I ask my father, who drives the lorry, to stop a little while. I jump out and go and buy a postage stamp to paste onto my letter to Hilde. I trust that the postal services to Norway are restored in the meantime. In my letter, which I have written during our voyage from Walvis Bay, I assure her that I am safe in Africa but that I will travel to Norway as soon as possible to fetch her. I express my wish that the birth of our baby went smoothly and that I often think of her and our child.

Soon afterwards, we see a sign against a big building: BANCO COMERCIAL PORTUGUES. The bank is still closed and a man and a woman are already waiting there.

The woman suddenly fires away in German: "Guten Tag, Herr Kapitänleutnant Strauss!" (Good day, Lieutenant Strauss!).

I almost falls on my back.

The woman: "We met in 1942 in Brest. I delivered four agents to your U-boat and you had to take them to New York."

Father-in-law Achim cuts her short: "I don't think we should discuss all these things here in public. Where can we meet in private to have a talk?"

The man: "We are staying in a guest house. We can give you the address. But, by the way, I also know Herr Strauss. He rescued me in July 1939 when my plane fell into the water."

After this encounter, I, my Dad, and father-in-law Achim enter the bank. I carry a bag with a single bar of gold and a handfull of golden coins. The bank manager is fortunaely available and he speaks English haltingly.

After father-in-law Achim and I have introduced ourselves as Swiss citizens and my father introduced himself as a South African ship owner, we ask the manager whether the bank would be interested in buying a quantity of gold. We show him the bar and the coins. He gives a whistle when he sees that it's Nazi gold and he immediately wants to know how we acquired it and whether we have any more. We promise him that we have gotten it quite legally without divulging any details and we add that we have more than a ton of it.

His eyes shine and he throws his hands into the air: "Dear Sirs, of course my bank is always eager to obtain such treasures. But we must sell it again on the international gold market at a profit and, therefore, I can only offer you seventy-five percent of the market value. Will that satisfy you?"

The three of us look at each other and smile. That was actualy very easy. We expected to have received an offer of merely fifty percent. We nod our heads to indicate our agreement.

Father-in-law Achim: "Is it in order if we bring the shipment tomorrow to the bank? It has to be offloaded first."

The manager gives a broad smile (perhaps because he plans to take part of the profit for himself): "Sim! Sim! (Yes! Yes!)"

Because the bank does not have enough dollars or pounds, father-in-law Achim has to open a bank account in his own name for the deposit of the money. He can then do with the money whatever he likes – transfer it to another banking account overseas, or whatever.

We take our pieces of gold and drive further. At the BANCO POPULAR PORTUGAL and the NOVO BANCO something similar happens, except that we promise that the crates with gold can only be delivered the day after tomorrow and the day after that respectively.

Later, during the afternoon, we join the German couple at their guest house. We are introduced to Major a.D. Karl Krause, previously of the Luftwaffe, and his wife, Major a.D. Sonja Schellenberg, lately from the Abwehr.

Sonja Schellenberg: "And what are you gentlemen doing here in Angola? Fleeing from the Nazis?"

My father-in-law: "We are here to do banking business, as you saw."

Karl Krause: "That's what we were also doing this morning."

His wife: "What type of banking business? Selling your submarine to the Portuguese? Or the contents of your submarine?"

My father-in-law: "Dear lady, my son-on-law told me earlier today that you were with the Abwehr. You, obviously, know a lot. And you also ought to know that there are certain things that ought not to be disclosed because it can bring danger to all those involved."

Sonja laughs: "You may tell us everything. You see, both of us are officially dead. We died in a plane crash almost a year ago. You are actually talking to our spirits!"

The three of us laugh and I say: "I didn't shake the hand of a ghost when I greeted you a little while ago."

Sonja: "Before we carry on discussing military secrets and war crimes, I will ask our landlord to bring us some coffee. He doesn't understand a word of German."

With her cup of coffee in her hand, Sonja continues: "Gentlemen, there is no need for secrecy anymore. The Nazis are on the run, if they haven't been apprehended yet. The only explanation for you presence here in Luanda, instead of being inmates in a prisoner-or-war camp, is that you stole a submarine and fled Europe. And now you are doing banking business in a Portuguese colony. Stolen Nazi gold, perhaps?"

Father-in-la Achim: "We won't admit or deny anything. Please, let's leave it at that. But what are you two doing in this corner of Africa? Did the Abwehr send you to spy on the Portuguese and faked your deaths?"

Karl Krause: "No. Our plane really crashed in Egypt during an attack on the Suez Canal. But we survived and stole a British fighter and fled to neutral Turkey. From there we got to Lisbon and now we are buying an airplane to fly to Windhoek. All above board. We didn't swipe anything from the Nazis. But I imagine that the Nazis were relieved that we are dead."

Me: "But why?"

Sonja Krause: "As a member of the Abwehr, I was indirectly involved in the assassination plot against Hitler. That's why we had to get to neutral Turkey in a hurry."

After we had swopped a few yarns abut our war experiences and had left, my father-in-law remarks: "That woman is sharp. Her service in the Abwehr taught her to be perceptive. She corrrectly guessed the reason for our presence her in Luanda."

My dad, who was silent the whole time, concludes: "Yes, we gave ourselves away by being visibly surprised by her accurate guess. But I think both of them of them also have secrets, although they told us that everything about them is above board."

Me: "Yes. Where did they get money to buy an airplane? Stolen from the Nazis before they defected to Turkey.? Despite their denial?"

Father-in-law Achim: "You may well be right. And I think we will see them again. They are on their way to South West, the same as us."

Southern Atlantic Ocean, Thursday, 21 June 1945

Today, we sail back to Walvis Bay – the submarine and the two fishing trawlers. We smuggled a ton or more of gold into the city during three successive nights each to deliver it early the next morning to each one of the three banks.

The offloading and onloading of the gold proceeded smoothly. Father-in-law Achim and I supervised the men taking the boxes and trunks to the deck. From there, they were carried by the crew members of the trawlers that were tied to the submarine on the deep sea.

A sample of the golden bars were weighed at each bank to ensure that all of them weigh exactly one kilogram. The mass of the golden coins was also determined. It was a rather lengthy process to determine how much the gold weighed and thereafter a price was calculated at seventy-five percent of $51 per ounce – the going price for gold nowadays.

Everything happened behind closed doors in the offices of the bank managers' offices. The gold was returned to the respective chests and containers and sealed. Thereafter, some of the banks' staff had to carry everything to their bank's vault, without knowing what they contained.

Father-in-law Achim requested each bank to supply him with thirteen guaranteed cheques – each one to an amount of one thirteenth of the money that was suddenly deposited in his three new banking accounts.

We agreed, furthermore, amongst ourselves that every submariner, as well as my father, Onkel Helmut and Simon would open new banking accounts in Walvis Bay at different banks and that the money of the various cheques would be paid into these accounts. Each one, therefore, received three cheques that had to be deposited in Walvis Bay into these new accounts. It wouldn't do to keep all the money in one place because that would only create problems with the banks in Walvis Bay.

I sail with my father and Simon in my father's trawler, back to Walvis Bay. I enjoy steering a fishing trawler again. The three of us cannot stop smiling because we are suddenly stinking rich. We cannot dare to discuss our plans with the money within hearing distance of the crew members. Each of them will receive a substantial bonus afterwards because they were gone from their homes for an extended period of time. If they are going to boast about seeing a mysterious U-boat, nobody will believe them because that submarine will disappear.

Something that I keep to myself is the fact that I have hidden twelve boxes in the torpedo room of the submarine while we were still sailing on the Atlantic Ocean. It is my plan to retrieve that gold at a later stage, very much later – long after the U-boat has sunk outside Walvis Bay. I want to share it with my family and my family-in-law – as well as with Hilde's folks.

Walvis Bay, Thursday, 5 July 1945

Our super submarine found her inglorious last resting place on the the ocean floor. After father-in-law Achim and the other crew members got onto my father's fishing trawler, I simply allowed the submarine to dive slowly by allowing all the air to bubble out of her ballast tanks and to leave the hatches on the deck and on the conning tower open so that all the air inside could escape. While she was slowly disappearing under the waves I also got onto the trawler. Father-in-law Achim, Franz, I and the other seven crew members gave the boat a last salute until she disappeared from view.

The sea bed is about seven and a half fathoms (forty meters) down and the submarine on the bottom ought not to be a shipping hazard. The height of the submarine is about twelve metres and that leaves another five fathoms (28 meters) above her to the surface – more than enough for passing ships. I mark the spot where she sinks clearly on my father's nautical charts of the Walvis Bay area. I also take note of the precise coordinates so that I can locate the wreck at a later stage.

My father, Onkel Helmut and Simon divide our submariners into three groups and we take them to Volkskas Bank, Barclay's Bank, the Netherland's Bank, Standard Bank, the Post Office's Savings Bank, and Saambou Building Society. Each one of us has received three cheques from father-in-law Achim and with those, each one has to open three different accounts at different banks. It could create problems if all the money was placed into a single account because the sudden riches would only draw unwelcome attention.

After the Portuguese cheques were deposited and the exchange rate was calculated, it became clear that each one of us thirteen suddenly owned a colossal amount in pounds sterling. I disguised myself with dark glasses while moving with Simon from one bank to another in the business district of Walvis Bay. We submariners all used our Swiss passports as proof of our identities and my parents' home or Onkel Helmut's home were given as residential addresses.

Each one of the Germans drew a few hundred pounds and declared that they wished to explore South West, with the object of settling perhaps somewhere.

Father-in-law Achim explains to me, my father and Onkel Helmut: "It is impossible for me and Franz to try and return to Germany. Our family estate on the border with Poland was surely expropriated or confiscated by the Red Army a long time ago and I will never be able to claim compensation. The Russians will see it as war booty – just as the Communists so-called 'nationalized' all the property of the nobility after the Russian revolution of 1917. In practice, that means that the important party bosses took those properties for themselves. I believe that the same has happened with my estate. Franz and I will, therefore, settle down in this country. We cannot dare to seek our fortunes in South America because the mob of crazy Nazis over there will certainly want to take revenge because their gold disappeared."

Me: "I wish you all the success with your search for a new future. I will miss you. After all, we were together again the last few months after you became part of my life twelve years ago. It is necessary for me to disappear before somebody recognizes me and I am arrested as a so-called war criminal or a traitor."

Directly afterwards, I stroll down to the harbor to see whether any ships are moored there. I find only one Argentinian freighter that is due to depart for Buenos Aires tonight. The captain is willing to appoint me as second engineer with my Swiss passport and my diploma from the Seefahrtschule in Bremen, although he cannot pay me. I am totally satisfied just to be able to get away. I have, after all, more than enough money.

5 July 1945

I go back to greet my family and my ex-family-in-law who found temporary lodgings with my folks. I ask my father to keep a big envelope of mine in a safe place. It is something that I will surely need later on, much later. He shows me where he deposits it on top of his wardrobe.

In town I buy myself new clothes and overalls with which I can work on the ship. I left my German uniform, together with my medals and decorations on the submarine. Perhaps I will salvage them some day.

Buenos Aires, Wednesday, 18 July 1945

The Argentinian freighter reaches Buenos Aires and I say good-bye to the captain. I thank him for the fact that I have, at least, had a place to sleep and something to eat while aboard.

I walk around in the harbor and try to find another ship to take me to Europe because I want to reach Hilde as soon as possible. If necessary, I can pay for my passage but I would prefer to sail as an anonymous crew member.

The first ship that seems to be a possibility is the Santa Isabella, a passenger liner registered in Portugal. The ship looks vaguely familiar, but then I have seen so many ships in my career that this is not strange. In English, I ask the first officer whom I encounter whether it was possible to speak to the captain.

I almost fall on my back when the man answers in German. He takes me to the captain who introduces himself as Kapitän Karl-Gustav von Lausewitz. It is clear that he must be ex-Kriegsmarine and I introduce myself as Korvettenkapitän Stefan Strauss, previously of the harbor protection flotilla at Kristiansand, Norway.

"Aaaah, are you perhaps one of those men who stole a submarine, just when everything came tumbling down?"

"Where did you get that silly idea?"

"I have already dealt with a few such people. I was a Kapitän zur See and in command of this troop ship till the end of April. Nowadays, we sail under the Portuguese flag and we help quite a number of Germans who want to get out of Europe to reach Argentina."

"That's interesting." I stay silent how it happened that I landed in Buenos Aires and what else I did before this.

"But, now I want to know: what can I do for you?"

"I'm looking for a ship to take me to Europe. If possible, I can pay for my passage, but I would prefer to sail along as a crew member. I have a diploma from the Seefahrtschule in Bremen and I can do the work of a ship's engineer. In addition, I'm an electrician, apart from the fact that I commanded seven armed trawlers."

"Wonderful! Fantastic! As a matter of fact, I need a second engineer. The pay isn't really much, but that will help you to reach Europe easily. We depart the day after tomorrow to sail to Portugal, Spain and Italy."

"Will it be in order if I disembark in Portugal or Spain?"

"If it really must be. I cannot prevent you from absconding. Do you have a valid passport?"

I laugh: "It looks valid enough. It's a Swiss passport. With stamps for Portugal, Spain, Argentina and Uruguay."

Captain Von Lausewitz also laughs – certainly because he realises that my passport must be a forgery.

I ask: "Herr Kapitän, what was the name of this vessel in the past? She looks somehow or other familiar."

"She was a passenger liner, the Usambara. Look here, I still drink my coffee from a mug with her name on it."

"I was a passenger on this ship in 1933."

"To or from Europe?"

"On my way to Bremen. From Africa."

"I know of other South Africans who also were passengers on this ship in the past."

"Interesting. May I make myself comfortable on the ship in the meantime?"

"Certainly. I am going to call the purser and inform him that you are a crew member from today onwards and that a cabin has to be assigned to you. Do you have overalls?"

Porto, Sunday, 5 August 1945

The war ended three months ago and I hope that the train system is working well enough again so that I can travel to Norway as speedily as possible. I want to reach Hilde as soon as possible and I think about her constantly.

I leave the Santa Isabella at the harbor of Porto and hastily go to the train station to enquire whether there are any trains to take me to Paris. There is an overnight train that leaves tonight at ten o' clock from Lisbon. I book a seat in the first class on that train and I buy a ticket to Lisbon where I have to transfer onto the train to Paris.

Captain von Lausewitz and I had a few friendly chats when I was off-duty. He revealed that he is, actually, part of an organisation that helps Nazis to reach South America where they can start a new life. Argentina has various German communities, which these people can join.

He wanted to know why I was so eager to go back to Europe. I explained that I wanted to join my fiancee in Europe to take her elsewhere. Our child must have been born by this time. It will be an ideal state of affairs if I could get a permanent position as ship's engineer on a large ship so that I can remain working at sea and so that my life partner can live with me on the ship and even be employed. Of course, I don't reveal that I cannot dare to settle in Germany, South West Africa, South Africa or South America and that it will be the safest to continue sailing on the open seas.

The captain: "We ought to reach Porto on 5 August. If you are able to get back there at the end of September, you will be able to encounter us there again. I can perhaps offer your present position to you again because I doubt if I will be able to find a suitable replacement for you in time."

5 August 1945

With this promise of the captain it seems as if my future, for the next year at least, may be secured. Perhaps circumstances may change later so that I and Hilde can return to South West. It is with hope in my heart that I start the long journey across Europe.

Oslo, Monday, 13 August 1945

It was a struggle of more than a week to get seats on trains. When I reached Oslo at last I noticed how many members of the Kriegsmarine were still waiting to be repatriated to Germany. They are, technically speaking, prisoners of war and they all have to be processed before their release. With my Swiss passport, though, I receive preferential treatment everywhere when I need help.

To reach Oslo I had to travel via Lisbon, Madrid, Paris, Amsterdam, Hamburg (which is almost totally in ruins), Kopenhagen, Göteborg in Sweden and Fredrikstad in Norway. At many places the tracks are only temporarily repaired and the trains don't succeed in keeping to their schedules. Trains are filled to more than capacity because much rolling stock has been damaged or destroyed during the war.

I spend the night in Oslo.

Bodø, Tuesday, 14 August 1945

While I am sitting in the train on my way to Bodø, I wonder how I will be received by the Freiberg family. To ease my reception somewhat I bought some delicacies in Sweden, such as sausages, cheese, chocolates and fruit to present to the poor people.

Fortunately, the rail tracks beyond Mo i Rana have been repaired after the retreat of the German troops and I can travel to Bodø. I reach my old lodgings, the dwelling of the Freiberg family, during the early evening. I knock on the front door and suddenly cold sweat appears on my forehead. It is possible that these people will chase me away because I brought shame on their daughter.

It is Hilde with a baby in her arms who opens the door. We stare at each other for more or less ten long seconds. I look at her from head to toe and I notice the baby who must be about four months old. She also views me from top to bottom with an expressionless face.

At last, she says: "Come inside." Just that.

While she is closing the door behind me I ask her whether I could hold the baby. She hands him to me. "His name is Johannes – as in the Bible."

I cannot help myself. My eyes fill with tears and I cannot see properly anymore. To think: here I'm holding my son! The moment overwhelms me.

Hilde just stands there, silent. Mister Fredrik Freiberg comes looking for his daughter to ask why she hasn't taken the guest to the living room. He stares at me as if I am an inhabitant of Mars with three heads and six legs.

"We didn't expect you so soon. Hilde received your letter of 18 June from Africa only last week. She has given it to us to read. You promised to come. We didn't think it would be so soon. Come inside. I see you're holding your son."

Me: "Thanks."

I sit down with little Johannes still in my arms. An uncomfortable silence descends upon the room. Missus Ruth Freiberg, Hedda, Hilde and Mister Fredrik all stare at me. My tears continue to drop onto the blanket of little Johannes. I remove the cap from his little head to have a better look at him.

Hilde says after a while: He takes after you."

I smile timidly.

Silence.

At last, I am able to regain my voice: "Thank you very much that you didn't chase me away. I certainly deserve that. I placed your daughter in a very difficult situation. I want to compensate for that. I ask permission to marry her – that is to say, if she wants me."

Her father: "What happens after that?"

Me: "I have an offer to work as an engineer on a passenger liner. The ship sails between Europe and South America. As an important officer on the ship I may take my wife along and she may even work on the ship, if she so wishes."

Her father: "And what happens to our grandchild? Are you also taking him away?"

Me: "But naturally. The child belongs with his parents. But we will visit you regularly."

Her father: "Hilde, what do you say?"

Hilde: "Far, I actually want him. He is the father of our child. It is clear that he immediately fell in love with his child. Look at his tears. I like that. Last year, when he left us, he also promised to come back to fetch me. I believed him. And now he has kept his promise. Yes, I want him. He's an honorable man."

Her mother: "Stefan, when you lodged with us a long time ago, you always behaved yourself like a gentleman – except when you seduced our daughter. But then, she participated willingly. You filled a gap in her life. We welcome you as a member of our family, as a son-in-law, even if you will only have a ship as a dwelling for the time being."

Her father: "We Norwegians are old seafarers. Our ancestors were fearless Vikings who sailed with small boats to Greenland and even to America. It won't be strange for Hilde to be married to a seaman. I give you our blessing."

I get up, return little Johannes to his mother and go and hug Hilde's mother and father. They also hold onto me tightly. Then it's Hedda's turn. She was silent until now and she says: "Welcome in our family."

After this, I take little Johannes again from his mother and place him in Hedda's arms so that I can embrace Hilde, the new love of my life. She presses her head against my neck while I stroke her hair. We remain standing like this for a long time.

After a while, I release her and I grab the bag with delicacies, which I have brought from Sweden: "Tonight, we celebrate, just like when the Lost Son returned to his father. Except, the Lost Son provides the food for the feast!"

The table is swiftly being laid. Suddenly, the stiff and sombre atmosphere is gone and the Freiberg family laugh and joke with me – just as it was last year while I was stll lodging here. After dinner, a short musical concert is held and I sing along the songs I can remember. This feast is regarded as an engagement feast.

Late at night I retire to the guest room – the same room in which I stayed in the past. Hilde slips into my bed as if it is the most obvious thing in the world to do.

Porto, Friday, 28 September 1945

The Strauss family – father Stefan, mother Hilde and baby Johannes – are sitting around in Porto, Portugal, awaiting the arrival of the Santa Isabella. The stay here is supposed to be our honeymoon.

We got married in Bodø ten days ago, on 18 September, during a low-key ceremony in the local church. A small celebration was held in the Freiberg family home with only the nearest family and friends present. Little Johannes was baptised the next day. We must still see to it that his family name be changed from Freiberg to Strauss. The Freiberg family agreed that it was better to take Hilde with me since the people in the area could not forgive her for the fact that she allowed a German officer to make her pregnant.

Something that increased the prejudice against the Germans are the tales of Nazi horrors during the war that are increasingly coming to light. The top Nazis who are held in custody are being prosecuted and the expectation is that a number of them will receive the death penalty. They are being accused of murdering millions of Jews, retarded people and war prisoners. My conscience doesn't trouble me anymore that I have helped to swipe the gold of the Nazis and any qualms I might have had evaporated quickly and swiftly. The bunch of mad Nazis who fled to South America certainly do not deserve to have that gold. By disappearing with that gold, I helped to prevent bad things from happening.

Hilde reminds me though: "During our journey through Germany to get here, it was very obvious that the Allies also committed all sorts of horrors. People on the trains told me that thouands upon thousands of civilians died during bombing raids. You also lost your family in that way. The Russians were especially cruel against civilians with their looting, rape and torture of civilians. We in Norway actually suffered much less than these poor Germans."

And today we notice the Santa Isabella entering the harbor in the estuary of the Douro river. I hurry to the ship to hear from Captain von Lausewitz if I am still welcome as second engineer.

"Yes, my friend, Herr Korvettenkapitän 'außer Dienst' (retired) Strauss. You are being offered the position of chief engineer. The man who held the position stayed behind in Spain. The Devil only knows why. Welcome back!"

"Thanks, a lot!"

"And is the new Frau Strauss here with you?"

"Yes. Also our little son."

"Would your wife perhaps be interested to accept the position of Kindergarten teacher aboard? Many of our passengers have children and they have to be cared for during the day."

"I'm sure she will be interested in such a position. She has a teaching diploma and knows how to deal with children. Then she can keep our little son with her the whole time."

Atlantic Ocean, Monday, 1 December 1947

Captain von Lausewitz was appointed as captain of a bigger and newer passenger liner. With my background, it wasn't a surprise when the position of master of the Santa Isabella was offered to me.

Something that constantly surprised me is the fact that the owners of the Santa Isabella, a gang of former Nazis in Portugal, never connected me with the men who disappeared together with father-in-law Achim in a super U-boat with a cargo of gold. That is perhaps due to the fact that father-in-law Achim never informed his superiors who the crew members on the last voyage of the U-3531 were supposed to be. I also never disclosed to von Lausewitz what my precise role after the war happened to be. The only thing in which the ship owners were interested in was my ability to be a ship's captain, even if I only have seven toes.

And so it happens that I am no longer a naval officer but the master of a big ship – although she is a rather old ship.

Bay of Biscay, Thursday, 1 July 1948

The Santa Isabella is supposed to reach the harbor of Bilbao in northern Spain this afternoon. We don't handle any fugitive Nazis anymore – all of them have, by this time, found holes where they can hide, in South America, the USA, Australia and so forth. The Santa Isabella is just an ordinary passenger liner that commutes between two continents.

Suddenly, the man in the crow's nest calls out: "Sea mine! Sea mine!"

The helmsman immediately throws the wheel so that we lean over to port, but unfortunately in the wrong direction and we collide with the sea mine in stead of avoiding it. A loud bang follows and I feel the vibrations of the explosion where I'm standing on the bridge.

I blow the ship's horn immediately to make alarm. Crew members jump to get the lifeboats ready. Passengers stampede to the deck. Some of them come carrying their valuables. I make sure that Hilde, little Johannes who is already three years old and his baby sister, Ruth, who is six months old, get onto a lifeboat. It is expected of me, as captain, to be the last person to abandon ship.

It takes more or less ninety minutes before the Santa Isabella eventually disappears beneath the waves. The hole caused by the mine was not very big and we didn't take on water at a rapid rate. She ship was, nevertheless, doomed.

The life boats reach a beach on the coast of northern Spain two hours later, just before the sun sets. The purser grabbed the list of passengers in haste and pressed it into a bag and we now use it to conduct a roll-call to find out how many passengers or crew members may be missing. It's a miracle that everybody on the list is accounted for.

Our radion operator has, as a matter of course, radioed our position and problem into the wide world. We expect, therefore, that help will arrive sooner or later, here where we are stranded on an isolated northern Spanish beach. Fortunately, there are emergency supplies in the lifeboats that we can use, if necessary.

Bilbao, Friday, 30 July 1948

Today, the board of investigation gives its verdict about the disaster that caused the Santa Isabella to sink. The captain of the ship – that's me – is commended for the fact that he stayed calm and composed and dealt with the accident with good leadership. Thanks to him, no loss of life was recorded, although the damage was considerable, namely a valuable ship that was lost, her cargo that disappeared into the depths and the passengers who have lost their valuables.

I attribute my so-called good leadership to the through training that I have received as an officer of the Kriegsmarine. I made a point of holding regular drills so that my crews – on all the warships that I commanded, as well as the Santa Isabella – knew how everything had to be done in case of a fire or an accident. It wasn't necessary to run around to ask anybody what had to be done; all the necessary procedures, actions, steps, and precautions were implanted into my subconsciousness by practice and repeated practice.

The board of inquiry finds, in addition, that ineffecient minesweeping after the war failed to remove all the mines from the Bay of Biscay. The anchor cable of the mine in question, which was apparently anchored to the seabed, seems to have weathered badly and disintegrated with the result that the mine rose to the surface and drifted with the currents, with disastrous consequences. It is unknown whether it was a German, French or British mine.

While the investigation was still ongoing, I and my family stayed in a hotel in Bilbao. The ship owners paid the bill.

Hilde and I often discussed our future while staying there. I proposed that I relinquish my career as ship's captain and join my father and uncle in Walvis Bay. Hilde, who hasn't met my family yet, was eager that I undertake such a step. I, therefore, wrote a letter of resignation as ship's captain – with immediate effect.

The shipping company enabled all the passengers to reach their destinations by other means. I and my family receive airplane tickets to a destination of our choice. We fly to Windhoek.

In the meantime, it became safe to return to South Africa and South West Africa. A general election was held earlier this year and the National Party with Dr Daniel Malan as leader won. One of the first things the new government did was to grant amnesty to people who cooperated with the Germans during the war. Therefore, it is safe to show my face in broad daylight in Walvis Bay again.

Walvis Bay, Tuesday, 3 August 1948

My parents await our arrival at the airport of Windhoek. We had to change planes in Johannesburg because there are no direct flights to Windhoek from Europe.

After both grandparents, first of all, greeted their two grandchildren, admired them, touched them, cuddled them, and made them afraid so that they cried, they are ready to be introduced to Hilde. I previously taught her a few Afrikaans sentences with which she greets her parents-in-law. For them, it is a pleasant surprise to have a Viking girl as daughter-in-law – one who can speak a little bit of Afrikaans.

The conversation switches to German almost immediately after the greetings, a language with which Hilde is familiar.

We take the train to Walvis Bay through the dry Namib Desert. For Hilde, who is used to the green and water-rich Norway, it is a new experience to see this arid expanse of sand and stones.

My father: "Stefan, you came as if you were called. I and my brother-in-law have decided it is high time to slow down and to retire. Simon needs your help."

Me: "I am more than ready to get involved with your fishing business. Do you still have that big envelope that I entrusted to your care, back in forty-five?"

"It's still on top of my wardrobe."

EPILOGUE

Walvis Bay, Monday, 3 January 1949

Every time, when I vist the harbor of Walvis Bay, I see an abandoned boat, a schooner, which is moored somewhere. She looks neglected and it doesn't seem as if anybody is using her. I inquire at the Harbor Police whether they know anything about the boat.

Constable van Rensburg of the Harbor Police: "Stefan, nobody really knows whose boat it is. A strange guy arrived with her from South America a few months ago. He was afraid that the Nazis in Swakopmund would steal the cargo. He was taken away by the Police and the Air Force flew away with him, the next day. Probably arrested. A while later, a ship of the Navy arrived for a short visit and removed a few items from the boat. Since that time, she just lies here and the harbor dues are piling up. Go ask the harbor captain if he knows anything more."

The harbor captain: "Man, if you pay the overdue harbor fees the boat is yours. She is just in our way. Repair her and sail around with her, if you wish."

I willingly pay the overdue harbor fees and I take the boat with the name of Atalanta in possession. I inspect the boat thoroughly and I find her navigational charts. I see that she departed from Buenos Aires in Argentina a few months ago and made a stop at the island of Saint Helena on her way here. I also find hidden documents that show that my old friends, David and Willie Scholtz, sailed on this boat in the past. I can only wonder: were they in any way connected with the Nazis in Argentina and then fled to Walvis Bay?

Walvis Bay, Saturday, 12 February 1949

In my spare times, I worked on the Atalanta after having hauled her out of the water at a slope. I painted her, cleaned her hull of sea grass and other accrued stuff, got new sails and replaced the ropes. Hilde eagerly helped me while my mother did baby-sitting with little Johannes and Ruth.

It's Saturday today and I and Simon and our families sail out on the Atalanta to try her. Simon got married to an Afrikaans girl in he meantime and they have a little boy of two years old. Hilde is a born mariner with her Viking heritage and I taught her how to handle the Atalanta.

While we are enjoying our outing I cannot help but to think back of the Nicoletta, the first schooner on which I sailed and on which I met Cornelia. My memories go back to the summer holidays we spent on the Nicoletta and where our love affair started and blossomed. I still miss my first wife, just as Hilde misses her first husband. But both of us agree that we don't see each other as replacements of our previous partners. Our present marriage is something totally new and we got married because it was the right thing to do.

Simon agrees with me that the Atalanta is an excellent craft and that I did an excellent job in restoring her to her former glory. I find that she is one way of continuing with my love affair with the sea – apart from helping to manage our flotilla of trawlers. Actually, Hilde also helps with the management of the business and she deals with all personnel matters.

Walvis Bay, Monday, 14 March 1949

Father-in-law Achim (I still cannot help to think of him as anything else) and Franz visit us in Walvis Bay. They are presently farming in the soutwestern corner of South West, directly on the border with the most northern part of the Cape Province of South Africa, north of the Orange River. Franz wants to visit a German girl in Swakopmund to see if a marriage between them will work out.

Father-in-law Achim, Franz, my strong Viking wife Hilde and I sail out on the Atalanta. My former German in-laws immediately liked my Norwegian wife and she immediately felt comfortable with them – especially since they can speak Norwegian. We also chat in German.

Father-in-law Achim:: "This reminds me of the Nicoletta. I miss her, actually."

Me: "What happened to the Nicoletta?"

Father-in-law Achim: "She sank. Blown to pieces. A bloody American bomb."

Me: "I need your help with an important project."

Franz: "Oh, yes?"

Me: "Ja. Only tomorrow, we are going to sail to the spot where our submarine sank and me and you are going to dive down to the wreck. There are a few items we have to recover from the boat."

Franz: "What items?"

Me: "That's a military secret."

Walvis Bay, Tuesday, 15 March 1949

Ex-father-in-law Achim and Hilde keep guard on the Atalanta while Franz and I dive into the deep water. Both of us have done the elementary diving course as part of our training as submarine officers and this experience of working deep under the surface of the sea is, therefore, not totally strange to us.

Each one wears diving goggles, oxygen cylinders, wet suits and flippers and we reach our old U-boat where she is lying on the bottom of the Atlantic Ocean. The sea grass has started to grow on her hull and it seems as if some fish have found refuge inside her as if in a submarine cave. Each one of us has a strong marine torch because it is dark inside the submarine, which lies askew on the bottom.

First of all, I open my old locker and take my medals and decorations out. I put them in the bag that I have fastened to my diving belt. Thereafter, I lead Franz to the place where I have hidden twelve trunks of gold. Because it is under water, we succeed reasonably easily in hauling the trunks through the hatches onto the deck. After all, the gold weighs much less under water.

Two long ropes with grapples are hanging down from the Atalanta right down to the submarine. We fasten a trunk's handle to a grapple and pull on the rope to give father-in-law Achim and Hilde the sign that they must haul the crate up. It takes a little more than an hour before all the boxes and crates are taken off the submarine.

Franz and I ascend slowly to the surface. To make sure that we don't get the bends we use more than an hour to move steadily upwards. The bends happen when nitrogen gets dissolved in a diver's blood as a result of the high pressure exerted by the mass of water above the diver and when that person ascends too rapidly the nitrogen forms bubbles in the blood and that causes extremely painful cramps.

When we reach the surface at last, we find that father-in-law Achim and Hilde have already arranged and stored the boxes.

Franz: "All right, now we know why you brought us here. What will happen with all these goodies?"

Me: "We are going to sell all of it again in Luanda. We take the Atalanta to get there. The three of us keep the money of one trunk each for ourselves and I want to donate the rest to my family-in-law in Norway. The poor folks suffered during the time we Germans occupied their country and I feel that we owe it to them."

Father-in-law Achim: "I rather like the idea that you, Franz and me are to get a little bit of extra gold. The three of us were, after all, in control of the operation to bring the gold here and we must be rewarded for that. I also believe that Hilde's family in Norway had a difficult time under German occupation. They ought to be helped."

Franz: "I would like to keep a hand full of golden coins and a bar of gold as souvenirs. They must remind me of our escape from Norway and the Nazis."

Hilde gets tears in her eyes: "Thank you for making me part of this little expedition. I am certain my folks will welcome your help. Stefan, this proves that you really love me."

Walvis Bay, Wednesday, 15 March 1950

My first new trawler is being launched today. With the money that I had made five years ago by selling the Nazi gold and the interest that has accrued, I was able to erect a small shipyard in Walvis Bay.

The big envelope that has been lying on my father's ward-robe all the time contained the building plans of the Kriegs-marine's armed trawlers.

Because I have found that these craft are very seaworthy when I commanded a flotilla of them, it is only natural that I would partially revive this design with the necessary adaptations.

It is known, in any case, that certain European countries, which captured the surrendered German war trawlers after the war, refurbished them as fishing craft by removing the armaments and fitting a hold for the harvest of fish.

My first effort is being launched today. She will be the latest addition to the fleet of Strauss & Stein Ltd. I already have two orders from elsewhere and I am confident that more orders will materialize.

Apart from the trawlers, I'm also going to build schooners. It's relatively easy to duplicate the Atalanta and adapt the design.

All the important people of Walvis Bay and Swakopmund were invited for the occasion and afterwards all those present will be treated with refreshments. The guest of honor is the administrator of South West Africa.

Other important guests are Kapitän zur See außer Dienst Joachim Graf von Czapiewski, his son Kapitänleutnant außer Dienst Franz von Czapiewski and his family, Kapitän zur See außer Dienst Karl-Gustav Freiherr von Lausewitz, my family-in-law, Fredrik and Ruth Freiberg with their daughter Hedda and son-in-law Rolf Trellevik and their two children, as well as as Doctor David Scholtz and Professor Willlie Scholtz. The distant cousin of the Scholtz twins, Gerrit, who became a newspaper editor after his studies in Europe, was also invited but he sent his newspaper's correspondent in Windhoek in his place with the instruction to write a story about my shipyard for the newspaper – which will be excellent publicity.

It just happened that the administrator was flown in by Lieutent Colonel Kurt Krause, the South African Luftwaffe pilot who was rescued by U-30 in 1939 on the North Sea and whom we met in Luanda after the war again. He is currently a pilot in the South African Air Force and commander of a transport squadron. He is accompanied by his wife, Sonja, the former Abwehr spy who delivered four saboteurs to my U-boat in Brest.

Another special guest of honor is the aged widow Sarah Stockhausen from Bremen who is housed in the best hotel in Swakopmund. She declared her delight in being able to see for herself this German town in Africa of which I've told her so much.

Everybody congratulates me with the fact that I have established a shipyard. It is only my family, as well as father and son von Czapiewski, who know how I have obtained the capital for this venture.

The new trawler is called the Hilde. The beautiful blonde woman after whom the boat is named receives the honor of smashing a bottle of champagne against her hull before she slips into the water.

During the reception afterwards, the Scholtz twins take me to one side. David says: "I notice a schooner over there, a yacht with two masts and her name is the Atalanta. Does she belong to you?"

"Yes. The harbor captain gave her to me after I had paid the outstanding harbor dues for this abandoned vessel. I repaired her and I use her regularly. And I know why you want to know because she is the boat with which you two escaped from the grip of the Nazis in Argentina. I found hidden documents on board that confirmed this."

"All right, then you know. However, we are not empowered to tell you everything that happened before that."

"It is in any case apparent that you spoiled the gruesome games of those nasty and nauseating and noisome Nazi nuts in Argentina in some way or other. Men, good for you!"

"We heard rumors in those times that you and your friends stole something from the Nazis. Is there any connection between that and the shipyard that you have built?"

"What on earth makes you think that way?"

"We only wondered. But anyway, if you and your pals managed to rob the Nazis then we salute you. You must've done something to prevent something bad, horrible, and ugly from happening. Yes, good for you!"

Somewhat later father and son von Czapiewski corner me and Hilde somewhere. Ex-father-in-law Achim looks concerned: "Just last week I received an anonymous letter with an Argentinian postage stamp and date stamp. It had my name and address correctly on the envelope. It was addressed to 'Kapitän zur See a.D. Joachim Graf von Czapiewski'. When I opened the envelope it contained only a clean white piece of paper. Here it is, I wanted to show it to you."

Franz: "It seems as if somebody wants to retrieve the gold that we smuggled here five years ago. They know who we are and where we are."

Me: "Are you worried?"

My ex-father-in-law: "Yes, rather."

I place my left arm over my wondrous wife's shoulder and I smile: "I don't think you have to be overly worried. I don't think they will be able to do anything. This is a futile effort to intimidate you. Nothing more. Just bravado and actually a cowardly deed. As we say in Afrikaans: 'Baie bek en min binnegoed' (a big mouth but no guts)."

Hilde: "Stefan told me everything about your adventures with your U-boat. According to my friends and family in Norway, these ex-Nazi's are on the run. The Israeli Mossad and the West German Gehlen Organisation are hard on their heels and they have nowhere to hide. The CIA and MI5 are looking for them as well. So relax."

Me: "You may listen to my wonderful wife. She has a very brilliant brain in her handsome head, here on top of her amazing anatomy."

GLOSSARY

GLOSSARY

The largest part of this story is situated in Germany, or in a German environment. For that reason, many German words and expressions are used. Their English meanings are given when they occur for the first time, but for the use of the reader a complete list of such, expressions and abbreviations, together with their translations, are given here:

Abwehr	The Germin Military Intelligence Service
Acht-Acht	Eight-Eight – the nickname given to the 88 millimeter anti-aircraft gun
Altstadt	Old city or central part of a medieval city
Amis	Americans (slang)
Außer Dienst (abr a.D.)	Out of service or retired
Behörden	Authorities
Bitte	Please
Dom	Cathedral
Ersatzfamilie	Surrogate family
Fischkutter	Fishing trawler
Frau	Woman, Missus, Madam
Fräulein	Miss
Freiherr	Baron
Führer	Leader
Gestapo (Geheime Staatspolizei)	Secret State Police
Gleis	Platform of a train station
Gnädige Frau	Litteraly: merciful Madam – the form of address for an important woman
Graf	Count

344

Gräfin	Countess
Groschen	Penny
Hauptbahnhof	Main station
Heiligabend	Christmas Eve
Heimat	Native town or region
Herr	Sir, Mister
Herrgott	The Lord God
Herrschaften	Sirs
Herzog	Duke
Kaffeeklatsch	Cozy coffee drinking
Kanzler	Chancellor or Prime Minister
Kapitän	Captain
Kombüse	Galley
Kompaniechef	Company commander
Kriegsmarine	German Navy
Kübelwagen	Litteraly a "bucket wagon" a military vehicle built on the chassis of a Volskwagen Beetle
Laus	Lice
Leutnant zu See	Emsign
Luftwaffe	Air Force
Marine	Navy
Marinebefehlshaber	Chief of the Navy
Marineintendantur	Office of the naval intendant
Marinelazarett	Naval hospital
Marinepfarrer	Navy chaplain
Marineschule	Naval school
Markplatz	Market place
Mutti	Mommy
Oberbett	Eiderdown
Oberfeldwebel	Sergeant Major
Oberleutnant	Lieutenant

GLOSSARY

Oberst	Colonel
Oberstabsarzt	Medical officer with the rank of a Major
OKM (Oberkommando der Marine)	Central command of the Navy
Onkel	Uncle
Pantzerschiff	Armoured ship
Personalausweis	Identity document
Plattdeutsch	Flat German
Reeder	Schipping owner
Reichsmarine	The Imperial Navy
Reichspräsident	President of the Reich
Reichsmark	The German currency till 1945
Reichstag	Parliament of the Reich
Ritter	Knight
Sanitäter	Medical orderly
Sanitätsdienst	Military Medical Service
Seefahrtschule	Nautical School
Seekommandant	Commander of a certain coastal district
Seeverteidiging	Coastal defence
Senf	Mustard
Sekt	Sparkling wine
Silvester	New Year's Eve
Staatsangehörigkeit	Citizenship
Stabsarzt	Staff surgeon (medical officer with the rank of captain)
Stollen	Almond cake with raisens
Sturmabteilung (abr S.A.)	Storm compay, the storm troopers of the Nazi Party
U-Boot	Submarine
U-Bootschule	Submarine School

GLOSSARY

Unterseeboot	Submarine
Vati	Daddy
Verstanden?	Do you understand?
Wachoffizier	Watch officer
Zwiebelturm	Onion-shaped tower

RANK STRUCTURE OF THE GERMAN KRIEGSMARINE
1935 – 1945

[Shoulder straps on summer uniforms or overalls and sleeves on winter uniforms]

Flag officers

Großadmiral (Admiral of the Fleet)	General-admiral (Grand Admiral)	Admiral (Admiral)	Vizeadmiral (Vice Admiral)	Konter-admiral (Rear Admiral)

Officers

Kommodore (Commodore)	Kapitän zur See (Captain)	Fregattenkapitän (Commander)	Korvettenkapitän (Lieutenant Commander)

Kapitänleutnant (Lieutenant)	Oberleutnant zur See (Sub-lieutenant)	Leutnant zur See (Ensign)

Midshipmen and cadets

Oberfähnrich zur See (Midshipman class I)	Fähnrich zur See (Midshipman class II)	Seekadett (Naval Cadet)	Offiziers-anwärter (Officer Candidate)
		No shoulder strap	

Non-commissioned officers

Stabsoberfeldwebel (Warrant Officer class I)	Oberfeldwebel (Warrant Officer class II)	Stabsfeldwebel (Chief petty Officer)	Feldwebel (Chief Petty Officer)

Obermaat (Petty Officer)	Maat (Petty Officer)

RANK STRUCTURE

Ratings

Oberstabsge-freiter (Able seaman)	Stabsge-freiter (Able seaman)	Hauptge-freiter (Able seaman)	Oberge-freiter (Able seaman)	Gefreiter (Able seaman)	Matrose (Seaman)

SOURCES OF ILLUSTRATIONS

Outside Cover
Type XXI U-Boat
https://3dwarehouse.sketchup.com/model/ub228ddac-893d-4fb5-8353-
0590c47ed43b/KM-Type-XXI-U-boat-Elektroboote

Prologue
Fishing trawler
https://www.enca.com/business/sea-harvest-group-reports-profits-
despite-pandemic

5 January 1933
SS Usambara
https://www.pinterest.pt/pin/451556300114880849/?amp_client_id=CLI
ENT_ID()&mweb_unauth_id=&amp_url=https%3A%2F%2Fwww.pint
erest.pt%2Famp%2Fpin%2F451556300114880849%2F&amp_expand=t
rue

17 January 1933
Market square in Bremen
https://monovisions.com/vintage-historic-photos-of-bremen-germany-
circa-1890s-19th-century/

18 January 1933
Main entrance to the Seefahttschule, Bremen
https://de.wikipedia.org/wiki/Datei:Infotafel_-_Hochschule_Bremen_M-
Trakt,_Neustadtswall_30_(Lage).jpg

21 January 1933
Boats on the Weser, Bremen
https://monovisions.com/vintage-historic-photos-of-bremen-germany-
circa-1890s-19th-century/

22 January 1933
Interior of the cathedral, Bremen
https://en.wikipedia.org/wiki/File:BremerDom-1.jpg

SOURCES OF ILLUSTRATIONS

16 June 1933
Seefahrtschule, Bremen
https://www.wikiwand.com/de/Hochschule_Bremen

20 June 1933
Yacht harbor on the Weser, Bremen
https://en.wikipedia.org/wiki/File:Bremen-Vegesack.JPG

Batleship: Kronprinz Wilhelm
https://en.wikipedia.org/wiki/File:SMS_Kronprinz_Wilhelm_in_Scapa_F
low.jpg

15 December 1933
Seal of the Seefahrtschule, Bremen
https://commons.wikimedia.org/wiki/File:Siegelmarke_Seefahrtschule_i
n_Bremen_W0355972.jpg

26 July 1934
Schooner
https://downeastwindjammer.com/activities/schooner-xandrielle/

28 July 1934
U-Boat of the First World War
https://www.mirror.co.uk/news/world-news/world-war-one-u-boat-
11201928

29 March1935
Battleship Scharnhorst being built
https://www.maritimequest.com/warship_directory/germany/battleships/s
charnhorst/scharnhorst_page_1.htm

15 June 1935
Adolf Hitler with generals and admirals
https://upload.wikimedia.org/wikipedia/commons/4/49/Bundesarchiv_Bi
ld_183-2006-0810-
500%2C_Flugzeugtr%C3%A4ger_%22Graf_Zeppelin%22%2C_Hitler_
bei_Stapellauf.jpg

SOURCES OF ILLUSTRATIONS

Launching of a U-Boat
https://www.bluebird-
electric.net/submarines/u_boats_german_submarines_world_wars_one_a
nd_two.htm

10 September 1935
Marinschule, Mürwik
https://en.wikipedia.org/wiki/File:MSM-hauptgebaeude.jpg

11 September 1935
Fregattenkapitän Kurt Slevogt
https://uboat.net/wwi/men/commanders/329.html

6 January 1936
Armoured ship Admiraal Graf Spee
https://en.wikipedia.org/wiki/File:Bundesarchiv_DVM_10_Bild-23-63-
06,_Panzerschiff_%22Admiral_Graf_Spee%22.jpg

1 May 1936
Marineschule Mürwik
https://en.wikipedia.org/wiki/File:Marineschule_Muerwik.jpg

3 July 1937
Old buildings in city centre, Bremen
https://www.jacobs-university.de/living-in-bremen

12 July 1937
Fregattenkapitän Werner Scheer
https://uboat.net/men/commanders/1071.html

13 July 1937
Armoured ships Admiral Scheer and Lützow
https://weaponsandwarfare.com/2017/07/12/deutschland-class-pocket-
battleship/

19 July 1937
U-Boat class VIIA in harbor

https://alternate-timelines.com/thread/2181/world-war-ii-real-time?page=15

12 August 1937
U-Boat in river estuary
https://www.pinterest.ch/pin/714453928358927849/

27 September 1937
U-Boat class VIIC in harbor
https://padresteve.com/2011/02/05/the-u-boat-type-viic-workhorse-of-the-kriegsmarine/

Admiral Karl Dönitz
https://prinxmaurice.com/2017/09/16/karl-donitz

3 September 1939
Kptlt Fritz-Julius Lemp
https://uboat.net/men/lemp.htm

Look-out on U-boat connng tower
https://www.youtube.com/watch?v=376q9QUezJU

14 September 1939
The Fanad Head seen from a U-boat
https://www.dingeraviation.net/skuaroc/fanad.htm

Blackburn Skua dive bomber
https://www.google.co.za/search?q=Blackburn+Skua&hl=en&authuser=0&tbm=isch&source=hp&biw=994&bih=429&ei=XwqqYO-XOqualwT04Z7oCw&oq=Blackburn+Skua&gs_lcp=CgNpbWcQAzICCAAyAggAMgIIADICCAAyBggAEAUQHjIGCAAQBRAeMgYIABAIEB4yBggAEAgQHjIECAAQGDIECAAQGDoFCAAQsQM6CAgAELEDEIMBULUGWOIsYKwva

28 December 1939
Battleship HMS Barham
https://www.wikiwand.com/en/HMS_Barham_(04)

SOURCES OF ILLUSTRATIONS

18 January 1940
Amiral Dönitz and Kptlt Fritz-Julius Lemp
https://en.wikipedia.org/wiki/Fritz-Julius_Lemp

4 May 1940
U-Boat class IIC
http://dubm.de/en/type-ii/

13 May 1940
Kvkpt. Hans Eckermann
https://uboat.net/men/commanders/235.html

11 July 1940
U-Boats in the harbor of Kiel
https://uboat.net/flotillas/bases/kiel.htm

3 August 1940
U-boat captain at periscope
https://www.youtube.com/watch?v=376q9QUezJU

6 September 1940
Volkswagen Kübelwagen
https://en.wikipedia.org/wiki/Volkswagen_K%C3%BCbelwagen

Iron Cross, First Class
https://ww2-medals.com/german-wwii-iron-cross-1st-class.html

10 February 1941
Kptlt Heinz Buchholz
https://uboat.net/men/commanders/145.html

21 March 1941
U-Boat class VIIC on the open sea
https://www.naval-encyclopedia.com/wp-content/uploads/2019/01/U101-color.jpg

21 May 1941
Battleship Birmarck

SOURCES OF ILLUSTRATIONS

http://www.navweaps.com/index_inro/INRO_Bismarck.php

24 May 1941
Battleship Bismarck's gun fire
https://www.wired.com/2009/05/dayintech-0527/

HMS Hood exploding
https://www.youtube.com/watch?v=4_jDaUSSPhc

6 June 1941
Konteradmiral August Thiele
https://en.wikipedia.org/wiki/August_Thiele

9 June 1941
Munkholmen
https://encyclopaedia.fandom.com/de/wiki/Liste_der_Marine-Flak-Abteilungen?file=Trondheim_munkholm_P9260550.JPG#Drontheim

17 June 1941
Junkers Ju-52 ambulance plane
https://line.17qq.com/articles/hgdjidhdz.html

Brest, Saturday, 23 August 1941
U-Boat in harbor
https://www.thestar.com/news/canada/2012/07/26/german_uboat_wreck_may_be_at_bottom_of_churchill_river_in_labrador.html

27 December 1941
Vice Admiral Eugen Lindau,
https://de.wikipedia.org/wiki/Eugen_Lindau#/media/Datei:Bundesarchiv_Bild_101II-MW-6416-10A,_Frankreich,_St._Nazaire,_Admiral.jpg

31 December 1941
Knight's Cross
https://en.wikipedia.org/wiki/File:DE_Band_mit_RK_(1).jpg

U-Boat badge
https://za.pinterest.com/pin/529806343654369602/

14 March 1942
Bristol Blenheim fighter
https://upload.wikimedia.org/wikipedia/commons/a/a3/Bristol_Beaufight
er_Mk.IC_1944.png

1 October 1942
U-Boat entering the Dora-1 bunker
https://www.klikk.no/historie/kriegsmarinewerft-drontheim-hitlers-
ubatbase-i-trondheim-6705766

1 February 1943
Admiral Eberhardt Godt.
https://en.wikipedia.org/wiki/File:RearAdmiralGodt.jpg

10 August 1943
Calalina flying boat
https://za.pinterest.com/pin/366480488408240089/

14 August 1943
U-Boat inside Dora-1
https://za.pinterest.com/pin/308989224436387158/

15 August 1943
Sanatorium for wounded and sick officers, Trondheim
https://www.flickr.com/photos/national_archives_of_norway/698360452
2/

28 September 1943
German fast attack craft
https://za.pinterest.com/pin/549368854524523170/

4 October 1943
American Dauntless dive bomber
https://www.pinterest.nz/pin/245938829627932198/

29 October 1943
S-Boat flotilla
http://www.s-boot.net/englisch/sboats-km-northnorway.html

15 Februarie 1944

German armoured vehicle in Norway

https://www.facebook.com/photo?fbid=10156893240997687&set=pcb.1
0156893243942687

30 October 1944

German S-boat badge

https://schnellbootnet.jimdofree.com/kriegsmarine-s-boot-waffe/

2 November 1944

German armed fishing trawler

https://maximodelizm.com.ua/viewtopic.php?id=4286

3 November 1944

Heavy coastal artillery

https://www.geocaching.com/geocache/GC63VGE_kystfort-meloyvr-
fort-kanon-b?guid=716abc62-a215-4bfa-9f64-5704f0f1c333

24 April 1945

Military funeral

http://www.s-boot.net/englisch/sboats-km-norway.html

30 April 1945

Flottilla armed fishing trawlers

https://www.wikiwand.com/de/Kommandant_der_Seeverteidigung

2 May 1945

German Class XXI U-boat

https://www.facebook.com/diedeutscheubootwaffe/photos/type-xxi-u-
boats-at-the-end-of-the-world-war-iithe-type-xxi-u-boats-also-known-
a/504937496250009

4 May 1945

German U-Boat Class XXI

http://dubm.de/en/typ-xxi/

18 June 1945

U-Boat class XXI near the coast

https://1.bp.blogspot.com/-v0t-
LCZLndw/VEvE74f8BLI/AAAAAAABTn8/oX7XJfcc-
Zc/s1600/Type_XXI_worldwartwo.filminspector.com_15.jpg

Bar of gold
https://www.proxibid.com/Firearms-Military-Artifacts/Military-
Artifacts/WWII-GERMAN-FANTASY-REICHSBANK-1-KILO-GOLD-
BAR/lotInformation/50609703

Golden coin
https://www.sbcgold.com/blog/archaeologist-digs-up-50000-of-nazi-
gold/

18 July 1945
Coffee mug with picture of SS Usambara
https://www.ebay.co.uk/itm/GERMAN-EAST-AFRICA-LINE-SS-
USAMBARA-MINI-STIEN-OCEAN-LINER-PURCHASED-
ONBOARD-2-/232968477173

1 December 1947
SS Usambara
https://www.trains-worldexpresses.com/webships/300/318.htm

12 February 1949
Schooner
https://za.pinterest.com/pin/237142736608540823/

15 March 1949
Diver with sunken submarine
https://www.dailymail.co.uk/sciencetech/article-8545711/Divers-capture-
stunning-underwater-video-German-U-boat.html

15 March 1950
Bar of gold
http://www.usmbooks.com/nazi_gold_bar.html

Rank Insignia of the Kriegsmarine
https://en.wikipedia.org/wiki/Uniforms_and_insignia_of_the_Kriegsmari
ne

End of List of Illustrations

Golden Nazi coin
https://www.sbcgold.com/blog/archaeologist-digs-up-50000-of-nazi-gold/

www.ingramcontent.com/pod-product-compliance
Lightning Source LLC
Chambersburg PA
CBHW051130030726
47504CB00004B/797